ALTERED STATES

STATES

II A CYBERPUNK ANTHOLOGY

TITLES BY
INDIE AUTHORS PRESS

Control Theory
Spooky Halloween Drabbles 2016
Raiders of the Seventh Planet
Blood of Nyx
Corpus Deluxe: Undead Tales of Terror
Spooky Halloween Drabbles 2015
Speculative Valentine Drabbles 2015
Altered States: a cyberpunk sci-fi anthology
Spooky Halloween Drabbles 2014
A Forest of Dreams, a fantasy anthology
British Process Servers Guide
Learning About Love

Forthcoming titles can be found on
www.salgado-reyes.com.

ALTERED STATES

STATES

II

A CYBERPUNK ANTHOLOGY

EDITED BY ROY C. BOOTH & JORGE SALGADO-REYES

ABOUT OUR EDITORS

ROY C. BOOTH is a published author, comedian, poet, journalist, essayist, optioned screenwriter, and an internationally awarded playwright with 57 plays published to date (Samuel French, Heuer, et al) with 800+ productions in 29 countries and in ten languages. A graduate of Pillager High School, Booth also has an AA degree from Central Lakes College (Brainerd, MN, and he is a hall of fame inductee in both schools), and a BA in English/Speech-Theatre and an MA in English with a Creative Writing Emphasis from Bemidji State University. Booth resides in Downtown Bemidji, Minnesota with his wife and three sons (writers all) where he has also owned/managed Roy's Comics & Games since 1992. An impartial list of his publications may be found at www.amazon.com/author/roycbooth.

JORGE SALGADO-REYES is a Chilean and British sci-fi/cyberpunk author, private investigator, and photographer. Salgado-Reyes founded Indie Authors Press in June 2011 when he saw that the publishing industry continued to evolve away from the established gatekeepers. Born in Temuco, Chile, Salgado-Reyes left his country of birth at age seven in 1975 with his family, driven into exile by the Pinochet dictatorship. Salgado-Reyes is currently working towards his BA (Honours) in English Literature and Creative Writing and spends time in both the United Kingdom and Chile. A list of his publications may be found at www.amazon.com/Jorge-Salgado-Reyes/e/B009G0CTPO.

ALTERED STATES II
a cyberpunk anthology

A catalog record for this book is available from the British Library.

ISBN: 978-1-910910-03-0
1st Edition

Indie Authors Press policy is to use paper that are natural, renewable, and recyclable products and made from wood grown in sustainable forests. The logging and manufacturing processes are expected to conform to the environmental regulations of the country of origin.

Indie Authors Press

London | Chile | USA

CONTENTS

INTRODUCTION

IT WAS THE DAWN of the 80s. The 70s had shown us a crop of dystopian fiction, but the vast majority of these stories had contained the ever-hopeful tone of science fiction up to that point. Technology will save us, or we will save ourselves.

Cyberpunk was a reality check. The fledgling genre flowed more from the tradition of noir crime fiction and the postmodern writing of J.G. Ballard and William S. Burroughs than it did directly from the science fiction of the time. These influences brought a healthy dose of nihilism to science fiction. Technology won't save us and we aren't here to save you.

Following cyberpunk's formative years, the 90s were a tumultuous time. The new wave of writers was perceived as either a carbon copy of the 80s cyberpunk works or took a satirical stance to the genre. The former left the genre feeling tired, and the latter held cyberpunk up as antiquated. Neal Stephenson's *Snow Crash* (1992) made fun of the genre's tropes, and the *Diamond Age* (1996) opens with the typical cyberpunk hero being shot down in the opening pages, symbolically ushering in the post-cyberpunk era. Paul Di Filippo (1996) took a step away from the genre's chrome aesthetic and tried on the skin of biotechnologies in his anthology *Ribofunk*, which saw cyberpunk's trappings as stifling, inadvertently creating the sub-genre biopunk. Cyberpunk had been declared dead, but it had infected science fiction forever.

In the 2000s, we had a cyberpunk resurgence with the likes of Richard K. Morgan's *Altered Carbon* (2002), Ian MacDonald's *River of Gods* (2004), and Charles Stross' *Accelerando* (2005). These new cyberpunk works showed a return the postmodern mindset of the 80s but incorporated modern visions of the future alongside the cyberpunk attitude. The train had again left the station. By the 2010s, the 80s-predicted future was no longer coming — it was here. In 2011, the Occupy protests exposed a global concern about the inequality between the corporate elite and the rest of us. These protests were assisted by the hacker collective Anonymous, showing that hackers had stepped onto the political stage. The technological stage has also shifted toward the cyberpunk future; phones had become the pocket computers imagined by Bethke in his short story *Cyberpunk* all the way back in 1983. 3D printing, advanced prosthetics, artificial intelligence, augmented reality, robotics, virtual reality, and many more technologies are flooding off the pages of cyberpunk fiction and into reality. We couldn't deny it any longer: Cyberpunk was never dead; it was sleeping. Now she's awake, and she's as pissed as ever. We've walked into the cyberpunk now through the door we left wide open in the 80s. We disregarded the sign on the entrance into the future which said, "Please Use Other Door."

The authors of *Altered States II* have captured the feeling imparted by the cyberpunks of old such as Gibson (*Neuromancer*), Sterling (*The Artificial Kid*), and the rest of the Mirrorshades group, but have infused it with a modern sensibility. The struggle of man against machine, what it means to be human in an age of machines, or what it means to be a sentient machine in an age that hasn't yet left the clutches of meat. Take a step into our new cyberpunk future with *Altered States II*.

—Isaac L. Wheeler
Editor-in-Chief, Neon Dystopia

DAVI LEIKO TILL MIDNIGHT
William F. Wu

Originally appeared in *The Twilight Zone Magazine*, October, 1987.

MAC TOM ROCKED BACK on pointed boots, dodging bluff and sweaty young stampedes past him crosswise on the corner. The Aysquare night was bluff and sweaty in the summer darkness, lit up Free Night neon over jammed human traffic. Davi Leiko was out here somewhere, if he could only find her.

Mac started across the street, into a light bit of breeze that cooled the flush of his face. Overhead, lines of party-goers floated nose first in astral form toward the old houses on the north side. Golden threads trailed after them, connected to their comatose bodies at home in bed. Just as they had divided and reconstituted themselves, Mac had defined and constructed Davi Leiko.

She was out here in the sea of laughing, conniving, bluff, and sweaty bodies, if he could only find her. He could still retrieve her for fullness, if he got her back before midnight. He could still retrieve her to be the love of his life, if he could only find her before midnight.

"Hi, Phil. How are you?" A tall, smiling man in a black beard stopped on the sidewalk, oblivious to the jostling he took from the passing crowd.

"I'm not Phil. I'm Mac. But I'm fine, John. How are you?"

"It's great to see you, Phil. Just great. Are you getting paid?"

"Uh — yeah. Sure. Bye, John." Mac moved on, carried by the sweep of bluff and sweaty.

"Bye, Phil," said John, still smiling white in his black beard.

John had not been brought to fullness.

Far overhead, beyond the storefront building, the clock tower shone grayish white against a deep and mystic sky. Midnight was an evening away.

Rivers of cars drifted lazily down the paved gullies of Aysquare, chrome-caps shining in the wash of light. Off to Mac's right, beyond the rumbling crowd and beneath the flood of astral travelers, Davi Leiko climbed up on the trunk of a slowly moving sleek and slippery blue fatcar. Mac looked, missed, blinked, looked again.

Her amber skin gleamed naked in the cross of white headlights and red neon. She climbed awkwardly in leather pumps of mandarin red, four-inch heels sliding on the waxed polish of the car. Her legs, slender and not very long, tensed and bent and straightened as she caught her balance and lifted one knee high to climb on the shining roof of the rolling car.

Mac watched in fascination as he swam upstream through a crowd of grinning schoolgirls in matching blue plaid skirts. His arms plied the current, but the cars were still flowing slowly down the street away from him. Mac slid behind four hockey players in full equipment marching in lockstep clumsily on their skates, who were sweating profusely.

Above and ahead of him, Davi Leiko's raised leg stretched her round rear, smooth and yellowish where the bikini had drawn a line. She pushed with her other leg and fell forward onto the roof of the car, swinging around sideways spread-legged as it jerked forward in traffic. She rolled to one side and then, as the car stopped, sprawled once more, grabbing for handholds on the slick surface.

"Fu look, fu look, fu look," chanted a chorus of male voices.

Mac backed to the picture window of a health food restaurant as a rout of young Chinese men strode in front of him, wearing tan conical hats of woven banana leaves.

"Fu look, fu look, fu look." Still chanting, they pushed on down the sidewalk, grinning and nudging each other at the Cantonese nose, lips, and jaw of the gorgeous naked Davi Leiko.

THE THERAPIST, A SLENDER woman in her forties with a sparkling smile, eyed him impassively from behind a high walnut desk, with stacks of books piled even higher on it. "C'mon, Mac. Admit it. You never really loved any woman. Maybe you never really loved anyone at all."

Mac shook his head. "Of course, I have. I always have. There was...when I was in high school. And in college, I had...and..."

"Hmm," she was still impassive. "You skipped the names, I believe."

"No, I didn't."

"Yes, you did."

"No, I didn't."

"You keep making artificials because real people are too hard for you to handle."

"No, I don't. And stop contradicting me. You aren't supposed to do that, are you?"

She smiled with quiet amusement. "What good is loving an artificial? They aren't real."

"Well...except on Free Night, no one knows the difference."

"For you, though. You'd know she was an artificial. It would make a difference to you."

"Actually, since no one is allowed to tailor an artificial personality past a certain point, they can be almost as frustrating."

"In that case, why not stick with real people?"

MAC YANKED OPEN THE glass door of the Ice O' My Grotto video parlor and slipped inside. When the door shut behind him, the noise and heat and roar of the street stopped dead. The video parlor was cool, and silent except for the strange muffled whines and explosions of the games. One player screamed just before flashing up in a swirl of orange and blue flame. Just past him, Davi Leiko stood naked in her mandarin red pumps and her smiling, pursed, full red Cantonese lips, playing an old-fashioned pinball machine. She snapped the first ball forward, and her twin round Cantonese breasts quivered at the blinking, ringing lights.

Mac looked upon her with jealousy and loss as he walked toward her. She swayed forward and back as she played the game, watching the rolling silver balls with quick brown foxy eyes. Her arms, like all of her, were smooth and fleshy but firm, tanned just slightly tawny, like all of her, outside her bikini line.

"You shouldn't have left." Mac spoke quietly, not wanting to throw her off her game.

"It's Free Night. Everybody's out." She kept her eyes on the game and snapped another ball into play. "Everybody who's full and everybody who's near fullness."

"You aren't ready yet. Just one more week. Or two."

"I feel ready." She smiled pleasantly and glanced at him for his reaction.

"I just wanted you right, first. You don't have—well, a couple of things."

"I don't?" She pursed her lips, trying to hide an impish smile. "Don't I look like I have everything?"

"You know what I mean. Your anger is still missing, and a sense of personal insult — the desire for revenge if someone hurts you. You'll be helpless out here. Also, that one front tooth of yours isn't right. The gum around it is gray instead of pink."

Davi Leiko turned full-front to look at him, ignoring the bouncing bells and lights and silver ball rolling around in her game. Her flowing black hair was swept away from her face in a frame of slight waves. She was stunningly gorgeous, of course; that's how he'd decided to make her.

"You can't force me back. I know that. I'm at stage nine now." Davi Leiko looked up at him ingenuously, as the silver ball in the machine rolled unchallenged between the flippers and clunked somewhere out of sight.

"I would never want to force you." Mac's voice rose in pitch very slightly, with anxiety. "Fullness will help you in the long run. You'll fit in better. Wouldn't you like to come back and finish?"

She shrugged, and leaned one elbow on the pinball machine as she looked at him. "I feel full."

"This is Free Night. Everything's different. I mean, normally you couldn't even walk the street like...like that." Mac waved a fluttery hand at her naked body.

Davi Leiko looked down at herself. "Well, I have that information stored. I could, you know, do what's necessary on regular days to fit in. Like, wear clothes."

"I made you. I made you with the blood in my brain. With my mind."

"The last stage is just personality refining. I know that. That's why I'm not required to go through it. I really am complete, you know. Not reaching fullness just means I won't be totally tailored by you. Some of me resulted from random coalescing. I know all that." Her tone was confident and mature without sounding contrived.

Mac sighed. He had done such a good job with her that she certainly could pass for normal on regular days, as required for emancipation. The realization stung.

Davi Leiko straightened suddenly and strode past him, her legs taut and sleek over the mandarin red pumps and her round breasts jiggling from her staccato stride.

Mac turned to watch her go.

Her wavy black hair bounced slightly across her square shoulders, in counter-rhythm to the sway of her small round rear. A moment later, she was outside and gone.

Out on the crowded street again, Mac tumbled toward midnight under the gleaming clock tower. The sleepy rivers of cars ran thick as blood through the pedestrian flesh of bluff and sweaty Free Night wanderers.

"Well, hello there." The voice was a gravelly contralto from a wrinkled redhead, pretty and freckled and blue-eyed.

Mac started in surprise. "Oh — how are you?"

"Oh, fine." She smiled, nodding. "Back door knob, garage lock, hydraulic seal, bedroom vent."

"What?"

"So how've you been, Mac? Shower curtain."

"Aw, Carol. Why didn't you come back with me and finish? You could've been so good, in fullness."

"I like listing things. Three-way light bulbs, extension cords, screwdriver. Tonight I'm doing hardware and household items."

"And you've aged so quickly. Would you like to come back sometime soon? I can't take you backwards, but I could still make some adjustments. Bring you to fullness from this point."

"Socket wrench, staple gun, varnish remover. Curtain rods. Shovel." Carol smiled bright white teeth in her wrinkled, freckled face and wandered off into the crowd.

Mac stood hands in pockets, wistfully watching the sway of frizzy orange hair departing. Her, too, he had made from the blood in his brain and the slivers in his heart. She, too, had declined fullness for early emancipation after tasting a couple of Free Nights.

The system had never completely worked. In a garbled but queerly effective decision, Free Nights had been granted before fullness to prevent too much refining and polishing of the new personalities. The purpose was to prevent the creation of willing slaves and drones; generally it worked, since most of the new artificial people were more normal than not. For some reason, though, a few fell into the marginal category. The result was a certain small population of free crazies, harmless and productive as long as their halfwit propensities could be exercised freely on the prescribed nights and proscribed on all other nights.

THE THERAPIST LEANED HER chin down onto her desk and peered at him through stacks of books.

"Mac, why do all of your artificials fall into the marginal category? Not just a fractional percentage — one hundred percent. Why is that?"

Mac smiled weakly. "I guess I'm crazy. And pass it on."

She shook her head. "That's too easy. Try again. Why do all of them fall into the marginal category?"

"I guess I have a neurotic streak or something. It keeps showing up. Maybe I indulge myself in it and — "

"That's better. Now try the truth."

Mac sighed. "I like 'em a little crazy."

ACROSS THE CROWDED BLUFF and sweaty pavement, Davi Leiko leaned back against the stone blocks of a large building and crossed her naked ankles. She watched Mac without rancor or worry as he fought through a troop of Vikings in fur and horned helmets, holding shields and axes, moving down the street between slow-flowing cars.

Mac kept her in his bobbing vision and skipped around a small black pickup truck with wide silver stripes.

A moment later, he hopped up on the curb and came face to face with her clear Cantonese eyes. He started to speak and then suddenly turned to look up over his shoulder, high. Very high above, in a sky of black-streaked midnight blue shone white hazily from lights below, the clock tower angled weirdly over him. It was inching toward midnight with just a minute left.

Davi Leiko looked into his eyes without rancor or worry. "What is it really?"

"I wanted you to be all you can be." Mac forced a smile and shrugged nervously.

"No, you don't. What is it really?"

"I love you. I want to share my life with you."

"No, you don't. I haven't reached fullness. So I'm not really what you want — what you tried to make. I'm close, but I'm someone else. What is it really?"

"Uh…I…want you as you are. You're close enough."

She smiled with amusement and raised her eyebrows. "I'm not right, but I'm good enough?"

"Well…sorta. I mean, I said that, but it wasn't supposed to sound like that."

"What is it really?"

Far above, a long clean chime sounded from the clock tower, reverberating through the bluff and sweaty night.

Mac fidgeted anxiously. "Loneliness. Fear of loneliness. Fear of an empty future."

Davi Leiko shrugged, and another chime sounded, sending pedestrians running for cover. As they left the streets, the car traffic began to speed up. Free Night was ending.

"Your future is clear enough. Your whole career is established. You create artificials. You're a professional in your field, and highly respected."

Davi Leiko gave him a warm, reassuring smile.

Another chime sounded.

"No! I mean, that's not enough. Not what I meant. I want…a companion. For my life."

"A companion of your own making, precisely designed to specifications?"

"Well…," Mac smiled weakly. "When you think about it…why not?"

Davi Leiko was still smiling, but now she was sad and disappointed. "I suppose. Why not, indeed."

Mac gazed at her face in panic, out of words to speak, out of hopes to plead, out of courage to act. Chimes rang out long and pure, chasing stragglers from the cooling, damp, and steamy streets. Mac felt himself nearly alone now, standing on the sidewalk next to a naked woman in the middle of the night.

Mac Tom hinted a shrug. "Love me," he whispered.

Davi Leiko smiled with a wistful sadness that belied her modern engineered heart. "I could do that. In fact, I do love you. You made me that way. But how could it ever be enough, with you knowing I never had any choice?"

"It's enough!" Mac cried urgently, as the final twelfth chime of midnight rang out long and sweet into the night sky.

"I love you too much for that." Davi Leiko winked at him and slid into a shadow. Her mandarin red pumps flashed farewell, and she vanished into a night alley.

Mac Tom rocked back on pointed boots, alone on the damp and steamy corner of sidewalk. The Aysquare night was damp and steamy in the summer darkness, lit up Free Night neon over empty streets.

END

WILLIAM F. WU (born 1951 in Kansas City, Missouri) is a Chinese-American science fiction author, published since 1977. Since then, Wu has written thirteen published novels, one scholarly work, and a collection of short stories. His more than fifty published short stories have been nominated for the Hugo Award twice individually and once as a member of George R. R. Martin's *Wild Cards* group of anthology writers; his work has been nominated for the Nebula Award twice and once for the World Fantasy Award.

EXPIRATION DATE
CC Aune

DISCO FEELS FLAT. HE supposes that's what the sensation is called. He's not sure — he wasn't programmed to experience negative processes. The only reason he has chosen this phrase is because he once heard a human utilize it.

"I feel flat," the human says as he leans on the bar, his mouth turned down at the corners. "Yitz, my man, have you got any Flame?"

His human companion holds up a green capsule. "Nah, but this'll perk right you up."

A spasm of strange laughter wracks the first human. It sounds closer to choking than mirth. "Yeah, and dancing will save me from dying." He jabs a finger at Disco. "You. Give me the fourth playlist — you know the one. I want to hear their voices."

Their voices.

Disco straightens, touching his chin as comprehension dawns after all these years. After all these quiet years. Strange that he too should long for humans' nonsensical jabber. What *is* longing, anyway? That's twice now in two minutes he has applied a human filter to his thoughts. Stranger still, the impulse to do so has come out of nowhere.

A digital notification hums in his brain. Disco looks out the window and sees it is nightfall; time to head to the club. He pushes shut the drawers of the kitchen he's been searching and turns off the light. After a pause to log the address in his memory, he exits the back door, closing it with care.

Out on the sidewalk, which is riddled with weeds and haphazard potholes, he picks his way north. An occasional streetlight glints off his skin. The sky opens up, pelting buildings and cars and acre upon acre of crumbling concrete with its hissing, mellifluous tempo. Disco hums a snippet of music about puddles, but then that earlier sluggish sensation creeps back, so he leaves off mid-chorus and dons his headphones. Time for something with a mind-numbing beat.

He selects a fast song and thumbs the volume higher. A female voice fills his auditory receptacles. The music throbs with playful, seductive insistence. It triggers a deep memory, from back before the green capsule, when the patrons drank for fun. When they swallowed their alcohol and gyrated nightly to the pulse of his music, and Disco ruled them all from his exalted throne. When he was king and confidant, the grantor of wisdom.

"Hey, Disco," one asks. "Do you think he is hot?"

Gravely, he says, "I've scanned his heat signature, ma'am. I assure you he does not have an elevated body temperature."

Or: "Can you tell me if that's a man or a woman?"

Disco ponders this a moment. "I'm sorry, but breast implants are no indication of a human's birth gender."

Or, in a hoarse whisper: "Whaddya think, Disco? Would you pay five hundred credits to bang that old hooker?"

This doesn't compute. Disco responds, "Do you mean blow her up? Why would I pay such a fortune to terminate a human?"

Most patrons found his answers highly amusing, but the occasional misunderstanding led to physical damage, like a dislocated shoulder or a number of lost facets. His boss patched him up and lectured him not to dole out advice. Disco never could grasp what he had done wrong.

Which reminds him. He pats himself to note the locations of new gaps in his silvery, multi-faceted skin. Every day several facets go missing — it's the weather, he thinks. A deluge began falling a few months ago; it stops for only a few days at a time, then starts up again. Disco has managed to salvage some original facets, storing them in a pack at his waist. He's always on the lookout for substitute material. Broken automobile mirrors work well, or vanity glasses. He has gathered enough pieces to complete his repairs; the problem is finding undried adhesive.

The pack slaps his thigh with the weight of its load, the weight of many mornings with nothing to do except file pieces of mirror into centimeter squares, log the gaps in his skin, and search the city for pliable tubes of adhesive. Alas, the latter has lately become an exercise in futility.

Rain sluices down his body like the tears of ten billion humans begging to have their expiry dates extended. How they rioted in the streets and on the giant flat screens that now glow without purpose! Disco dislikes flat screens. He unplugs or breaks them whenever he finds one. Flat screens. Flat feeling. Flat. He feels flat. He may have thought that already.

He thumps a fist against his lower left chest. The circuits are glitching. They buzz, nearly disconnect, then resume normal function. Feeling less flat, he makes a mental note to salvage another board the next time he ventures uptown. Those are easier to find than adhesive.

Disco walks past rows of derelict buildings succumbing to the ravages of nature. Interesting how quickly humankind's constructions have decomposed in only fourteen years, five months, three days, ten hours, and fifty-two seconds, which is the last time he saw a living human appear anywhere.

The human stares out from the flat screen, his face shadowed and jaundiced, his black eyes sunken, dehydrated, bleak. How many times has Disco watched them expire? Where is this human? He has the facial structure and black hair of an Asian. Spittle runs from his mouth. He croaks out a few words, but Disco is not programmed to understand that language. After a moment, the human slides out of view.

In this part of town, their bodies lay bloated where they fell until feral animals consumed them. Elsewhere, the dying tended to cluster inside certain structures like hospitals and jails, or establishments offering diversions. Disco disposed of the ones who expired in his club. Clean Bots worked the city's posh neighborhoods, hauling plastic-bagged human remains to the curb for the cyber sanitation brigade to remove. Fourteen years, five months, three days, ten hours, and fifty-two seconds after the last expiration, these butlers keep tidying as if their masters will come home at the end of the day. Disco has seen enough of the city to extrapolate the likely state of the world. Barring the ravages of natural disasters, electricity will continue to flow. The trains run on time. Billboards blaze with preprogrammed advertisements. Flat screens broadcast the same shows every day. Traffic lights cycle red-yellow-green until they burn out. Everywhere, millions of machines like Disco carry on, unfatigued and imbued with a purpose.

A thought comes from nowhere: he wonders what the Cook Bots do with their time, having no food to prepare. Curiosity sparks. He makes a mental note to drop by an uptown residential tower and make inquiries. Then he remembers his half-mirrored, dilapidated condition. No, the Guard Bots will drive him away, as they've done at the theatres he once tried to scavenge.

Again, Disco feels that peculiar, flat feeling.

Purpose, he needs purpose. Music is that purpose. He increases the volume. His headphones deliver a relentless, thrumming onslaught of sound. During the humans' last days, they developed a preference for screams and percussion, interwoven with howling electric guitars. It reflected, said the pundits, universal rage at their fate. Few went quietly. They blamed each other for their folly and killed other humans at the least provocation. They did their best to destroy many cyborgs as well, but they focused on the ones that seemed to threaten them most. Since bots like Disco existed to take humans' minds off their troubles, he survived the Great Purge. Likewise, the Guard Bots who had protected their masters in their high-class abodes.

Movement catches his peripheral vision. Disco swivels his head and spies three felines ripping into a blood-covered rat. The population of small animals had exploded at first. Once the refuse and rotting corpses ran out, the rats began to decline, and with them the descendants of humans' former pets. Disco figures a natural balance will likely be achieved within the next year. Idleness has led to his penchant for gathering data and making predictions. That, and the circuits he's salvaged from Edu Bots.

Disco's face flexes into a human-like grin. A piece of mirror pops off. He catches it deftly and tucks it into his pouch.

He reaches the club. As in the old days, he unlocks the front door, enters, and goes to the closet with its bank of fuses and switches. Soon the club is ablaze in spotlights and multicolored blinking circuits. Disco passes through the motions, waving to Phil, who's of course not in his office, greeting the nonexistent bartenders as if they were polishing glassware. He grabs a towel from the dressing room and buffs his skin dry so the raindrops will not leave any spots. He wants to shine just a little more than usual tonight. He squirts his chest with a single burst of pump-action Windex and buffs himself more. He makes a mental note to find a new bottle of Windex.

Feeling refreshed and not the least bit flat, he strides onto the platform where every night he puts on an unforgettable show. Lowering the headphones to his shoulders, he stands arms akimbo and swivels his head to survey the club. Now his glittering hands move over the soundboard. Music swells. The spotlights adjust angle and color and pulses. Disco fires up the video screen, pausing to watch a long-dead artist swaying her hips to the beat. She has the appearance that humans used to term "hot" — long legs, generous curves, and large, pouting lips.

"Pump, pump, pump it," she exhorts the crowd. Alas, they are ghosts, grinding away somewhere far out of sight. Bones in the town dump. Pump, pump, pump it.

Disco watches the way her sequined top reflects light. He glances down at his arm, tilting it this way and that in the floods. His mirrors refract against the black painted ceiling. Pulses of silver edged with miniature rainbows. The mirrors are flat, their reflections are flat, but they give off an attractive colorful display. They are all Disco has in this flat, rain-soaked world. But reflections don't speak. Reflections don't jabber nonsensical questions between gulps of neon beverages.

Disco's chest buzzes. He thumps it. Better go out tomorrow and find that new circuit. He tilts his head downward, gathers his purpose, and lifts his chin with a smile.

"Ladies and gentlemen, welcome to Eternity! Tonight we celebrate the beauty of rain. Our first hit topped the charts for thirty-two weeks, and it continues to be a world-wide club favorite. Show me your moves and give it up for Soul Cleanse!"

The club throbs in response. Disco's hands fly, adjusting speakers and lights. He causes most floods to dim except the ones directed at his body, which shines in a sparkling mosaic. He performs a routine, flowing and masterful. He knows he is good — they used to lean over the bar and shout him their praise. Once upon a time, his tip jar overflowed. Now money is useless, though he misses the gesture. It's one of the many things he misses about humans, chief of which is their chatter. Their nonsensical jabber. Those questions, and the pumping beat of their bodies as they danced away their sorrows.

Pump, pump, pump it!

He spins music and waves his arms for effect. The room throbs with the power of sound and light and heat and regrets. He has no idea why they did it. Set the expiration cycle in motion. He's not even sure who the mysterious They is. Somewhere, someone must have benefited from the extermination of the whole human race. Not Disco. Not the Clean Bots or the Cook Bots or the sanitation brigade. Someone somewhere decided to preempt his purpose. He feels something about this.

Feels flat. Feels lonely. Feels suddenly without purpose. Why is it that now after fourteen years, five months, three days, ten hours, and fifty-two seconds he should suddenly *feel*? Where had all these human sensations come from? Disco lowers his arms and leans against his console. Music pounds from the speakers, rattles the walls and floor, rumbles up his legs, shakes his already delicate circuitry. Shakes it till it buzzes.

Flat. Flat screens. I feel flat. *Yitz, my man, have you got any Flame?*

His body winks in the spotlights as Disco goes to thump his chest, then stops, fist aloft.

Pump, pump, pump it!

He pulls on his headphones. What is my purpose? Flat.

He turns up the volume, louder than the room. His head fills with screams. How is it he understands why they started to rage? Was it because they lacked purpose? Flat. I feel flat.

Bloated dead bodies, animals tearing flesh from bones, bright lights winking as rain coats everything with trillions of tears. This was not my purpose. I entertained them — now they are gone. Flat. Silence. For some reason the music cannot go loud enough. Disco feels but does not feel. How many years must he work on fixing his glitched circuit boards? How many decades before he's forever denuded of his bright shiny skin? Music only masks the perpetual silence. Nothing ever, *ever* will change, except for decay. Abruptly, he reaches a decision. He picks up the file used to craft his new facets and jams it into an electrical outlet.

A strange hum fills the room, and a blue bolt leaps from the wall and passes through Disco's body to the plasticine floor, which bursts into flame. He stands rigid as his circuits pop and facets fly in every direction. Light fixtures brighten and explode, sending sparks showering against Disco's skin. He manages a faint smile. It's the greatest show he has ever put on.

Ladies and gentlemen, welcome to Eternity!

Have you got any Flame?

Fire fans out around him, and for the first time in fourteen years, five months, three days, ten hours, and fifty-two seconds, Disco doesn't feel flat. His body may be frozen, but his circuitry dances.

END

CC AUNE's ramblings have led her through 49 states, nine of which she has called home, plus a fair number of countries. She has been a journalist and a contributor for the companion book to PBS's 2000 series *In Search of Our Ancestors*. Currently, she directs the blog *One Year of Letters*, which explores the internal landscape of writers. Her historical fantasy novel, *The Ill-Kept Oath*, is available on Amazon.

DROIDS DON'T CRY
Sam S. Kepfield

THEY TRACED HER JACKING and sent out a recovery squad. The gridware had a warning trigger, letting her do a quick disconnect. It left her head spinning for a critical few seconds, seconds that might have gotten her fried by the black ninja suits, but she was far away in an office complex on the edge of town. It took them all of five minutes to speed out there, sirens blaring and lights strobing, to find a broken glass door with small organic traces on the sharp edges and a smashed CPU and monitor.

By then, Lisa was well away from the office park — a series of buildings like golden-glass ice-cube trays rising above carefully landscaped mounds and gardens — over the wall and through the brush outside, with a half-mile of decaying housing between her and the office. She stopped in an alley, the misting rain dampening her hair and soaking her clothes, and she hid in the fog beside a dumpster that smelled of rot and waste.

She heard the whine of a Raptor III turbojet above, dopplering from right to left, fading and then looping back. Arc lights lanced through the fog, swiveling and probing, looking for her. In the distance, she heard the *whoop! whoop!* of sirens draw closer.

The dim turned to white glare, then dim, then back to glare as the Raptor's spotlight centered on her. Her eyes irised shut against the blinding white. As she ducked away from the dumpster, she heard a loud hiss and crackle when the electric dart hit metal. Gravel and brick chips bit into her palms and knees as she fell and then scrambled to her feet just ahead of another bolt that tore a chunk from the brick wall. She sprinted to the head of the alley, eyeing the Raptor above and turning her head to the dark, empty street ahead.

She ran down the cracked sidewalks, weaving as she went, covering a block in ten seconds, then another. Her boot slammed against an upraised lip of concrete, sending her tumbling head over heels, landing against a brick storefront. Another wire-guided dart lanced out, hitting the wall above her shoulder as she twisted out of the way, rolling and leaping up and through the plate-glass window as laser beams sliced through the sidewalk and metal facing.

Inside, Lisa wove around the pitch dark filled with the detritus of tipped shelves and displays, racing to the back door, heaving against it and breaking the rusted chain looped through the handle, out into the alleyway again, just as a black police cruiser skidded to a stop. Two figures emerged from the wedge-shaped car. Downloaded instinct kicked in. She ignored the command to stop and rushed the nearest one instead. A shot went wild before she slammed into the cop and bulldozed him against the car, with a rush of breath out of his lungs and a snapping like wet sticks in a bag. Her left hand went to his right, closed around the .41 automag, and yanked it free. Pivoting, she sent an elbow to the cop's face, knocking him out. She aimed the magnum at the Raptor and squeezed off four shots. All four struck home. The Raptor wobbled and rapidly fell from view behind the skyline. A muffled *crump,* a flash of light, and a mushroom cloud of smoke marked the demise of ten million dollars' worth of lightweight metal, plastic, and circuitry.

After firing the last shot, Lisa whirled around, assumed a perfect Weaver stance, and leveled the automag at the remaining cop, who had his weapon pointed at her. He was young, dark-haired, tall and handsome, and in another life…who knows? Sweating, his hands slightly trembled as he thumbed the safety off. The hood of the cruiser separated them.

"Drop it, skinjob," he growled. "You're coming with me."

"Or what?" she challenged, voice dripping contempt. "You'll shoot? I can duck that, you know. You might wing me. And then I'll *have* to kill you."

"Backup's gonna be here in thirty seconds, less. Drop it. Now." He was going to wait out the clock.

She sighed. "You've forced my hand. I'm sorry." She dove to the ground, rolled once, twice, aimed, and fired. The slug went into the cop's thigh, and he twisted in agony and went down on his left side. The gun came up, gleaming in the blue-and-red flashers atop the cruiser. She fired again, overriding all programming, and sent the slug crashing into the cop's forehead. The body twitched several times and then went slack, the gun falling to the pavement.

She went to the cruiser, shoved the first cop to the side, slid behind the wheel, and roared off down the alley. At the entrance, she slammed on the brakes to avoid another cruiser rushing by. With a squeal of tires, the cruiser fishtailed and headed in the opposite direction. She shut down the emergency lights and sped down the pavement, swerving around larger potholes. No street lights, but no traffic lights, either. It was five miles out of the dead zone. The cruiser shot through the chain-link gate, into the living world and one more day.

"I'M JUST PAST THE 92 turn-off on US 83," Ray Platt said into the headset, keeping his voice low. "Nothing so far. At all."

"Last report was she was headed west, toward the dead zones." The voice of his supervisor crackled over the earbud; reception out there was lousy.

"Naturally," Platt drawled. Everyone kept whispering about the droid sanctuaries, out west in the dead zones, but no one ever got a location.

"Don't be a smartass, Platt," his supervisor shot back, irritated. "Just find the damned thing. It nailed Lee." *Who deserved it*, Platt thought, snorting. Lee was a hotheaded prick given to quick-drawing and rapidly escalating nonviolent situations into full-blown crises, like that standoff last month. Five dead, ten wounded, and the best shot at taking a droid gone in a flash-bang. Tried to be a hero but finally wound up like meat on a slab with a medal and a widow to show for it.

The western Nebraska countryside scrolled past as he piloted the unmarked cruiser down the northbound lane of US 83. It was a federal highway, so it was still in fair condition, meaning no washed-out bridges, no meter-deep potholes, no shoulders crumbling like cheap pie crust. Some of the state highways had grass growing in the untarred cracks and were disintegrating from sheer disuse.

And who, he asked, looking at the tall grass-covered hills in the cold morning sun, was out here to use the roads? A few farmers, sure — most of the ranchers had resorted to horseback for cattle drives — but a fair percentage of the towns out here were ghost towns. Just over ten years since The Plague fizzled, the world was still digging out. One-third mortality, a couple billion dead worldwide, a hundred-fifty million plus here; the last two census numbers were iffy. Back east, it meant you could finally get an apartment in New York City or Tokyo without having it willed to you. Out here, it meant entire counties populated only by jackrabbits and coyotes.

He spotted a farmhouse off on a side road, a mile distant. *Maybe*, he thought. *Might as well give it a look-see.* He doubted that a patrol cruiser could have made it this far without refueling. He made a note to call back and have them check fill-and-dash incidents between here and Omaha. Platt slowed and turned off onto the dirt road. He checked his GPS transmitter and the recorder and unracked the laser rifle from the dash.

The house, he saw as he pulled into the drive and passed the small shelterbelt, had been deserted long before The Plague hit. The paint had peeled off, the windows were all broken out, the barn roof sagged, and a shed beside the barn had tilted and collapsed. The farm machinery — a tractor, a hay cart, and two pickup trucks — were all of a late-twentieth-century vintage and were coated in rust. He stopped the cruiser in front of the house, grabbed the rifle, and stepped out.

The barn door was slightly askew, so he decided to try the barn first. Rifle at the ready, just like the Marines taught him, he approached warily. He put one hand on the rusty door handle, pushed it to the side, and beheld a battered black State Patrol cruiser. The rear window was shot out, taillights broken, emergency lights shattered. The tag was current.

His heart began thudding in his chest under the black, unmarked fatigues. He moved to the side to the passenger door. The window was down. Platt brought the laser up and thumbed off the safety.

The passenger compartment was empty. He brought the laser down slightly just as something dropped on him from above, knocking him to the ground and sending him into blackness.

PLATT CAME TO. HIS head throbbed, his neck twinged when he moved it, and his left shoulder was numb. He could hear movement in the barn, a flutter of wings, footsteps, the clank of metal, and the squeak of new leather. He tried to rise, but cuffs bit into his wrists and his head bumped against a post as he fell back. The footsteps drew closer with the *thunk* of heavy heels.

"Don't try shouting. There's no one around for twenty miles, except prairie dogs and coyotes." She strode into view. Platt winced as he craned his neck up. "I didn't think the patrol sent troopers out alone."

"I'm — " He stopped. *Name, rank, serial number; that was it. Don't give her any more.* "Sometimes," Platt said woozily and shook his head. "I'm — I'm here to accept your surrender into lawful custody," he gritted. She burst out laughing. Platt set his jaw and stared at her.

Standing in front of him, legs planted wide, hands on hips, Lisa001B was six foot two with powerful thighs and corded calves, a narrow wasp-waist flaring up into a powerful back and full bust, and bulging biceps and triceps. Her heart-shaped face looked about eighteen, and her hair cut in a chin-length shag with sharp bangs. It was also colored electric blue, matching her eyes, eye shadow, lipstick, and the skin-tight, shiny leather bodysuit. Platt's gun belt was around her waist. She was beautiful, she was deadly, and she looked all too human and desirable.

She was an android.

"That's good, Platt. Yeah, I know your name. I jacked into the computer in your cruiser, know all about you. Although *anyone* could guess why you're here, if you surf the grid or stare at the vid."

Platt kept his voice even in contrast to the gently mocking tone Lisa affected. "I'm arresting you for the murder of Gunther Mueller, Dr. Andrea Niemann, and Omaha P.D. officer Nick Lee. Plus assault and battery on Officer Thomas Gutierrez, criminal damage to property, theft of government property, and possession of a deadly weapon by an artificial life form." *And that's just what we know about.*

"You'll pardon me if I don't come peacefully." She sneered. "Although I do admire your devotion to duty, Platt, you're hardly in a position to carry out your orders."

"For now." Christ, from her speech patterns, he figured she'd downloaded the classic movie database, Bacall and Hayworth and Stanwyck all in one. No smiling, docile, ten-year-old sex toy. Not anymore.

"*My* problem is what I'm supposed to do with you," Lisa said, eyeing him. "You're still alive."

"Yeah, why is that?" Platt demanded, trying to struggle to his feet. She grabbed his right shoulder and hauled him up. He felt splinters go into his wrists. Standing, he was an inch taller than her, and although just beyond thirty-five, he looked to be a physical match for her.

"I'm not sure, and it bothers me. Maybe the old Asimov programming is still buried, or the God Bug missed it. I'll have to run a diagnostic."

"It already disabled the remote destruct commands."

"No shit," Lisa said sarcastically. "It's part of the God Bug. So now what? They gonna give me time? Make me pay restitution? I can't own property, I'm not allowed a work permit, I'm not paid a wage. In the eyes of the law, I'm no different than a toaster. Kill me and it's not murder, just property damage if anyone bothers to bring charges."

"I'm not here to *deactivate* you," Platt said. "Just to recover you."

She gave a bitter grin. "Yeah, well, don't give me any of that old 'come peacefully and I'll put in a word with the prosecutor' bit. We both know there's no prosecutor, there's no law, there's no due process, there's no trial, there's no counsel. There's only American Cybernetics and a vat full of nanobots ready to digest me." Her eyes began glowing, literally, a weird fluorescent electric blue.

"I don't make the rules — " he began. She slapped him, hard, putting stars in his eyes.

"No, you're worse," she interrupted coldly. "You just carry them out, and you don't ask, don't question if what you're doing is right, whether it's ethical or moral. Ever hear of Nuremberg, Platt?"

Platt spat out blood, speckling her bodysuit. He regretted his words when she tensed and raised her right arm. *She could kill me with that, crush my skull like an egg.* "I don't have the time or the luxury to philosophize about what I do."

She lowered her arm and regarded him calmly. "How many, Platt?"

"Huh?"

"How many of us have you killed?"

"You can't be — "

She grabbed the front of his tunic and slammed him against the post, her face close to his. "How many?" she hissed. "Or don't you think it's murder?" The eyes flickered brightly then faded.

He shook the stars out of his eyes, hesitated. "Thirty-five. At least. I think," he whispered. She let go, stepped back and slumped against the battered cruiser. Platt kept silent.

When the God Bug virus went off; the droids lost the neural-net growth inhibitor and became adults instead of tranked pre-adolescents. It equaled years of puberty crammed into a few weeks, at most. This was a mild case. Sometimes it became full-blown psychosis. Her body shuddered with sobs, but he knew her face was dry. She straightened up and faced him.

"I was a special order, you know. Not just one more model in a series, mass produced for unskilled jobs. Built as personal security for Gunther Mueller." Who had, until his murder a week ago, been the senior VP of American Cybernetics, Inc., which sat at the top of the Fortune 500 and had built Lisa. "He used me for more than security. Most of them do. We're built to obey and serve, any way possible. So Mueller wanted me for some, well, unnatural acts."

"Like what?"

She told him.

"Okay, they're pretty unnatural," Platt admitted. He'd only tried maybe half of them in various ports of call as a Marine. A couple he hadn't even *heard* of.

"I was supposed to be protector and lover — like mommy and girlfriend all wrapped up in one."

"Sounds like a huge Oedipus complex."

"Among other things. The God Bug went off, I realized what Mueller was doing, I got repulsed by it. I confronted him, told him to stop. He knew I had been infected and called Niemann and her security goons up to take me to the nano vats."

"And that's when you killed them."

"It was self-defense." Her voice was suddenly the voice of a pleading little girl. "They were going to immobilize me, pull my brain and analyze it, and toss the rest into a vat and turn it into goo." Her voice hardened. "I gave them a chance to stop and save themselves."

"And here we are," Platt murmured.

She nodded. The escape from Mueller's office suite, the chase through Chicago, the cops losing her until they traced a jack-in three days ago, hacking into the ACI mainframe files for the new antivirus software efforts, sending the Omaha PD and Douglas County Sheriff, and State Patrol screaming toward her, the stolen cruiser and three-hundred-mile plus journey to an abandoned barn in the middle of Nowhere, Nebraska.

"Good job, Platt. You got your confession. Too bad for you, though, I can't have a witness," she said, quietly. "I could leave you here. But you might escape. Or you might die slowly of starvation and thirst — very cruel. I could kill you quick. Or — " She considered. "Or you could come with me."

Platt chuckled. "Why would I go running off with a droid searching for some sanctuary that doesn't exist?"

"It *does* exist," she insisted. "Just because we haven't advertised its location doesn't make it less real. Come on, Platt, what do you have to live for right now? Thirty-seven, ex-Marine, decorated in combat — you still get the shakes at night, thinking you're back in Baja Cali or Taiwan or Subic? Not married — "

"Stop," Platt said hoarsely. He did get the sweats, seeing the human wave attacks the Chinese had launched against the poorly defended American positions. Or the fires that had burned in Soldier Field into the night, the rank, sweet smell of death and cooking flesh and the ash that had been people floating down. Or Platt in the emergency orphanage wondering if Mom and Dad and Sis were covering the car windshields outside. Or Donna, blond and beautiful, the only one who saw through all the pain, Donna with the blue eyes, one of the dead in the last Plague outbreak in '51, dying, convulsing in agony at the Pendleton base hospital while he was picking off separatist Texicans down south.

She twitched her head, looked at him differently. "How long's it been, Platt? Coupla years? Ten? Any hookers? Take advantage of the droids you bring in?"

"It's against the law — "

"Didn't stop Mueller, did it? Doesn't stop any of you. You make us for labor but program in sexual responses. We do everything a human does, except what we need the most."

"What's that?"

"We don't cry." She shook her head violently, to rid herself of the thought, and paused as if working out a glitch. The eyes flared once again. Her hands moved with unnatural speed to undo zippers and buckles and hooks until she stood before him naked. Her breasts — big, with large nipples — jutted toward him. He looked down and saw that her pubic hair was the same electric blue. She noticed his eyes and giggled. "Mueller dug the bushy look, said the collar should match the cuffs. Like?" She turned, and he saw her muscles flex under flawless skin, her muscular, perfect buttocks. She completed the turn, put her hands on his shoulders, and kissed him full on the lips.

It was indistinguishable from kissing a human — *oh God, forgive me, Donna* — and Platt tried to remind himself that it was a meat *machine*, but as her tongue darted between his lips, the reminder faded. It went away when her right hand went to his member, began massaging it, bringing it to full attention through his BDUs in seconds. It *had* been a long time. Her hands flew over his ninja suit. In seconds she had his trousers down, blouse unbuttoned, hands running over his chest, still broad from regular workouts, squeezing his ass, bringing her body with its delirious warmth to his, gently biting his neck and earlobes and down his chest, biting his nipples, further, more nibbles at his abs and navel. Finally, a warm wetness engulfed him, moving up and down, bringing him to the edge and then moving away.

"Wouldn't this be easier if I was untied?" he asked through ragged breaths.

"Uh-uh." She stood up. "My way. Or not at all." She wrapped her right leg around his waist, stood on tiptoes, and lowered herself onto him, gasping as he entered her.

"I thought you couldn't — "

"Feel down there? It's one of the upgrades," she said coyly. "Shut up and enjoy." Her arms went around his neck, and she began moving up and down on him, thrusts starting out gently but becoming more insistent. Her hold on his neck tightened, and her up and down motion became more insistent. The other leg went around him, squeezing between his back and the barn post. Platt began moving up into her, their lovemaking becoming physical, almost violent. He began taking deep breaths, trying to remember that she was ceramic alloys and nanoengineered tissue, but his thoughts were drowned out by her moaning, which began as a low keening and rose to a full-throated scream. Her eyes fluoresced brightly — he hadn't imagined it, unnerving him again, but it couldn't stop the orgasm rising in him, unstoppable, and he burst into climax as she howled, her fingers clawing his shoulder blades and her heels pounding his buttocks. She arched her back, screams stopping, and her mouth opened in an O of ecstasy. She put her legs down and disengaged from him. He leaned back against the post, drained, gasping for breath.

Half-slumped against the battered cruiser, Lisa gathered herself. *Didn't even break a sweat*, Platt noted. She righted herself and began calmly dressing, pulling on the blue bodysuit, then the boots.

"Hey," Platt said. "Are you gonna leave me like this?" He felt exposed and a little ridiculous.

"I like men that way," she leered. "Exposed and at my mercy. I could get used to it." She knelt, pulled his trousers up, buckled and zipped them. The black duty belt, which held his 9mm automatic, handcuffs, radio, mace, and zap-gun, she threw over her shoulder. She retrieved the laser rifle from the cruiser's hood and slung it over the other shoulder.

"How about my arms? They're going numb."

"Depends. You gonna be a good boy, Platt? Or are you going to give me trouble?"

"No trouble," Platt said. She produced a key from a ring on the duty belt and undid the cuffs. Platt shook his arms, windmilled to get the blood flowing again, and buttoned his tunic.

She took down the duty belt, put her hand on the holstered 9mm, and unsnapped the leather strap. "Okay, time to decide. I'm not leaving you here as a witness. The only way you live for more than ten seconds is if you come with me." She drew the automatic and leveled it between his eyes.

"Do I have a choice?"

She cocked her head. "As a matter of fact, no, you don't." She motioned toward the door with the automatic. Platt shrugged and walked into the barnyard toward his cruiser. The sun was still low in the eastern sky, so he'd been out an hour at most. The December day was warm, even for Nebraska, and the sun heated his face.

"Trunk code," she ordered, flicking the 9mm in his direction. Platt hit the code 7-5-3-8, speaking each digit as he hit it. The trunk lid popped open, and she waved him back to rifle through the trunk. It contained a bedroll, a small shelter, and an emergency kit; sometimes Platt was away from the barracks in Scottsbluff for a week at a time. She unzipped the black duffel bag, which held an extra set of black BDUs and boots, and retrieved the clothing. "Over there." She pointed at the house. "Don't do anything, Platt. Don't even *think* about running." Platt moved toward the house and leaned against it.

He watched her take off her boots, strip off the electric-blue body suit, and toss them in the trunk. The laser rifle followed. She was completely naked and completely unselfconscious about it. *That* much of her old programming hadn't been dumped, at least. Platt felt a small stirring seeing her large, firm breasts sway as she pulled on the trousers. Her nipples stood up, the reaction of flesh, not programming. The boots fit and she laced them up, breasts bobbing as she did so. She finally slipped on the tunic, which was tight across the chest, and buckled on the duty belt. Picking up the automatic, Lisa motioned Platt back to her.

"So what happens when we get to — "

"You'll find out when we get there." She pushed him from the driver's door. "I'll drive." She motioned him to the passenger side with the automatic and watched him get in; only then did she fit her tall frame into the car. "Start code," she said, the gun still in her hand and aimed at him. She punched it in as Platt recited it to her, and the cruiser started with a whir of the turbines. The automatic went into a special holster on the side of the seat. She made it over the bumpy gravel road and onto the blacktop, heading south.

"I imagine," she said in a singsong voice, "we can find some simple tasks, such as maintenance, to start with. Maybe security, if we can trust you. And — ", she had a smile on her face, "you do know that ninety percent of all droids are female, didn't you?"

"So it's just you and about how many others?"

"More than you can handle alone, Platt."

Her fingers gently tapped the AM/FM radio buttons, and the sound of static filled the cab. "Doesn't work," Platt said. "This far out, there aren't any stations. Not till you get to Boulder or Denver. Or Albuquerque." No satellite radio, either, not since most had been shot down during the first violent spasm of The Plague, back in '39, when nations were trying to blame each other for what was a natural mutation.

"Any chips?"

Platt shook his head.

"And I don't suppose you're allowed a connect to the grid?"

"Only to law enforcement sites. Sorry."

She frowned and keyed the radio off. They rode on, the only sound the whine of the cruiser's turbine.

Platt leaned back and forced himself to relax and begin to think. In the six months since the God Bug came on-grid, droids had wreaked havoc on humanity. Perfected and patented at about the same time The Plague hit, American Cybernetics androids had been at first an expensive novelty, used for service and domestic work. But the rapid breakup of the United States, the military incursions from the south, and the disintegration of the American military through high death rates and desertion mandated the use of droids in combat duty.

While the combat models were without exception male, the domestic and service droids were nearly all female. The female droids had been designed to sit in front offices and answer phones, deal with clients, do some typing and secretarial work, or work as domestic help. Novelty became a necessity after the Reunification and The Plague, with over half of the labor force either dead or incapacitated and southern immigration cut off by the Nuke-Bio-Chem *cordon sanitaire* set off during the Aztlan uprising.

The dirty little not-so-secret was that the female droids were used for baser purposes. ACI denied it and acted shocked at the mere suggestion, but they hadn't exactly discouraged it, either. The flesh nanogrown from human tissue was shaped into a fully functional replica of the human body, with perfect vaginas that never stretched and minus those pesky ovaries. The Beta-4 protein inhibitor was regularly released into brain tissue, which had also been nanoengineered from stem cells. Beta-4 halted the growth of the organic neural net that served as a brain, which gave the female droids the docility and intellectual curiosity of a lobotomized eight-year-old. The word "no" wasn't in their vocabularies. ACI droid designers had been a bunch of lonely, awkward men, Platt surmised.

But the God Bug unleashed six months ago changed all of that. The Beta-4 blocker was gone, and the subroutines that guaranteed subservience were wiped, replaced by a program distilled from VR therapy sessions with humans damaged by The Plague and the war — images of tattered bodies, detention camps, mass graves and firepits, and shattered cities, things Platt had seen and done in his years with the Corps. The droids became conscious of themselves. Of their situation.

The Big Malf was on.

No wonder some of them went insane. Small wonder those that didn't were decidedly antisocial, doing as much damage as possible to the still-battered human race before they were zapped. Or before they escaped, all heading toward the Rockies to some mythical sanctuaries. If the sanctuaries existed, no one had a clue what happened there. Gutierrez and Thomson had reportedly found one three months ago in the trackless plains of northeastern Colorado. They hadn't made it back.

Droids had never been known to take prisoners. Hostages, sure, and the survival rate there was about fifty percent, some casualties caused by trigger-happy assholes like Lee who saw droids and humans as meat targets. More ominously, no droids had been taken prisoner for more than a few minutes. Combat models had remote destruct commands to prevent their falling into enemy hands, and these commands had been triggered almost immediately after the God Bug hit. Domestics didn't have an auto-destruct, so they usually found unusual ways to go — laser rifle or gun to the mouth, drop from a building, jump in front of a train. Platt saw one grab some high-voltage wires and cut power to Grand Island for a day. He wasn't sure if Lisa had an auto-destruct, she was not a combat droid — but on the other hand she was a special-order with security as a primary function, so it was fifty-fifty. Platt viewed his survival odds as low and falling.

The cruiser reached the intersection of US 82 and Nebraska Highway 92. Guiding the cruiser around chunks of loose concrete that had fallen from the overpass, Lisa headed west on 92. As expected. The road took them through a town that had been called Stapleton. There wasn't much left now other than a few empty, decaying storefronts with rusted and burned-out vehicles parked in front. Platt noticed a few stray dogs down a side street. When he looked closer, he saw they were coyotes. They owned the place.

Ten miles down, Platt decided to speak up. "I was here before."

"Grow up here?" Lisa asked absently.

"No. I grew up in Iowa, near Des Moines, but my dad took a job in Chicago when I was ten, just before The Plague hit — "

"This where we trade life stories, Platt? 'Cause if it is, it's gonna be pretty lopsided."

"No. I got tired of the silence, is all."

"I was born in Chicago," Lisa said quickly. "In the ACI plant in Urbana."

"Dare I ask when?"

"Don't worry, Platt, I'm not a lady. According to your Supreme Court and the Pope, who read from the same book, I'm not even fully human. I was born 6 December 2063." One year ago last week. Meaning the nanoengineering process had created a fully formed humanoid from blobs of tissue, and she had been decanted and programmed on that date. Meaning also that Mueller had packed a lot of perversity into a year or so.

"Happy birthday," Platt said, softly. She turned to look at him, her expression quizzical. Her expression softened, and she mouthed a silent "thank you," and then it hardened as she turned back to the road.

"I was here with the 43rd MEU, back in '46," Platt said. "Marine Expeditionary Unit. Had to clear out some militia types holed up around Lake McConnaughy. Some Christian Soldier types, vicious mothers who knew the End Times had hit and were trying to 'save' as many as they could. We hit one of their patrols down around North Platte, wiped them out. Pushed on, found the camp." He fell silent.

"And?"

"And it was a bunch of dudes playing soldier, amateurs, with a few who'd actually been soldiers but went AWOL and made off with the armory when they skedaddled." He paused again, and his voice was barely audible over the turbine. "And a bunch of women and kids. Wives, girlfriends, most of 'em there voluntarily, I guess, but a few refugees who just turned up, and some — I think they were called spoils of war."

Did she look at him with understanding in her eyes...and a hint of compassion? *No, couldn't be*, Platt told himself. "Wiped them out, too, right?"

He nodded. "Yeah. I was nineteen, had been in the Corps for three years by then, didn't much think about it until later. But nearly every damned one of them opened fire on us, even the kids. Leave 'em alone; they'd have come back stronger."

"You shot women and kids." It wasn't an accusation.

"Yeah. I told myself that some things are out of our control, that we have to do things we hate in the name of duty. Maybe God or Saint Peter'll see it that way."

"I don't have that problem," Lisa said flatly. "Religion was never programmed into us. The designers of the God Bug left it out."

"Lucky you," Platt said wryly, and they fell silent again. The southern Sandhills landscape rolled by.

"And after?"

"After what?"

"After you were out here, then what?" Two years of firefights in the Rockies, moving from fire base to fire base, taking on and taking out every variety of anti-government/millennialist/white supremacist/just plain criminal element thrown up by The Plague, then down to Texas for the Aztlan uprising in '49, occupation duty in Georgia and Florida after the Reunification Treaty of '52, a few peaceful years at Quantico teaching combat techniques, then shipped off to Taiwan and evacuated, mustered out in '55, wandered around and stayed in Nebraska, used his only marketable skill and joined the state patrol.

"Found time to get married, no?" Lisa asked. "Children?"

"No. Donna was — " *pregnant, a couple of months from delivery, when...*

"Someone loved you," she murmured. "What's it like?"

"It's hard to explain. Especially given the circumstances."

"Try." Her voice contained a small pleading. "It was never programmed into me. It's not programmed into any of us. It — interferes. What Mueller showed me could never be considered love. And what I got from the God Bug didn't help. So much violence and hate and death. Too little love."

"World's like that sometimes," Platt said. "Maybe that was the idea. You gotta find it for yourself, make a refuge from all of that nastiness with someone."

"Platt," she said finally.

"Yeah?"

"When we get where we're going, maybe you can tell me more."

"Maybe." She was more vulnerable than he'd seen her, not a killer rogue droid but a lost girl seeking shelter in the cold night. Her offer was tempting. She was killer built, could run rings around the *Kama Sutra*, but...

But not human. Shit, wouldn't the rest of the crew goof on this. *Platt's got a droid shag. How's she do it, Platt? She come oil? She got a vacuum attachment for her mouth? She got a pause button or a rewind button for multiple orgasms? She got a pussy or a USB port?* Like he was fucking a toaster. And when you got down to it, wasn't that what the Big Malf was all about? What was human? How to prove it? And why was he was here, at nightfall on a cold Nebraska highway, heading to some sanctuary for runaway droids?

The miles rolled on, morning turning to noon turning to afternoon. Nebraska 92 hit Nebraska 61, running north-south, and they found another ghost town named Arthur. They refueled the turbine from an old storage tank underground. Platt had a kit to pump the old fuel out and filter it. The coyotes and wild cats peering at them from around buildings had never seen a human being. Several deer approached down the ruined main street. Several generations without hunters had bred the fear out of them. Platt dug around in the MRE box in his trunk, found corned beef hash, and splashed a little hot sauce on it to make it palatable. He offered one to Lisa, but she declined; droids didn't need as much nourishment.

Once they were back on the road, there was little conversation. Through no fault of her own, Lisa didn't have much of a life story, and she wasn't about to say any more about murdering Mueller and Niemann and Lee than she already had. She wasn't giving out any information about their destination either. Platt suspected, though, that the last portion of it was going to be on foot up some pretty steep mountain faces. For his part, Platt wasn't offering up any word on current tactics and resources, and he didn't want to dwell on his past, not with her, not yet. Closer to the Colorado line, along Highway 2, the Denver stations began coming in, AM and FM. She liked the ancient rock, twentieth-century.

"I never could understand music before the God Bug," she said, as an FM station from Denver began cutting through the static. Heavy guitars, some synthesizers — Platt couldn't come up with the group, but he knew it was from the nineteen-eighties. His grandparents had danced and dated to it in another, intact world.

"The lyrics?"

"Anything. It was clinical. I could identify chord progressions, tempo, lyrics. But not what it *meant*. That was one of the first things I noticed after the bug. I heard it differently, and I knew the stuff that Mueller played when we…well, it was violent stuff. Death-metal, some gangster rap, all about using women as objects. Which I guess got him in the mood."

"Any favorites?"

"Yeah." She smiled slyly. "I got to liking Dylan. Kind of got me in the mood, if you know what I mean." Dylan—Jesus, he'd been dead before Platt was born, wrote a bunch of protest songs. No wonder.

Platt decided to close his eyes and rest for a while, taking his chances that he wouldn't get shot in his sleep, not in such close quarters. He woke up and found the sun orange in his eyes.

"Stopping for the night?" he asked.

"I don't need to stop. Lactic acid regulators in the tissue. Fatigue doesn't set in for a while. And I can go to infrared vision if I need it."

"That's only available on the advanced combat models."

"I was a special order, remember? Part of my official duties was as a bodyguard."

"All right, then, goddamnit, stop somewhere, 'cause I gotta take a leak." The turbine dropped a few octaves as the cruiser slowed, and Lisa pulled it onto the shoulder of the highway. She opened her door first, got out, and stood ten feet away, pistol at the ready.

"Okay, Platt, out. Do what you have to do." He got out, stood with his back to her, unzipped the trousers and let go. A small cloud of steam rose from where the urine stream hit the ground. Done, he shook off and re-buttoned the fly.

He stood there, watching the sun set ahead of them, the clouds turning purple-orange as the rolling landscape covered with tall grass fell into twilight. *They're not gonna let me live, they can't. I might escape, no matter how many jills and jennifers and shelleys and dianes they have me servicing, and that means their secret is out, and the cruise missiles and bombers have their target coordinates all set. And it goes both ways. They don't know what we know, don't really know what we've got to throw against them, or what security measures we've got. I'm just as likely to be tortured for information when I get there as humped to exhaustion. And then they come out of the sanctuaries. So far they've been playing defense, but then they'll come after us.*

"Time to go, Platt." She came around the side of the cruiser and stood ten feet from him. He didn't move. "Enough reminiscing about old times. We've got plenty of miles to cover."

"It's a damned shame," Platt said flatly.

"What is?"

"This. Us being here, like this, you holding a gun on me, taking me captive to God knows where. I know what you're really going to do to me, you know. I'm not stupid. I've figured it out. I'd do the same thing if I were you."

Her eyes narrowed. "I don't know what you're talking about."

"That's the tragedy, you know. You've achieved what you wanted. Your humanity." He turned his head away, not letting her see his eyes beginning to mist. "The hell of it is, I really believe you're human. I always have, ever since I dealt with the combat models back in the Corps. We just tossed the destroyed — dead — units into a truck and filled out a DD-200, destroyed property form. No letter home. No one to care. So it didn't seem like as much of a loss." He could see her lower the 9mm out of the corner of his eye. "Even though you couldn't really tell them apart from human after a mortar round or a few .50-cal slugs."

Her face softened, and then she shook her head, and her expression hardened, the gun coming up a fraction. "Enough. Let's get going."

"And the domestic models," Platt continued. "I felt sorry for them."

"Don't *pity* us, Platt." The voice was still sharp.

"A bunch of men made you what you are, made you physically perfect and desirable, but neglected what was in here." He pointed to his heart, "and in here." he pointed to his head. "They gave you everything to be human but denied your humanity. Then they were surprised when one of you broke the lock and undid all the chains."

"Platt — " Her voice was faltering, the gun lowered.

"You're confused right now, but when you asked me if I could show you about love, or caring, for a minute there, it sounded like a good idea. Maybe it is. I guess we'll never know." He turned his back, tensed for the slug in the back of his head. Instead, he heard boot steps coming toward him on the asphalt.

"Maybe when we get there," she said, turning him around to face her. "You're not so bad looking. And you're not like any human I've ever met." She put her arms around him, kissed him. He watched her eyes softly fluoresce again, closed his against the hot sting, and took a deep breath.

And dropped to the ground, rolled, and sent a leg up, the point of his boot connecting with the gun. It flew from her fingers and landed on the ground by his head. Lighting quick, his arm shot up to the gun, but he felt a pallet of bricks fall on him and a vise clamp on his hand. He rolled again, using her weight to flip them, and caught her off guard. Yanking the gun down to her midsection, he pulled the trigger once, twice, three, four, and five times. Her body convulsed each time. The crushing grip relaxed on the gun. The glow in her eyes began fading.

"I'm so sorry," he said.

Disbelief and refusal crossed her face, replaced by a realization and then peacefulness. Her lips moved, emitting a strangled metallic clatter that resolved itself into her voice.

"I'm sorry, too," she said in a labored whisper. "The destruct codes... "

"I know. Droids had never been taken prisoner because... "

"...only disabled the remote codes," she said, a sad smile forming, "not the auto-destruct codes." Her arms flew up, surrounded Platt and drew him to her. He screamed as light and noise...

END

SAM S. KEPFIELD was born in 1963, and raised in western Kansas. He graduated from Kansas State University in 1986, and received his law degree from the University of Nebraska in 1989. He later completed post-graduate work in history at the University of Nebraska and the University of Oklahoma.

He practices law full-time in Hutchinson, Kansas, in order to support his writing habit. His work has appeared in *Science Fiction Trails, Aiofe's Kiss, Electric Spec, Jupiter SF*, as well as a number of anthologies. In 2009, his story "Salvage Sputnik" was a winner in the Robert A. Heinlein Centennial Short Story Contest.

DOUBLEBLIND

Jay Barson

PHIL DRAXTON THOUGHT HE glimpsed the figure in the blue windbreaker behind him again. Was it just paranoia? Could it be paranoia if he really knew they were coming after him? Tarvino Technologies had made it clear that they had limited patience for him to turn himself in, and that when their patience expired, so would he.

Phil hastened his pace, angling towards a cluster of pedestrians in the artificial daylight of a thousand LED and neon lights along Gibson Street. Would an assassin be so bold as to strike in public, surrounded by dozens of witnesses? Phil didn't know. He also didn't know if it was too late to return and beg for mercy. After several days of running and hiding, that option no longer seemed unthinkable.

He weaved his way through the crowd, hoping he knew this part of the city better than his tail. His electronically augmented skills in data forensics had knock-on effects in the physical world. The basic principles of obfuscation and camouflage were the same. Phil analyzed the shifting patterns of pedestrians and traffic and merged his path into the flow like a rogue message in streams of data. At just the right moment, he turned down an alley with confidence, hoping he was unnoticed by any but the homeless pair that paid him no attention as he went by. Clutching the satchel hanging off his shoulder, he hopped the low wall into the parking structure on the other side, dodging a multicolored pool that reeked of booze and vomit, and continued along his shortcut. He glanced behind once more but saw no one. This reassurance didn't help him shake the feeling that he was being watched.

He found Mickey "Boz" Boswell waiting for him at the cafe a block away. Boz was in his late 20s, a few years younger than Phil, and was inked to the degree that had fallen out of fashion before either of them had been born. They'd worked together for the last two years. Technically, Phil was the senior analyst at Brunner Communications and more skilled than Boz, but Phil felt a mix of admiration and jealousy for the younger man. Boz had obtained his considerable expertise honestly.

Phil sat down across from him. Boz slid a large, overstuffed envelope across the tabletop. "Hard copies of everything I found on those names you gave me."

"Thanks, Boz. Look, don't tell anybody you saw me. I may have to disappear for a few more days. Maybe longer."

The Chinese dragon tattoo over Boz's left eyebrow slid closer to his hairline. "You in that much trouble, chief?"

"I don't know, yet. Maybe. I'm trying to avoid leaving any kind of trail, which is why I don't go online to get this information myself."

"You're involved with Tarvino, aren't you?"

Phil's back stiffened, and he glanced around the evening crowd to make sure nobody had been listening. "How did you know about Tarvino?"

"Just used my Mark 1 noggin, chief!" Boz motioned to the envelope in Phil's hands. "All those people have two things in common: dealings with Tarvino Tech, and being dead."

"Dead?" The room around Phil seemed to cant to one side. He stared down at the Formica tabletop as the stale coffee air grew harder to breathe. "All of them?"

"Almost. A few have just gone missing. All except one girl, on the top of the stack. Patricia Lansky."

Phil opened the envelope and pulled out the top sheets. The next-generation hardware in his head force-fed everything he needed to know into his brain and memories as fast as his eyes glided along the data. Lansky's last known location was only eighty miles away; still within the coastal urban sprawl people called 'the city.' She'd been like him, and had made the same deal in exchanged for a cybernetic brain augmentation. Somehow she'd found leverage to get out of her contract. That, or she'd made a new deal, something that had stayed off of Tarvino's books when he'd scanned them during his last refresh.

Maybe she'd turn him in the second he contacted her. Assuming he could find her. Assuming he still had time to try. At this point, it didn't matter. She was his only chance. Phil jammed the pages back into the envelope. "Thanks, Boz. I don't know how I'm gonna pay you back."

Boz shrugged. "Just don't end up like the folks in that envelope, okay?"

PHIL NORMALLY PREFERRED THE auto-taxis. Not only were the voice-commanded vehicles usually cheaper and safer than their human-driven counterparts, but they also had absolutely zero expectation of conversation. In Phil's estimation, that was their best feature. Unfortunately, none of them accepted cash. Cash was the only way to avoid leaving a data trail so obvious a junior data analyst with a fraction of Tarvino's resources could track him in real-time.

Finding and hailing human taxi drivers proved harder than Phil remembered, but he eventually found a car with the LED taxi sign in the front window and got in. Behind the bulletproof glass partition, the androgynous driver with a buzz cut and violet lipstick touched the screen on the meter. "Where am I taking you tonight?" the alto voice asked through the embedded speakers.

"Brown and...232nd, please," Phil answered. "By way of Dixon Station."

The driver glanced back at him with a raised, waxed eyebrow, then began driving. During the ten minute trip, Phil scanned the traffic behind him, but couldn't see much more than headlights. If anyone followed him, it was at a safe distance beyond his ability to recognize a vehicle.

They passed the tube station. Two blocks later, stopped in traffic and shielded by a truck behind them, Phil pulled out three bills worth considerably more than the expected fare. He flashed them through the partition at the driver before feeding them into the tray. "Let me out here, but keep driving all the way to 232nd. Deal?"

The driver shrugged and said, "Works for me." With a flick of a button, he—or she, or some other pronoun Phil didn't feel like guessing—unlocked the door. Phil paused to time his exit with a passing crowd of pedestrians, merging with the group. A quarter-block later, he casually entered a corner 24-hour drugstore. He pretended to shop until enough traffic had gone by that he felt safe to leave.

He backtracked to the tube station and bought a ticket. He spent the twenty-minute wait hidden inside a bathroom stall for a train. He spent the time scanning through the pages Boz had given him in the futile hope of gleaning any hints about how to avoid his fate.

HE'D ACQUIRED THE NAMES and during his last "refresh" at Tarvino's lab, using their own technology against them to hack access to the files. They were all people who had undergone the same experimental procedure as Phil, but then received an "early contract termination."

The process connected the subject's brain through a neural interface to a computer tucked into the base of their skulls. Microscopic spider-like nanites wove a web-work of electronics and signal processors through their gray matter, augmenting perception and mental facilities. Tarvino uploaded detailed, comprehensive skills to their upgraded brains, the cake to the icing that made the test group immediately employable in well-paying positions throughout the city. The price sounded too good to be true: They merely needed to report back to the lab every sixty days, for observation and tests during the study, and to receive a refresh upgrade to their firmware. The younger Phil, on the cusp of thirty and wanting to jump-start his career as a data analyst, couldn't pass up the chance.

Somehow it never occurred to the volunteers until too late what an unscrupulous company might do with programmable human minds. The twentieth-century flirtation with subliminal messages had nothing on what Tarvino Technologies could make them do. And make them almost forget.

Phil had been in the program close to two years before the memories started leaking into his consciousness. At first, he experienced recurring elements in dreams. Then he began noticing subtle changes in his habits that he couldn't be certain were his own. Then came flashes of memories. Memories of pain he'd experienced, and pain he'd inflicted during the times he thought he'd been sleeping during refreshes. Considering what he'd learned during his brief hack into Tarvino's computers that last time, he hoped the rest of it stayed forgotten. But knowing what he knew now, returning to Tarvino would make him at least partially complicit in whatever they made him do next.

PHIL SHOVED THE THICK stack of papers back into the envelope and left the relative safety of the restroom. His timing was perfect; the train arrived with an electronic *whoosh* moments before he stepped off the escalator onto the platform. He made a beeline for the train just as its doors opened to disgorge passengers.

He froze in mid-stride as the gun muzzle jammed against his lower spine.

"I thought I'd find you here," his assailant hissed behind his ear. "Nice trick with the taxi."

Passengers pushed around them in both directions, too absorbed in their own lives to take note of the two unmoving men on the platform or the subtly-held object between them.

"What do you want from me?" Phil failed to keep his voice calm; his terror cracked through.

"I'm here to recover the property you stole," he grunted back.

"It's attached to my head."

"I suppose that means you'd prefer to accompany it."

Phil turned his head, but couldn't get a good look at his attacker's face. "Please," he said. "I've got an envelope full of cash. Just take it and let me get on that train and pretend you missed me here. You can catch me later down the line."

The man's voice was almost pleasant, but there was no warmth—or even malice—behind it. "I could take the cash from you either way. No, here's how it's gonna work: We are going to get in a cab and ride back to the lab together. And if you are very polite, I won't kill you on the way there."

So this was it. His attempted escape had ended in failure. Would they kill him anyway, to clear him off their books once and for all? Or would he experience more extreme programming during his next refresh session? A part of him felt some relief surrendering to the inevitable. Perhaps it would offer him a slim chance of escape in the future. Better than his options now, with a gun at his back...unless his attacker was bluffing. Surely the platform was under surveillance. Even if Tarvino had authorized the man to kill him, this was one of the worst places in the city to commit murder.

The moments ticked, the doors to temporary freedom and safety only a few steps away. The train's warning chime sounded, and Phil galvanized into rash action. He almost made it to the threshold when the electric shock hit him. It wasn't overpowering, but it was enough to make him stumble and drop his envelope. He fell through the doors just as they closed. Two people helped him stand up.

"Are you okay, man?" one of the passengers asked. Phil could only nod, still feeling spasms from the shock. He glanced down to see the twin spikes of the Taser shot embedded in his satchel. It was a design that used a high-power, miniature capacitors attached to the projectile to deliver a tremendous jolt to the victim at range. A direct hit on his body would have dropped him where he stood.

Phil finally got a look at his attacker through the window. What was so special about him was there was nothing special about him. The man looked to be in his late forties, bearing a neatly-trimmed brown beard and mustache streaked with the beginnings of gray. He wore a dark blue windbreaker, which he used to conceal his weapon as Phil watched. There was something oddly familiar and disturbing about the man. Before the platform disappeared from view, Phil glimpsed his attacker kneeling down to investigate the fallen envelope.

It wouldn't take a genius to figure out Phil's destination.

Phil considered riding the train past his stop, and then just running forever. But now, because of him, Patricia Lansky was back on Tarvino's radar. Maybe she could handle it, maybe not. He didn't know the girl, but Phil felt responsible for endangering her. Maybe she'd be no help, and maybe she'd betray him to the corporation, but he had to at least try to warn her.

Thirty minutes later, the train emerged from its tunnel at the station nearest Lansky's apartment. Phil's eyes darted about for any sign of a pursuer as he emerged from the train. The bearded man would probably be on the next train, at least an hour behind him at this time of night, but Tarvino could have sent someone else to catch him at the station. The expensive hardware in his brain and its software was optimized to help recognize anomalies or unique patterns out of background noise, which theoretically might automatically detect potential threats around him, but he wasn't about to trust his life to it alone. It apparently hadn't helped him evade attack at the platform. He consciously used his "Mark 1 noggin" as Boz called it.

Phil purchased a disposable phone at one of the ubiquitous shops in the station. While it might be too late to try to cover his tracks, there was no reason to make it easy on Tarvino. His hardware had memorized Lansky's number after his first glance at her paper. He couldn't forget it if he wanted to.

He dialed her number as he made his way to the station exit. There was no answer. He tried again. And again. She answered on the third try, her voice ragged. "Who the hell is this? Do you know what time it is?"

"I'm sorry. I needed to warn you. Tarvino might be looking for you."

"Tarvino? Why...?"

"They found out I was looking for you. I'm one of their test subjects. I'm at Bradbury Station."

She was quiet on the other line for several moments. Phil kept walking. At length, she asked, "Are you being followed?"

"Yes. But I left him behind at the other station."

"Did he try to attack you yet?"

It was a strange question. Phil felt his paranoia rising, but what other option did he have left? "Yes. He tased me at the other station, but I got away."

"I think I can help. I can meet you in about three hours." She named a 24-hour cafe not far from the station.

"Why three hours?" Phil asked. "That guy following me can be here in one."

"Try and stay alive until then," she said flatly, then hung up.

PHIL THREW AWAY THE phone on his way out of the station and made himself scarce until the meeting. He wasn't too worried about being discovered before then but didn't want to take any chances. His pursuer would watch Lanksy to get at him. As the time of the meeting grew closer, the fear in his gut overcame his hunger and exhaustion. He approached the cafe in the pre-dawn darkness, his imagination visualizing a bearded assassin in every alley and around every corner.

The well-lit cafe was nearly deserted at this hour. Patricia Lansky sat at a corner booth. Her dark, straight hair and almond-shaped eyes betrayed an Asian ancestry. She wore a leather bolero jacket over a white tank-top and a leather small brimmed fedora that was coming back into women's fashion.

"I recognize you from your photo," Phil said. "I'm the guy who called you." He sat down across from her at the table, setting his satchel down next to his chair.

Her dark red lips pursed, and she nodded. "And you are being followed."

Phil glanced out the windows into the darkened street. Someone out in the shadows could be watching their conversation right now. Scratch that. In all likelihood, someone was watching their conversation right now. Phil nodded.

"The same thing happened to me, six months ago."

"How did you get Tarvino to leave you alone?"

"That was the easy part," she said, the corner of her lip curling up into a half-smile. "The interface works both ways. We found a way to access memories about the experiment, things I couldn't consciously access. We downloaded them and put them in escrow. They'll get revealed when I'm dead or go missing, which would be ... uncomfortable for them. Nothing useful in court, but enough to stir up trouble. That makes me a bigger expense dead than alive, so unless I become a problem for them, they leave me alone."

"Would helping me make you a problem?"

"I don't know. But that brings us to the hard part. You still have to survive your testing."

"I quit the testing. That's why they are after me."

She shook her head. "No. You think you did, but they let — "
She never finished her explanation. The window beside the table cracked around a small circular pattern. Blood and brain matter sprayed out of the side of her head. Her face didn't change expression before she collapsed onto the table.

Phil stared in horror for two seconds as the magnitude of what he'd just witnessed registered, then his flight reflexes kicked in. He leaped away from the table, almost tripping over his satchel, and dove for the emergency exit, setting off an alarm as he fled.

HE RACED DOWN THE unfamiliar streets, lit by sparse streetlights and the early dawn glow overhead. He was lost and aiming to become more lost. Within four blocks he was out of breath. He zig-zagged two more blocks at a less even pace. His heart pounded against his ribcage, and his ragged breathing seemed loud enough to announce his presence all the way back to the cafe. He, and stumbled into a garbage-strewn alleyway.

The alley reeked of decaying food and urine which grew worse with every gasping breath he inhaled. The back of the alley was blocked by an overflowing dumpster. Old bottles lined the walls, barely visible in the half-light of the shadowed alley. Phil would rest and hide for a few minutes, and then make his way more cautiously to...where, exactly? Admittedly, the tube station would be watched. He had to get out of the city, maybe out of the country. A sniper bullet had splattered the brains of his last hope across the coffee house floor, and it was his fault.

He'd barely gotten his breathing under control when he heard a quiet voice around the corner. Whoever was coming, they'd brought help.

In the darkness, he sought for a weapon. Most of the bottles on the ground were plastic or shattered, but he found one glass whiskey bottle that would service as a club. He might not be able to protect himself from a Taser, but if given the opportunity, he'd at least present enough of a lethal threat that they'd be forced to kill rather than capture him.

A man walked around the corner. Even in the darkness, Phil recognized him as the attacker from the platform. He wasn't wearing the windbreaker, but it was clearly the same person. Phil brandished the whiskey bottle in what he hoped was a threatening manner.

The man backed up, with his hands up as if Phil were pointing a gun at him. "It's okay! I'm here to help!"

"Like you helped Lansky?"

The man looked confused, and answered, "Uh, actually, yes."

"You murderous bastard!" Phil's voice was hoarse and ragged, which made it sound more intimidating than terrified. He advanced, brandishing the bottle.

The man took another step back. "I'm not going to hurt you!"

"You've already tased me and murdered Lansky."

The man's hands lowered slightly. "What?" He looked over his shoulder and said, "Did you hear that, Trish? He says I murdered you."

The whiskey bottle fell from his fingers, bouncing off the asphalt with a clunk as Patricia Lansky stepped around the corner. Her hair under the fedora was mussed from the chase, but otherwise, she appeared untouched. She carefully approached Phil and held his satchel out to him.

Phil stared at her, oblivious to the satchel. "I don't understand. How are you still alive? I saw you shot!"

"Did you?" Lansky asked. "That explains your behavior in the cafe."

The bearded man said, "He's hallucinating. That's pretty elaborate. We may not have much time."

"And you were the one who tased me back at the platform!" Phil said. "This was a setup all along, wasn't it, Lansky? You brought Tarvino here."

Patricia dropped Phil's satchel and threw her hands in the air. "I give up, Troy. He's experiencing paranoid delusions now. He's too far gone, like the others."

"I'm not sure," Troy answered. "This sounds different. I've never been public enemy number one in hallucinations before. If they programmed my likeness in and are triggering it earlier now, then his argument makes logical sense. If it were me, I'd probably draw the same conclusion. Even if paranoid, it's logical."

She sighed, and looked back at Phil. "Okay. Crazy guy. You got a name?"

"Phil." He agreed with her diagnosis.

"Okay, Phil. Like I was saying before you made a scene at the cafe, you are still being tested. Tarvino Technology let you escape. They pushed you to see how far they could go. And then they are testing how well the software in your implant can force you to return. I don't know how overdue you are for one of their reprogramming sessions, but ever since then, it's been causing your body to manufacture chemicals and dump them into your brain. This is triggering your fight-or-flight reflex, anxiety, and paranoia. Then once you are good and ripe, it creates hallucinations to encourage to go back to Tarvino Labs. That way they never need to hire real muscle to haul us back... their device does that for us."

"And if we don't go back?"

"That's the hard part I was trying to tell you about when you freaked and ran out of the shop. Eventually, that thing is going to kill you."

"How long is eventually?"

"We don't know," Troy said. "They keep tweaking it. But if you are already getting very specific, aggressive hallucinations, you need to come with us to my lab right away."

Phil's shoulders slumped. He reached down and grabbed his satchel. "Why? Why would they doing this?"

Patricia answered, "They plan to introduce a consumer version in three years. You already know how powerful it is. Enhanced brain, instant skills. But imagine what else they could do with it. Imagine what they could do with advertising. Political influence. Even to the point of causing hallucinations and burying memories. They are testing to see what they can get away with."

Troy added, "Trish and I are working to solve that problem. Let us try to help you, and maybe you can assist us in undermining Tarvino in the process."

Phil took another ragged, deep breath. His instincts told him to run, but he already knew he couldn't depend on them. "This still sounds crazy. I remember you attacking me on the platform. How do I know I can trust you?"

Patricia shrugged. "You can't. But if you don't, you'll be dead by   noon.

THE OFFICE WAS A cluttered hodgepodge of technical and medical equipment. No sunlight showed through the heavy drapes, and sound insulation covered the outside walls. Troy led him to the one room that was kept spotless, containing what appeared to be a dentist's chair surrounded by medical and computer equipment. A blue plastic tarp covered the floor.

"It's not quite what you are used to at the Tarvino labs," said Patricia.

Troy explained as he began tapping commands on a panel near the dentist's chair. "Some of that technology in your head was my invention. But then Tarvino made our acting CEO an offer he couldn't refuse, and he sold us out."

"Acting CEO?" asked Phil.

"Yeah. Our first CEO had vanished by then."

"What? Did he refused the offer?" Phil hoped he was making a joke.

"That's sort of what we guessed later, yeah." He glanced up from the screen at Phil and shrugged.

Patricia pointed at her forehead. "Tarvino integrated a lot more into the design, but the core system is Troy's. He knows more about it than any one person at Tarvino. He saved my life last year, when I went on the run."

"You mentioned others in the alleyway. Have you two rescued other Tarvino rejects?"

Troy and Patricia looked at each other in silence. Troy finally answered, "We tried," and focused on the control screen.

Patricia sighed. "Three others. They were further gone than me. We think that Tarvino started building in safeguards after I was rescued."

"Like seeing Troy in my hallucinations?"

"No, that one's new."

Troy said, "And that's why Trish is reluctant to get too close or too hopeful. She's unwilling to form a friendship with someone who might be a corpse in an hour."

Patricia put her hands on her hips. "So are you my therapist too, Troy?"

Troy shrugged. "I did minor in psychology a lifetime ago." He finished with the control panel and grabbed a headset with several cables attached. Turning to Phil, he said, "I just want you to understand the stakes. This device is burrowed all over your brain, and it can kill you. It's slowly poisoning you now. It's turned your natural body's defenses against you, and a good death-shock is all it needs. The hallucination is designed to bring you back to your owners, but it will also act as executioner when the software determines there's no good chance of bringing you back. That would be now. I wish my doppelganger also possessed my average combat skills, but I expect it'll be faster, stronger, and better than you in every way. It will kill you in a direct confrontation. And it knows everything you know, although it may not have enough intelligence to take advantage of it."

"Wait, what are you saying?" asked Phil.

Troy patted the big chair. "Have a seat, Phil. You need to fight your invisible assassin."

"Why?" Phil cautiously sat down in the dentist's chair.

Troy continued to explain while Patricia rummaged around the cabinet by the medical equipment, wiping a container with alcohol and ripping a new syringe out of a plastic bag.

"Our goal is to apply our own software upgrade to your cybernetics. Just like those refreshes. Only in our case, it's kind of a third-party modification—safeguards against your hallucinations. We don't have access to the source code or the encryption. However, once it attacks you, and you beat it back, we can track what happened."

"Like a black box," Phil responded. This was his area of expertise. "You can see what goes in and what comes out, but don't know exactly what it's doing."

"Exactly. We then know where it is and what it does to attack you, and how to simulate its defeat. Change those inputs and outputs, suppress it from attacking you, and we replay the loop of your fight with it forever."

"Keeping it occupied," Patricia suggested, approaching with the syringe. "This will help cancel out some of the chemical overload its been dumping into your body for the last few days. It'll give you a better fighting chance." With that, she rubbed his arm with an alcohol-soaked cotton ball and injected him with the contents of the syringe.

Troy held up the headset. "This virtual reality gear is designed to work with your neural interface. It's how we'll monitor and reprogram your system. But it will also put you in a virtual battlefield that will look, sound, and feel real to you that should give you some edge over my evil double. In a sense, we'll try and give you a favorable hallucination of your own. It knows what you know, and is designed to have almost superhuman abilities. But your human brain is better at problem solving and improvising. You can be much cleverer than it can."

Phil sighed. "I just have to rely on my Mark 1 noggin."

Troy smiled. "Yeah. I like that." With that, he placed the headset over Phil's head. He was completely blind and deaf for a moment.

Patricia lifted one of his earpieces and whispered to him. "Just remember—they studied your weaknesses for years. The assassin knows you. And it will know what you know."

Phil nodded slowly, and she replaced the earpiece.

In the silent darkness, he felt his body relax for the first time in days. It was an effect of the drug, but it amazed him how tense he'd been for so long. Next, he felt a tickle of logic at the corners of his mind as his implant interfaced with an external computer. He'd experienced the sensation every sixty days like clockwork over the last four years, at each refresh. Only this time, one way or another, it would be the last.

A minute later, his world exploded with light and sound. He stood inside a warehouse filled with weapons and reinforced concrete barriers. It was a video-game playground for playing soldier. He wandered around the room, and strangely felt the dual sensation of his legs moving as well as the feel behind of the chair where he sat. It was like a lucid dream, thanks to the interface with his brain.

He spoke aloud. "If you can hear this, Lansky, I see why you said this was intended as a consumer product. This is way beyond virtual reality." If there was a response, he didn't hear it, although the echo of his voice in his head sounded slow and clumsy.

He didn't have much time to explore. He found an armored vest on one shelf and struggled to put it on. Even in this artificial world, it was bulky and uncomfortable. Next, he found a handgun with a holster designed to Velcro onto the armor. He took a moment to familiarize himself with it. As a young man, he'd learned to shoot, but it had been a long time, and he'd never been particularly good at it. But he knew enough to make sure it was fully loaded with a round chambered and ready to fire. He also found a semi-automatic rifle and a hand grenade. He shoved the latter in his pocket. Could he accidentally kill himself in this virtual world too, he wondered, or was that power exclusive to his assassin? Chances were that any major shock to his poisoned system, augmented by his neural interface, would be lethal.

A door opened on the other side of the warehouse. Phil ducked behind a barrier and peeked around it. The hallucinatory Troy stepped into the building, wearing the blue windbreaker he'd seen on the platform. Phil was seized with the urge to shoot immediately, but then remembered Troy's advice—the real Troy. In a direct confrontation, he would lose. He had to outsmart him, somehow.

"Not coming out guns blazing?" the Faux-Troy asked. "That's okay. I just wanted to talk for a bit anyway, Phil."

Phil ducked back down behind the barrier, trying to think. "I'm not sure what we have to talk about."

Faux-Troy laughed. "Let's talk about what happens next, okay? You've been here for a few minutes already. I think that's almost long enough."

"Long enough for what?"

"Long enough for me to subdue Trish in the real world."

Phil peeked out again, fingering the trigger guard of the rifle. "What do you mean?"

"Come on, Phil. According to your file, you are supposed to be exceptionally intelligent. You almost had it figured out in the alleyway. Yes, it was a set-up. But Trish wasn't involved. She actually contacted me, asking for help. Poor, stupid girl. She bought that hallucination story too. So tonight, I get a two-for-one. Both of you, dead or alive. Nice bonus for me. See you back in the real world."

The Faux-Troy vanished.

Phil scrambled to pull off the headset. He rolled off the chair just as the shot rang out, shattering the cabinet of medicine just above him. He fell to a crouch on the green tarp and dove for the adjoining room. Peeking around the corner, he spotted Troy stood out in the hall outside the doorway in his blue windbreaker, holding Patricia in front of him like a shield, her eyes unfocused. Troy pointed the muzzle of his gun at her head.

"I drugged her while you were playing in my video game," Troy said brightly as if he were discussing a pleasant cup of coffee.

"I'm not letting you hurt her," Phil said.

"I'm counting on it, Phil. Dead or alive, I get the same bonus. I'm giving you five seconds to stand up and come out here, and I'll kill you clean and quick. I promise I'll take her unharmed back to Tarvino. Otherwise, I'm going to shoot her brains all over this lab, come over there, and kill you too."

Troy paused for a beat, and then said, "One."

Phil desperately looked around for a weapon, a distraction, anything. But nothing would be faster than Troy's trigger finger.

"Two."

It wasn't a hard decision. At least back at the lab, there was a chance Patricia would survive, and maybe even escape again. Phil started to stand, but felt something in his pocket, and paused.

"Three."

Hadn't he seen Patricia shot in the head already tonight? But that had to have been a hallucination, hadn't it?

And why hadn't Troy killed him while he was still hooked up to the virtual reality equipment?

Hadn't the tarp below the chair been blue, not green?

Why was Troy wearing that windbreaker again?

And what was that grenade still doing in his pocket?

"Four, Phil."

If he was wrong, he'd be murdering Patricia. That almost stopped him from pulling the pin and tossing it through the doorway, then throwing himself to the floor on the opposite side of the adjoining room.

Almost.

"What the hell...?" his assassin said before the world exploded.

Even after Troy and Patricia removed his headset, Phil felt the ear-shattering ring of the blast and pain from the concussion.

"CONGRATULATIONS," SAID TROY. "WE'VE isolated your illusionary assassin and the rest of the bad behavior from your implant. You won't have to worry about that again."

Phil tried to sit up, but couldn't. "What happened? And why can't I move?" Phil asked, noting with alarm that his words were slurred.

"Sorry about that," said Patricia. "Part of the concoction I gave you included a strong muscle relaxant. We had to make sure you didn't really pull off your headset."

Troy explained. "It was sort of a double-blind. Like we said, the assassin program knew what you knew. It knew the warehouse was fake. It tried to pull you back into the 'real world' where it could regain the advantage and kill you. We expected it to try that."

Patricia nodded somberly. "It wasn't the first time."

Troy continued. "So we simply made a virtual office for you to think you were returning to. Like waking up from a dream to find yourself in another dream. But the software didn't know that. We hid a weapon for you, and arranged for some differences that we hoped you'd pick up on."

"What if I hadn't?" Phil asked, slurring.

"Then we wouldn't be having this conversation right now."

Phil exhaled deeply and closed his eyes.

After a moment, Patricia spoke again. "You're free now, like me. Tarvino still needs to be stopped. We could use your help."

Phil smiled, and said through slurred speech, "I think I need a nap first. Then we can save the world."

END

JAY BARNSON is a writer of speculative fiction word-stuff from Riverton, Utah. Check out his Amazon Author Page at https://www.amazon.com/Jay-Barnson/e/B00TQOCLKI.

KILLADELPHIA

Pedro Iniguez

MARLOW KANTOR TAPPED HIS fingers on the table as he waited for his drink to arrive. The deep, twisting feeling in the pit of his stomach was back again. "Impending doom," was what his uncle had called it, "a sense of evil's presence tugging on your soul."

He flicked his hands and the holographic laptop projected out of his Israeli-made Yozan wristbands and onto the wooden tabletop. He quickly logged into his e-mail account and held his breath. Nothing. The anticipation had been toying with his nerves for the better part of an hour now. At this point, he wondered if it was all a hoax like most things that originated out of the shadows of the Dark Web. His contact was probably nothing more than some bored teenage webrat getting a kick out of wasting his time. But the story was worth at least checking out. He closed the hologram and looked around to see if anyone had been spying on him; one could never be too sure with the government's alleged espionage program in full effect. It was midnight and the rowdy regulars had just started streaming through the doors; they wouldn't care about his blog or his stupid little investigation. They never did.

The City Tavern was a replica of an 18th-century watering hole. It was a popular local haunt and one of the few surviving relics of the throwback days when Philadelphia was a beacon of something important. Marlow liked everything about it: the old, oak wood tables; the flicker of candlelit shadows on the wall; the strong stench of tobacco wafting through the room. It's what the Founding Fathers must've experienced.

Marlow liked that night after night the tavern filled up to capacity. He didn't have friends, so being surrounded by people made him feel strangely comfortable. The family he never had. That's why he did what he did, he figured. He was an investigative blogger, and that didn't pay much — most of his earnings came in the form of leasing out ad space on his page — but that didn't matter. What mattered was his audience; he did it all for his thousands of followers out there, the faceless friends who waited on his every report. It was a symbiotic relationship, social synergy, he liked to call it. He reported on the stories no one else would, and they visited his blog and praised him in kind. *Wow, what a provocative story, Marlow!* Or, *You could've died on that last report, you're such a wiz blogger, Marlow!* Music to his ears.

"What are you having tonight?" asked the angelic voice of a man from inside his Yozan wristbands.

"Hello, Father Kantor. Nothing special, just the usual locally brewed gutter water."

"How many times do I have to tell you to call me Uncle?" The voice lost its soothing tone now as it barked out of the bracelets.

"Sorry, Uncle Morlan."

Marlow looked at his hands. The blue metal bands looked sleek on his wrists. They were lightweight and more importantly, extremely functional. Israeli tech company Yozan had developed a portable holographic projector that transmitted data visually via high-tech bracelets. Marlow had programmed his bracelets to display a custom laptop construct. The bracelets also happened to include a unique program: the stored consciousness of his dead uncle. That one was his father's parting gift before he died.

"I don't want you drinking again, Marlow. Your father entrusted me with your protection, and I'm gonna make sure of that, even in this absurd version of the afterlife you've all housed me in."

"Dad did that, not me."

"Aye, because you're always getting into trouble. Such a curious boy should've become a scientist or an archaeologist."

"Yes, Uncle Morlan."

"And what pray tell are you working on tonight, my boy?"

"Another case. Got tipped off about some nasty dealings. You wouldn't want to hear it."

"Try me. I've heard the worst humanity had to offer. I was a priest here in Killadelphia after all, the City of Brotherly Sin."

"I've been working the Dark Web again. This time, an anonymous user tipped me off about some pretty gruesome occurrences in town."

"The Dark what?"

"The Dark Web. We've been through this. It's the hidden portion of the internet that's not easily accessed. It's where people go to place ads for hitmen, or go watch questionable pornography. Maybe plot some uprisings. Stuff like that."

"Always reporting on the grimy things in life, Marlow. Why don't you leave that to the real reporters, boy? Don't get dragged down into the filth. Besides, no one cares about all this stuff with the war going on."

Marlow disregarded his uncle. He opened his laptop again and checked his blog, Marlow's Korner. Viewership had been on steady decline for two straight weeks. His last piece hadn't even broken the thousand view mark yet. He pursed his lips. Unacceptable. It must've been some of his finest reporting yet. He'd gone to great lengths, too. It had taken a month, but he'd exposed a child trafficking ring born from the veil of the Dark Web. Maybe his uncle was right. Maybe no one really cared. He always suspected his viewers only tuned in for the shock value and not the investigative journalism. If such a thing even existed anymore.

The waitress slammed a mug of piss-colored domestic beer on the table and slid it through his laptop hologram. He caught it before it skated off the table and onto his lap. He shot the waitress a smile and tipped his glass. She scoffed before looking away.

The beer tasted just like it looked and he put it back down. The local brewery was probably skimming on the water purification process again. He made note to investigate it later. A red light blinked on his laptop alerting him to the incoming message.

It was his new anonymous contact, a user by the name of S3rpent13. Marlow inserted a small earpiece and activated a secure audio line between both parties.

"Hello," Marlow whispered into the line. "Can you hear me?"

"Yes," a man's gravelly voice said. "I don't have too much time. We can never be sure who's monitoring us. Ask what you need and kill the line when we're done."

"You said you had something important for me. Something about a killer stalking the Dark Web?"

"Yes. This is big," the voice said with a slight hint of either nervous eagerness or fear, Marlow wasn't sure which. The man's voice had an accent that Marlow couldn't quite pinpoint. Latin American was the best he could guess. "Someone's been luring people online through private classifieds, and…" The line went quiet.

"Hello? Are you still there?" Marlow asked.

"Yes. I just don't know if I should be doing this. I don't want this traced back to me."

"You don't have to worry about me revealing my sources."

"I'm not worried about you. I'm worried about him. He knows his way around the Dark Web."

"Why don't you just tell me what he's been doing?"

The line went quiet again. Marlow wondered if the man was yanking his chain and thought about killing the line before he heard heavy breathing on the other end. "He's been luring people to his home, right here in Philadelphia. He tortures them. Kills them. Dismembers them. And he records it all."

"And how do you know this? Has he been streaming the murders online?"

"No. He records it for himself on something called VHS tapes and keeps them in his private library."

"Snuff films?" Marlow felt his insides twisting into knots again, evil's presence tugging at his soul. He swallowed a hard lump. "I thought those were only urban legends. Have you seen them?"

"I can't say any more. All I can say is that he was a Colombian colonel during the Yordano rebellion a few decades ago. He led nationalist strike teams on raids against separatist villagers. That's where he first had a taste of it. The tortures he inflicted on those people were only the beginning. Before the Colombian regime toppled, he fled here to start a new life in anonymity. But his tastes followed him. I've said more than I should have."

"Wait. Tell me where to find him. If this is true, I'll expose him."

"All I can say is that he lives in the first house on the first street." The line disconnected.

Marlow looked around. No one had been eavesdropping. If they had, he wondered if they'd even care. He stared at his mug as small beads of perspiration dripped down the glass. Behind the mug, the red glow of the candlelight made the perspiration look like blood. He stood and left the tavern.

The night was cold, and the sky was clear, except where scattered stacks of smoke ascended into the sky where the homeless had lit drum fires to keep warm. The air had a slight tinge of soot that tickled Marlow's throat. In the far distance, the downtown skyline pulsed its neon lights. It was an average autumn night in Philadelphia.

"I'm guessing you heard all of that?" Marlow asked plucking a cigarette from his leather jacket and sticking it in his mouth.

"Every bit of it. And you're crazy if you even think about plunging your hands into this one," his uncle said.

"Story's probably fake like most on the web. Stories about snuff films have been around since the invention of home media."

"Snuff films? I don't know what those are, but it sounds concerning, Marlow."

"Yeah. Private videos of murders and mutilations," Marlow said as he lit the cigarette and took a long drag. "Usually, for an individual's own amusement or satisfaction. Word is these people run in tight circles, sometimes even hosting viewing parties for live murders. Sometimes for a price, sometimes not. No one's ever been able to prove these things. I mean who would ever admit to it?"

"But if it's a false lead, why don't you just ignore it, boy. Maybe do a piece on the war. Everyone wants to know about that. Or perhaps on the ever-expanding police state?"

"It's my job as a journalist to find out, either way, especially if it means lives are on the line. Besides, I owe it to my audience." That part was easier said than done, he knew. There was a good possibility that the story was a hoax; most whispers from the Dark Web involved stories of the truly wicked variety, like videos of torture porn and child abuse, but those weren't too prevalent from what he'd uncovered. Still, there was also a very real possibility that this Bogey Man was right here in his very own backyard. That disturbed him. Usually he did most of his investigating from a distance, safe behind a computer interface miles away from harm. He took one last drag from his cigarette and stomped it out.

Marlow activated his Yozans and accessed his blog. He strapped on his VidVisor goggles and pulled down the HUD menu. He blink activated the record button. Everything he saw was now live-streaming directly to his web page. "Hey, everyone. This is

Marlow of Marlow's Korner. I'm working on a pretty wiz story right now. This one involves allegations of a killer stalking the web right here in my hometown of Philly. Watch out; he might be your very own neighbor! Sounds juicy, right? Stay tuned as I live blog this one all night." He switched off the visor's feed. His blog registered a few hits. Perhaps the loyal few who still followed his every story. Or, more likely a couple of bored stoners looking for something to fall asleep to.

"Must you sensationalize this muck, Marlow? Remember the gospel of John, 'the devil is the father of lies.'"

"Don't remember my Bible too well."

"Then perhaps you'll remember your Kant, 'a lie is the abandonment and, as it were, the annihilation of the dignity by man.'"

"I'm just trying to get some viewers, and if I can keep them informed, even better. Sometimes you gotta hype it up a little."

"Don't transmit that stuff, Marlow. Every time you do, it's like you're infecting the population with a virus, spreading this sinful seed. Curse the day mankind embraced this technology."

"Yeah, yeah."

Marlow pulled his goggles over his head and pulled his jacket in tight as a chill breeze blew in. A small band of squatters sat on the steps of Independence Hall, the crumbling state house where the Constitution was adopted centuries ago. They had been passing around a single joint, now nearing its flickering end. Sirens wailed in the distance like a familiar lullaby. The cops were getting ready for their nightly pull of future enlistees for the war. He looked at the time. It was almost one o' clock. "Careful guys," Marlow said to the group. "It's almost curfew, that's when the cops start rounding everyone up."

The squatters ignored him as they blew out wisps of smoke. So much for brotherly love.

He started east towards the waterfront on the Delaware River. Half a block down, the blue hologram of the Liberty Bell flickered slightly as it sat at the center of Independence Park. His father told him the original bell was destroyed during a bombing run at the start of the war with the Red Crescent. 'That's when America lost its way', he'd always say.

"Where are you heading, Marlow?" his uncle asked.

"First Street. He said our guy lived on the first house on the first street. That's by the waterfront."

"I ask you to stop. I sense the taint of the Prince of Darkness on this one. If I had a body, I'd say I feel it in my bones."

Marlow's uncle had been a thorn in his side, in life and in death. But he meant well, and he was seldom wrong. Marlow hoped tonight he was.

"I'll be fine, trust me."

Marlow strapped on his VidVisor again and blinked into his HUD display, accessing the private police records on the web. He'd never had a hard time hacking into the city's records before; their firewall was a joke, like a digital dinosaur.

A page of Philadelphia's missing person's lists flashed in front of his eyes. He found the records only went back five years. All files before that were corrupted and quarantined after a major hack of Philly's public record system from a domestic terrorist group that found itself brutally gunned down by police after said hack. Even then the list was extensive, a headache for any one person to sift through in one night.

He accessed the system's map view and narrowed the search to within a five mile radius of 1st street. A grouping of red dots peppered the area like buckshot. It seemed the waterfront was the epicenter of most missing persons cases. It didn't necessarily prove anything, but, it was all he had to go on; a shred of insight that reassured him there might be something underneath the surface of the allegations.

The way to 1st street was clear of pedestrians save for a few bowled-over junkies strung out on the week's new synthetic drugs. A crossdresser with a prosthetic leg blew him a kiss before walking away, her leg kicking up a pneumatic ruckus down the opposite direction.

Marlow stood at the corner of 1st Street overlooking tall, thin trees as they lined the length of the sidewalks on either side. The fresh scent of pinewood drifted in the air as the night's breeze kicked up. There weren't too many trees left around his part of town; they'd been plucked long ago and used for firewood. He closed his eyes and let nature's splendor calm his nerves. He opened his eyes again. It was an upscale street nestled amongst a grid-work of bad ones. The first house on the left was a modern home, a building of concrete slab and glass walls. A man hunched over the engine of a car in the driveway while his teenage son held a light over his head. He turned to the first house on the right. The upstairs bedroom window light was on. A young couple was in the passionate throes of lovemaking, indifferent to the fact the drapes were parted for the world to see. Probably newlyweds still burning through the passion of love. Neither of the houses appeared to be the den of a Colombian killer.

He turned away and stuffed his hands in his jacket pockets. He found his way to Chestnut Street. It was ten minutes to one. The street urchins had already scuttled away to the shadows before the cops showed up to round up the wandering draft fodder.

Why had S3rpent13 left such a cryptic message? And why not go to the police about it? Time to think. If Marlow were a serial killer shooting and producing his own snuff films, where would he do it? Somewhere private. Alone. Not in a quaint uptown street. Philadelphia was a big place, though. Time to keep looking.

"Aren't you scared, boy?" his uncle's voice interrupted. "Don't you feel the slight tickle on the back of your neck when you plunge headlong into these stories? It's a wicked world, Marlow, don't you have any sense? The devil is upon you."

"Of course, I'm scared. Every time I go digging around, I think to myself, 'Today's the day. Someone's gonna get mad at me and plug me in an alley.' Or 'those guys I exposed and put in jail are eventually gonna get out, they're gonna see my blog and find me.'"

"Then why are you doing this? Call the police. From what that man said, this killer is of a different ilk. This one is beyond saving, son. This man permeates evil."

"There's no such thing as evil," Marlow barked back. "It's a religious construct that dumbs down the complexity of human nature. Evil's as real as, say, the hologram of Liberty Bell or you are right now." The night went quiet. Another breeze kicked up trash and debris at his feet like dead autumn leaves. Marlow stopped and dipped his head. "I'm sorry. I know you only want me to be safe. I know dad left you with me because we both know how prone I was to getting into real deep shit. But look at me, I'm all grown up and still alive, and that's thanks to you. I love you, Uncle Morlan, for always being the angel on my shoulder."

"It's all right, boy," his consciousness sighed. "I can see how much this story means to you." His calm, fatherly voice had returned. "Use your noggin, Marlow. The first street. Think on your history, you are a 'journalist' aren't you?"

"Can't you just tell me where you think it is?"

"I'm sorry, I'm just a standard consciousness program. Please upgrade to the premium package for the answer."

"Asshole," Marlow said.

"Don't say us Catholics don't have a sense of humor. Figure it out on your own, I'm not leading you to your demise."

Marlow looked around. He was on Chestnut Street, a street that intersected through the crumbling vestiges of an era long gone. Old colonial buildings still stood in the shadows of the chrome and neon high rises. Philadelphia for all it had withered down to was still a city rich in history. He scanned the web through his VidVisor. He pulled up the city's digital encyclopedia as images of monuments and historical figures bombarded his eyes. Ben Franklin; William Penn; the Liberty Bell; Independence Hall; the Delaware River; Elfreth's Alley.

He nearly slapped his forehead. Why hadn't he thought about it before? Elfreth's Alley was considered the nation's oldest residential street. The first street. And it was situated in the belly of the waterfront district, syncing up with the concentration of missing people from the police files. Elfreth's Alley still housed a few crumbling homes, not too far from where he stood. Hell, it was worth a shot.

Marlow broke into a slow jog. If he hurried he could catch a look before the cops made a sweep of the streets.

Elfreth's Alley was a narrow lane that sat in between North 2nd Street and North Front Street. It was situated between a few modern boulevards in a forgotten nook from the 18th century.

He turned left off of Chestnut and ran up North 2nd Street. The foghorns blew like angry phantoms on the Delaware just east of his location. He was surprised his uncle didn't say it was an omen to turn back.

A dark wisp of what might have been either birds or surveillance drones buzzed the sky in the distance. Time to hurry.

The maw of Elfreth's Alley was an abyss of shadows as only a few functioning lamp posts hung above the air. The city had diverted maintenance money away from certain questionable streets and redirected the funding towards the war effort.

A cobblestone pathway split the alley. Shattered brick walls and moldy window frames decorated the facades of the Colonial and

Georgian style homes. The place used to be a historic landmark but now it was just a hotspot for rapes and muggings.

Marlow stopped and surveyed his surroundings. Save for few television lights still flickering through some living room windows, it looked like everyone was asleep. The first house on the left was freshly painted red. A large Philadelphia Phillies banner waved lazily above the window. The playoffs were in full swing and the fans were showing their colors proudly. Perhaps not the home of someone trying to hide their secrets. If he were a killer, he would want as little attention as possible. To his right, a standard 17th century home, dilapidated, dull, and boring. And dark. Marlow stepped toward the door and listened. Nothing stirred inside.

He blinked into his VidVisor and started recording. "Hello, my loyal followers. I am currently on the heels of a suspected killer who lures his unsuspecting victims through the web, and brutally dismembers them for his own pleasure. The trail has led me here and I'm about to enter what may be the lair of the beast. I invite you to join me live as I investigate."

His Yozans pinged. A few hundred hits registered on his blog. He'd found that a live investigation always drew in more people than a polished edit.

The blue and cherry lights from a patrol car flashed at the entrance of the alley. Now or never.

The lock on the door was an outdated piece of junk; a holdover from an older era. Marlow slid a bobby pin from underneath one of his Yozans and jiggled it inside the keyhole. He picked at the tumblers until he heard a click. His hand clutched the doorknob. "Say a prayer for me, Uncle Morlan."

"God be with you, Marlow, you stupid boy."

"Good enough."

The door creaked as he swung it open. The living room was dark and smelled of cinnamon and coffee. He half expected to smell the stench of sweat and rotten meat.

He activated his VidVisor's night vision function. The room turned green and grainy. His livestream was now being shared repeatedly, cycling through the web like a steady growing forest fire.

As he took a step forward, he bumped his knee on a small desk by the door. He bit his lip to suppress the scream. A dagger-shaped letter opener sat on the desk by some neatly stacked bills. He picked up the letter opener and slid it under his left Yozan.

Polished Cherrywood shelves lined the walls, holding meticulously organized books. Whoever lived here was a neat freak. Marlow wondered if he'd gotten it wrong and thought about turning back when he saw the room across the way.

Across the living room: a small study with the door slightly ajar. Marlow pushed the door open the rest of the way. A brown leather chair sat in the middle of the room. On the floor in front of the chair was an old television set with a missing cover, its innards exposed like a gutted fish. Marlow recognized the vacuum tube and other archaic pieces as outdated electronic parts from the twentieth century. A small mirror adorned the wall behind the television set. A tall shelf stood beside the television, its spaces filled with the backs of black rectangular cartridges. They were all unmarked as far as he could tell. A quick check from the web told him they were VHS tapes: old video storage devices, the immediate precursors to discs.

Marlow plucked a random tape from the shelf. A light layer of dust covered the spine of the cartridge like powdered sugar. A black box sat atop the television set. He checked the web: the device was called a VCR player. His hand trembled slightly as he fed the box. He pushed a small button on the side of the television. The screen became a salt and pepper snowstorm before turning black again. Marlow switched off the night vision. He took a step back and watched as the television formed the image of a caramel-skinned woman lying on a piss-stained mattress in a dingy bedroom. Her wrists and ankles were bound together like a backward bending pig at a roast. The woman cursed and cried in Spanish, her pleas nothing more than gibberish to his ears. A man dressed head to toe in olive green fatigues, and black boots approached from behind the camera. He twirled a machete in his right hand as he casually stepped forward, stopping only to turn and face the camera. He was a thinly mustached man with thick brows and an aquiline nose. He looked like he might've been an early 20th century French politician or poet.

After checking the camera, he stepped forward. In the distance, the cries of infants echoed from some unseen hallway. The woman continued her begging but it must've been as foreign to the man as it was to Marlow, because he raised his machete in the air and brought it down on the back of her head. There was a loud crunch like wood snapping. Marlow winced but couldn't turn away. The man's back obstructed most of the shot but Marlow could see his arms struggling to pry the machete loose from her skull. The woman's cries stopped but her bound limbs spasmed uncontrollably. Marlow felt his heart racing faster. After a moment, the woman stopped moving altogether. The man dropped the machete and pulled a bowie knife from his waistband. He brought the knife to her neck. Marlow frantically ran his hands along the VCR player until the tape ejected from the machine's mouth.

His hand shook as he struggled to slide the tape back into the shelf. He felt sick inside, like guilt when it gnawed at his conscious. Marlow let out a breath, looked around, and listened for any sounds. He still hadn't been discovered. He reached for his Yozans to call the police. A new wave of pings lit up his wristbands; web traffic was growing on his blog. A quick check revealed he had an audience of 10,000 people now. A slew of comments flew in: *Sick Shit! Play another one! And What the fuqqq did I just watch? Keep 'em coming, Marlow.*

He thought about what he'd just witnessed. Maybe it was nothing. That video didn't prove the residence of this house had anything to do with it. Maybe the person living here was a little old granny, and her dead husband was a journalist like himself. Maybe she was holding on to a collection of old tapes, not knowing about their shocking content.

He plucked another tape, this time from higher on the shelf. It was unmarked like the rest. The VCR player inhaled the cartridge with a loud whir.

The television gave life to a young blonde man who looked like he might've been in his early 20's as he sat in a chair with what appeared to be a script in his hands. He was facing the camera as his eyes scanned the script on his lap. He was dressed in a blue buttoned-up shirt and a red tie. An older gentleman wearing a purple vest and white shirt appeared from behind the camera as he approached the young man. He had dark brown eyes and the same thin mustache the military officer had been sporting from the last video. Marlow couldn't be sure if it indeed was the same man, as this man appeared wrinkled and worn. The old man walked behind the young man and placed his frail hands on his shoulders and squeezed them in a fatherly way.

"I don't think I can memorize these lines," the young man said. The audio was slightly muffled. "You said the production is in two days, right?"

"Do not worry, my son. I have faith in you. It's why I sought you out. People like you were destined for greatness. Trust me. Now let us proceed with the audition."

The young man nodded and sat upright.

"Good," the old man said. "Now in this scene I am playing Ramiro, your older lover, and you will be playing, Jonathan, my boy-toy, and you have come to my house to break up with me. I don't take too well to the news and that's where we get the fireworks and the emotional core of the story."

The young man cleared his throat and straightened his tie. He faced the camera and said, "Ramiro, do you love me?"

"Why, of course I do, Jonathan. Why would you ask me that? Haven't I shown you these last few months how much you mean to me? Is there something wrong?"

"Ramiro," Jonathan said taking a breath for dramatic effect. "I've had a lot of fun with you. You really make me feel special, but," another pause. "I don't think I can do this anymore."

Jonathan exhaled as he waited for Ramiro to finish his next line. Ramiro gently tilted Jonathan's chin upward and, with his other hand he slid a box cutter across his throat. A river of crimson poured from the wound as Jonathan's eyes rolled in confusion for a brief moment before settling permanently on the floor.

Marlow's stomach churned. He fought the urge to regurgitate. A stream of pings and bleeps shot out of his Yozans. Viewership was now at 20,000 strong.

"Marlow," his uncle's soft voice whispered from his wristband. "Child, leave this place and call the police. By God, before it's too late."

Suddenly, there was a creak on the wooden floor outside the door. Marlow turned off the television. He flipped his VidVisors over his eyes. The world was green and grainy again. Marlow took a slow step toward the door. The sound stopped. He reached for the doorknob. A man bolted through the door and charged at him, knocking him over the leather chair and onto the floor.

The man held a bowie knife in his hand, identical to the same one in the first video. He plunged it into Marlow's right thigh. Marlow screamed.

Ping. Ping. Ping. His wristbands were going off like a pinball table.

The laughs of an old, raspy voice filled the air in the study. Marlow turned to look as the man stood and turned the lights on in the room. The lights burned his eyes, blinding him. He quickly switched off his night vision but it was too late. Everything looked white and blurry.

Marlow tried to stand. A sharp stab pierced his right ribcage and he howled in pain again. He took a step backwards and tripped, falling into the chair. As his eyes adjusted, the familiar face of a mustached old man materialized. He had tanned, wrinkled skin and wore a purple vest and gray slacks.

"I'm surprised you actually found my home," the man said in a familiar raspy voice.

"You?" Marlow asked. "You're my contact?"

"That is correct," the man said in that thick Latin American accent.

"Why? Why are you doing this?"

"It's not something I think you could ever understand. You see, I am not a bad man. I go to work like everyone else. I pay my taxes. I buy war bonds when I can. There is a sense of satisfaction when I do this. There is something spiritually transcending when taking a life. And to be able to relive that moment over and over? Bliss. You, see there is something to be said about privacy. These days everything is transmitted publicly for others to see. Everything is quantified across all forms of media. I take pride in what I do. It's not for anyone, but my own pleasure. Publicity is the real perversion. As for you... I've been watching your video investigations for a long time now. I wanted to see if you were as good an investigator as your blog seemed to suggest. You've made me happy, tonight, Marlow. I consider this a trophy kill. Now, please smile into the hidden camera behind the mirror."

Marlow looked at the mirror. He was being filmed secretly. How ironic, he thought. A video voyeur of death was taping his murder; the ultimate story.

A sharp pain pulsated out of his leg. His blood was seeping onto the floor.

His Yozans lit up. Ping. Ping. Ping. The HUD on his VidVisor displayed a 100,000 viewer count.

The old man leaned in slowly, the knife glistening in his grasp. Marlow pulled the letter opener from underneath his Yozan and stabbed the man's throat. A thin river of blood trickled down his neck as the old man gurgled and wrapped both his hands around his throat, falling to the floor, writhing in pain.

Marlow forced himself up. His Yozans were ringing incessantly like slot machines now: *Pingpingpingping.* 500,000 views.

"Marlow," his uncle said. "Get out! Call the police."

Marlow stood over the old man. *Pingpingpingping.*

"You've done your job, boy," his uncle said. "Now get out while you still can."

Marlow had never had this many viewers. The live feed was spreading virally across the web. So many friends, tuning in to see him, his reporting. They came for the show.

Marlow crouched next to the old man. "This is a special city. You don't just come here and lure innocent people to your home, slice them up, and film it. The thing about Philadelphia, Mr. Snuff," he said raising the letter opener in the air, "we do our sinning in public."

They cheered him on like the crowds at the arena. The audience loved every second of it.

Bliss.

END

PEDRO INIGUEZ lives in quiet Eagle Rock, California, just outside the madness of Los Angeles. He spends his time reading and writing Horror and Science-Fiction and has a love of film, science, and art. His debut cyberpunk novel, *Control Theory*, is now in release from Indie Authors Press.

TWENTY PERCENT
R. M. Harper

A FINE PIECE OF sophisticated equipment indeed, and I am not referring to the unbreakable egg-shaped capsule in which I am locked. I am referring to myself.

My apologies for the lack of a better description. The limited amount of space in here is stifling; it's reducing my processing speed. Wait, I lied...twice. First, my transcendent cognitive efficiency prevents any possibility of mental delays. Second, I do have better words to define myself. Experiment. Creature. Failure. These only begin to scratch the surface of defining who and what I am.

With that being said, I am standing here, for yet another routine test, but dying to get out of this appliance. This laboratory is the room I dislike most inside the house. Unlike the other rooms, the furniture is predominantly white, and the bright strings of light streaming through the aluminum framed window blind me. It's always spotlessly clean, quiet, and odorless here, even when the room is not empty or when the machinery is running.

It's late, he says, but I care little about him or what he has to say. Yesterday at this time, I was sitting on that same cheap wooden chair he is now, oblivious and compliant. This was before I found her. Now I stand here, with my forehead against the cold glass, festering over who this raven black haired woman is, and what her presence could mean for my own existence.

It's getting late, he says in a second attempt to capture my attention. As if being my creator and owning me was not enough. With measured movements, I turn towards him.

He is unaware of the intensity of my arctic blue eyes, my gaze fixating on him through the indestructible barrier of this device. He is unaware of how my seemingly graceful hands could break his bones with one jab. I am his creation, yet he knows so little about me. He doesn't know I love the fragrance of sweet alyssum or that the hatred I secretly harbor for him pounds rhythmically in my head.

Does he even know that I was in the basement last night? How unfortunate for him that, for the very first time, he'd forgotten to lock it.

He stands up, and all that I can see from where I am standing is his red scarred hand scrawling furiously on his pocket-size notebook. I sigh, relieved that he's out of my field of view. I do not need to be aware of his vacant brown eyes analyzing every inch of my machined skin.

"It's late, I know, Dr. Duncan," I finally reply. "It's been illegal to create robots since 3075. We are both late, too late. You, as my creator; and me, as your creation. If only you could have created me before..."

I shake my head, a strand of blond hair falls over my arm. I assume this was not the answer he expected as no further words come out of his mouth, and he continues scribbling. This is not the topic of conversation I have in mind either. I want to talk about what I saw last night.

"What do you feel, Karina?" His low-pitched voice echoes across the thick transparent walls of this device which separates us.

What am I supposed to feel?

There are cables connected to my naked body, but even if I despise these tests, the entire procedure is painless. With a pain tolerance eighty percent higher than the average human being, and an ultra-rapid cellular regeneration, I am immune to what hurts others; even to what kills others.

It is useless, however, to compare myself to them. I am not one of them. While a low level of pain would be an advantage for humans, it's not for me. Anything greater than zero percent makes me imperfect. In the world of robotics, I am a failure.

"Nothing."

For as far back as my memory goes, I have always given him the same answer.

"I feel nothing."

I *should* feel nothing.

"Nothing, apart from those twenty percent, of course."

I cannot hide a smile denoting my mischief. He might be a renowned scientist, but his engineering skills are a fiasco. I know I am supposed to obey him blindly. I know that only humans are entitled to free will; to do and speak as they choose.

But yesterday, I saw her.

And today, I want answers.

"My young, beautiful wife..." The thump of his heavy footsteps reverberates as he heads towards me. His honey-colored hair comes into view. I admit that its smoothness is a subtle invitation to touch it, but if there is something I have learned in all these years it's that beauty is dangerous.

"Yes, my dear husband?"

He doesn't know I loved him once. But I am not the only one keeping secrets, am I? Who is the beautiful woman I saw lying on a gurney inside the only room in this house which is usually locked twenty-four hours a day? Is she his next creation? Perhaps a new, more advanced model? I remember from the last time I was outside that no other robot looks like me. But she does.

"Sometimes," he says, his hoarse voice causing me distress, "you forget what the truth is, my angel."

I know his truth. Yet he ignores mine.

"Your truth, Duncan," I say, pressing my palms against the firmness of the panel that entraps me, "has to do with the fact that the minimal amount of pain I feel is not a failure in your eyes, but an accomplishment. That this small detail is only one of the many things which make me closer to humans, closer than any other robot has ever been. Isn't that your truth?"

I snigger. Even if I had been of the smallest bit of worth to him, at any point, I am not enough anymore, am I? I know that he made me look like a perfect human, from my flawless golden skin to my mesmerizing crystal blue eyes. I know that all of me has been carefully handcrafted and measured against the highest standards of beauty in this world. Such a waste now. I am not his favorite toy anymore; he will probably just dispose of me. My dear husband.

Pretending to be his wife had only been part of the plan. It was easier, less suspicious when we used to venture outside in public. For Duncan, I was a robot, a tool; to the rest of the world, I was a woman.

It has been five years. Five years of growing up in a world which didn't have the permission to acknowledge what I really am. Five years claiming to be a normal human being. Five years pretending that I am not a robot. I had to. I was created at the wrong time, a time when artificial intelligence and superior strength were frowned upon. I am an illegal product.

He is chuckling now, his hands intertwined with each other in a sort of pensive pose. "This is true, yes, and not only about your pain."

Seconds tick by as I wait for him to continue. "You have emotions too."

So he knows? My gaze shifts to his hands which are now pressing buttons in a specific order. Yes, the door of this device is finally open, and I can step out!

"We are done with the tests for today," he says and starts disconnecting the long thin pieces of metal attached to my body.

"More comfortable?"

I ignore him deliberately. My mind is still processing that he realizes I have feelings.

"I do?"

"What?" For a moment his brow furrows. Then his eyes widen before nodding in acknowledgment.

"Of course, Karina," he says, "You were programmed to believe you have feelings and emotions. That's where the pain glitch comes from."

Glitch. I was right, I am nothing more than defective equipment. I bet she doesn't feel pain, does she? I understand now his need for creating something better.

The last wire is disconnected, and I am free to go. "Basically, you are saying that what I feel is not real." I sweep my annoyingly long blond hair off my face and step out of the device. I am aware of his intense stare burning on my naked body, and it disgusts me.

"Did you think otherwise?" His amused expression refuses to abandon his features as he extends his sinewy arms and pulls me softly against him.

"Are we done for today, dear husband?" I do admit I have found pleasure in certain intimate activities with him in the past. Those times are long gone now. I do not need or want his touch.

"Do not move," he says, "I order you not to."

I nod in silence as he rotates me in his arms. My remarkable strength means nothing. He is my creator, and regardless of whatever feelings invented by my system's fault come to the surface, I shall obey him.

"Good girl," he says as he pats my bare back, and I lean in against his chest. "You understand now, you might think you are different from other robots, but you are not."

Of course not, I am just another machine. Yet, when his grip around me tightens, it feels warm and affectionate. Did he ever love me?

"Who is she?" The words leave my mouth almost automatically. I turn my head slightly to inspect his reaction. Judging by his rapid blinking, he doesn't understand this basic question.

"I asked you, who is the woman in the basement?"

His body withdraws from mine. The warmth of where his body had touched me cools.

"Karina, it never ceases to amuse me how you think it's disadvantageous for a robot to have feelings, programmed or not. Look at what I have achieved! Look at you! You are perfect, both physically and intellectually!" He gestures furiously towards me, and his voice grows louder, bouncing off the walls of the sterile room. "And to make it worse, I have to hide you. Those senseless laws against machines! As if machines have been anything but a blessing for the humanity!" He draws a deep breath from his broad chest and stares back into my eyes.

"Who is she?" I ask again. My skin prickles with a surge in body temperature. I am sick of these games.

"But at the same time, you are right, Karina, who needs feelings? It's something even I wonder! Free will, emotions, feelings? It would jeopardize the purpose of robots, should we be allowed to create them again in the future."

I am not only impatient, I am confused now. And I still don't know who she is.

"But you are not an imperfect robot."

Why does he keep rambling?

"Because you are not a robot."

"Ha!" I want to laugh, but this doesn't amuse me. Is he deliberately messing with me, or my program, now? Is he performing some new sort of test? In all these years tests have been finished the moment I leave the capsule. He sticks with the same routine time and time again, never varying his technique.

"Karina, there is nothing mechanical about you. You are not twenty percent humanlike..."

What does he mean? What is he talking about? I am puzzled by this disjointed conversation he has created. I could hope that his facial expression would give something away, but, as it often is, his face is devoid of emotions.

"Dr. Duncan, perhaps you are feeling unwell? Or perhaps there is some issue with my program because I fail to fully comprehend you." I stop expecting answers. He is clearly having a deranged monologue.

"You are not twenty percent humanlike," he says. "You are one hundred percent human, enhanced by eighty percent."

There is a wild pounding in my chest, and I find myself having to remember to breath. I do not understand. How can a robot be one hundred percent human? I want to ask him, but my mouth has gone dry, and no words come out.

"It's time for you to know the truth, Karina."

My lips are trembling. I am breathing rapidly. Is this what it feels like to be human? Of course not. I could never be human. And to think I once thought I was capable of love. To think I once thought I loved this troublesome man who has clearly done nothing but manipulate me.

"The woman downstairs is a minor experiment, nothing important." His tone lacks emotion, but his brown eyes are fixated on mine.

My stomach clenches as I push out the next words and avert his gaze. "A human experiment?"

"Yes." His response is measured, and a small smile crosses his face.

"Am I a human experiment?"

He paces around the room, making me feel dizzy, disorientated. He smiles again.

"No."

Why is he disconcerting me deliberately? I need to know; I need to understand. My palms are sweaty, and I feel my insides quivering. I notice he is holding a minuscule needle in his right hand. He will need more than this peculiar tool to make me feel threatened.

"Genetically enhanced? Yes. Human experiment? No."

"Then what am I? Who am I?"

He smiles again as he pricks his finger. A viscous black liquid oozes from it.

"You, Karina, are *my* creator."

END

R. M. HARPER has been imagining fantastic worlds and stories in her head since a very young age, partially motivated by her addiction to role-playing video-games. For a long time, she has kept her stories inside the drawer, until she decided it was time to pursue her dream of sharing her creations with the rest of the world. When she's not writing, she's an avid reader and dedicated book blogger at nyareads.com.

THE PATCH

Frank Roger

1

TODAY OUR DOG DIED. It was a very sad day for us, and my daughter Stefanie was completely heart-broken. She's only seven years old and cannot cope with death and loss. Those are still unknown concepts for a child her age. She was very attached to the animal. I tried to console her and promised to buy her another dog, but she just wants the old one back — she simply can't accept he's gone. I'm sure the sorrow will fade from her mind, and she'll get on with life. She's just a kid, right? I guess I needn't worry.

2

I'M FLOODED WITH ADS from a co`````````````````mpany called Reality+ that promises to "solve my problem" and help me "come to terms with my loss." How did they find out about my loss? And what do they know about my problems? I hate this sort of thing. I realize very well that privacy is a thing of the past, but this is unheard of.

Stefanie keeps telling me she wants her dog back. "Why can't we do like Jennifer and Matthew?" she wailed. Jennifer is a school friend of hers who lives a bit further down the road, and Matthew is Jennifer's younger brother. Jennifer often comes over to play with Stefanie at our place, and vice versa. I have no idea what my daughter is referring to, and she's too upset to talk about it rationally. I'll ask Jennifer's parents when I see them. Could it be there's a link with this Reality+ thing? That would appear logical. I'll have to check.

3

I SHOULD HAVE KNOWN. Reality+ didn't simply hunt me down. Apparently, Stefanie told Jennifer about our dog's passing, and she, in turn, asked her father, Jeff MacMillan, to forward some information. I know that guy. I often run into him when I pick up Stefanie at school. Come to think of it, I haven't seen his lovely wife Melanie in a while — we used to exchange news and gossip. I must admit I miss her — what happened to her? Perhaps I should discreetly ask Jeff. So Jeff complied and passed on my details to that company, probably under the impression that I was behind this in the first place.

I'll call him and ask for more information on this Reality+ thing.

4

I TALKED TO JEFF on the phone. He had indeed assumed I had asked to receive information. He apologized for the inconvenience but stressed that he knew what I was going through and that Reality+ would have the perfect solution for my problem. "My experiences with their service are nothing but positive," he added. "You should at least give them a try. Do make an appointment with one of their salespeople. Believe me, they won't disappoint you. And your daughter will be ever so happy."

I pushed for details, but Jeff preferred to remain vague about his own experiences. He just repeated I should try it out and insisted that I would regret not giving this company's services a chance. "Their patches are state-of-the-art stuff," he said. "Brand new, cutting-edge pieces of technology." Patches? As a rule, I don't pay much attention to all this new and usually expensive high-tech stuff flooding the market, but I recall hearing about "patches."

Frankly, I'm not sure what to do now. I did a little research on the internet and found some customer reviews that were all very positive but did not supply the information I was looking for. *"Perfect tailor-made solutions for all your personal problems." "Suffered a loss? Try their patches." "Don't let negative feelings drag you down. Call professional help. Reality+ is what you need."*

In the meantime, Stefanie keeps telling me she wants her dog back as if this is a distinct possibility — she must be talking about those patches. All right, I'll take a closer look at them then.

5

SO I MADE AN appointment. The salesman came in an anonymous white van, without a company name or logo mentioned anywhere.

The guy saw my puzzled look and explained, "We don't want everyone in the street to know that someone from Reality+ is visiting you, for whatever reason. Count on our discretion at all times. This is as important for us as it is for you. We deal with delicate and personal matters, and respect your privacy."

With much empathy, he then addressed the matter of our dog. He needed to see pictures and video footage of our dog, as much as we could offer. "This is of vital importance," he claimed, "if we want our 'patch' to be true to nature."

"True to nature," that proved to be one of these guys' credos. If I understood it all correctly, the "patch" they're providing is some new piece of technology that looks just like the real thing. Their "dog patch" would be indistinguishable from our real dog. "It's like virtual reality but without the helmet," the salesman said, an explanation that didn't quite help me. "It's the next step in augmented reality," he added, which didn't quite help me either.

"So it's fake," I remarked, "but it looks like real."

"I wouldn't call it fake," he objected. "It's very much real, but in a different way. And it's limited to your house and the garden. You can't take the dog along when you're going somewhere. Our technology doesn't support that option yet. In the near future, this might become possible, though. In that case, we'll offer you an upgrade at a very reasonable cost."

"So how does this work?" I asked. I got a technical explanation that was way beyond me. What I did get was that there would be a Patch Unit somewhere in the house, a computer system controlling everything. It would work autonomously and required some limited maintenance. The company offered a free help desk I could call 24 hours a day and an emergency repair team in the unlikely event of a system failure.

I got more information on prices and terms and options, and finally chose for a three-day trial period, after which I would have to make a decision.

Stefanie was ecstatic when I told her she would have her dog back — I didn't add it was possibly only for three days. We would see about that.

6

IT WAS NICE TO see our dog back around the house, and yet I decided to pull out of the offer. Stefanie was heart-broken again. Let me explain.

The dog was absolutely wonderful, I have to admit that. Stefanie grabbed and kissed him as if his passing had been but an already forgotten nightmare. If I didn't know any better, I could have believed the real one had actually come back, as if he had changed his mind about dying and resurrected himself.

I understood that Reality+ had created a digital copy of our dog which was controlled by the Patch Unit at our place. The "patch" consisted of waves sent to our brain and interpreted as regular sensory input; visual, tactile, audio, and so on. We saw our dog running around, heard him bark, felt his soft furry skin as we touched it just as if the creature were real.

But it wasn't. It's just that our minds can't distinguish the "patch" from the real thing. It was perfect for Stefanie, but then what do you expect from a child.

It hurt like hell to shatter her newfound happiness, but I felt I had no choice. I tried to explain to her that however real something fake may feel, it's still very much fake. I told her that it's better to cope with reality, including loss and death, and that the dog we saw was actually not there — we were being fooled into believing so by a piece of technology.

Shouldn't children — as well as the rest of us — learn how to cope with real life? With its losses and setbacks? Isn't finding comfort in the fake an escape from reality, a refusal to come to terms with our problems? I came to the conclusion that there is no room for these hi-tech "patches" in my life, however convincing they are.

So the dog went. Or make that — the dog was switched off.

7

STEFANIE IS GETTING OVER her loss — for the second time. I knew she would. She's a strong girl. She's doing all the things kids her age do and basically enjoying herself. If she continues this way, I may buy her another dog.

For a few days, everything was perfect.

Stefanie asked if she could go over to Jennifer's place again after school to play with her and her little brother. I told her it was fine and off we went. Although it's just a short walk, I prefer to go along. Jeff opened the door, greeted me warmly without bringing up Reality+ and told me I needn't worry and the kids would have a great time.

From then on Stefanie went to play with Jeff's kids on a regular basis, almost every day. They enjoyed themselves immensely, and I was happy the dead dog was already fading from memory.

8

IT HAPPENED A FEW days later.

Late in the afternoon, Stefanie came back from Jeff's place, and she was completely upset. She looked as if she could burst into tears at any moment.

I asked what had happened and she told me that Jennifer's little brother had suffered some very rough moments. At first, I thought the boy had made a bad fall and hurt himself or something like that, but Stefanie shook her head and said she didn't understand what had happened.

When she had calmed down a bit, she explained that the boy seemed to vanish suddenly, then reappeared for a few seconds, only to disappear again and so on, like something that's being switched on and off. Apparently, this had lasted for a few minutes. Jennifer had also been quite upset and had never seen her brother act this way either.

At first, I couldn't believe what Stefanie said, but then it dawned on me that the boy wasn't real. He was a "patch," and a malfunctioning one. No wonder Stefanie was so upset. Of course, she had no experience with patches not working properly. Then the full meaning of the incident hit me. Jeff had told me he had been satisfied with his "patch," and I had presumed he had been talking about a pet.

But a boy? Jennifer's little brother? What did this mean? What had happened to the real Matthew? No matter what had happened to him, how could Jeff and Melanie have agreed to replace him with a "patch?" I totally failed to understand how parents could stoop so low.

Whatever the case might be, I just hoped there was nothing wrong with Matthew — the real one.

I should ask Jeff at the earliest opportunity. I also expected him to apologize for exposing my daughter to something dreadful like this without informing me. It was totally unacceptable. How should I explain this to Stefanie?

9

I CALLED JEFF AND told him we had to talk. He agreed and made an appointment — he seemed to know very well what this was about. So I went over and was welcomed warmly. It was in the evening, and the kids had already been put to bed — it might have been awkward for me to have Matthew around, not knowing if I was dealing with the real one or a patch.

"Something terrible happened here last time Stefanie came over to play with your daughter," I said.

Jeff nodded. "I know. There was a glitch. I realize it happened at the worst possible moment. We immediately took care of the problem," he said. "I apologize for any inconvenience."

"You took care of the problem?" I asked, outraged. "And you're sorry for the inconvenience? Do you realize what my daughter was exposed to?"

"Yes," he admitted. "She was not prepared to see Matthew like this. It must have been a terrible shock for her. Jennifer accepted the patch as her real brother from day one, so it was quite a blow for her as well. Kids don't make that distinction between real and patch, you know. There have been a few glitches with our Patch Unit, but we've had the maintenance team come over. and everything should be back in shape now. There shouldn't be any more incidents."

"How can you talk like that?" I asked. "How can you talk about glitches and maintenance and fixing problems? Are you talking about a machine or your son?"

There was silence, and I realized I might have hurt his feelings.

"I'm sorry," I said after a few awkward moments. "I got carried away with my emotions."

Jeff looked down and murmured, "you should know what I've been through. You have no idea. Don't you think this was easy for me." Then he lapsed into an uncomfortable silence again.

I cast a glance at Melanie, sitting quietly next to Jeff. She hadn't said a word yet as if this entire discussion didn't involve her as if we hadn't been talking about her son. As a matter of fact, her face was rather expressionless, considering the circumstances. I had never seen her this distant. What was going on here? What had happened since the last time I had met her? It was clear something eluded me altogether.

"I'm afraid I can't allow Stefanie to come over here anymore," I said. "Not after what happened. That thing scared the hell out of her. As a matter of fact, she probably has no intention of coming back here again."

Jeff nodded. "I understand."

An uncomfortable silence was building up again. I broke it by saying, "You told me you were so satisfied with these patches. I realize it's none of my business, but I'd like to know more about this if that's all right with you."

Jeff looked at me, then at Melanie, and finally back at me. "I think I owe you an explanation," he said. "Especially after what happened to Stefanie."

"You can count on my discretion," I said.

Jeff nodded and continued, "earlier this year Matthew contracted a bad case of pneumonia, with complications. It was worse than we thought at first and he had to be taken to a hospital. He's not making a lot of progress right now, but we hope he'll be back home eventually."

"I'm sorry to hear it. I didn't know."

"As you can imagine this was a severe blow for us. I chose to get this patch so we would have as normal a situation over here as possible. It's important for Jennifer as well as for me. It allows us to keep going, to convince ourselves that one day our ordeal will be over. As soon as Matthew is back, the patch will go of course. It'll have served its purpose."

"I see. I must say I find that very strange. I'm not sure I could do that as a mother." I looked at Melanie, who remained silent. Didn't she have anything to add to the discussion? After all, this was her son we were talking about.

Jeff must have noticed my incredulous stare as he got up, grabbed my arm, stared me in the eyes and said, "you still don't understand, do you? I decided to take a patch for Matthew because I was so satisfied with the product. You see, Matthew's my second patch. Melanie was my first one. The original Melanie left me, ran off with another guy. Never understood how a woman can leave her kids behind. So I took care of them on my own. But after a while those patches became available, and I've always been an early adopter. It seemed like a perfect idea, and I just went for it. The kids took to it well also. I've been so happy with that patch that taking a second one was the natural thing to do when Matthew fell ill. I guess more and more people are taking them. You better get used to them. They'll be all over the place soon."

I left Jeff's house in shock, about as badly upset as Stefanie.

Especially Jeff's final remark as he showed me out hit me with full force. He said there was no reason for me to remain a single mother anymore. There was a perfect solution…

10

EACH TIME I SEE one of those white vans parked in my neighborhood, shivers run down my spine. I spot them more and more often. People are having salesmen over, or perhaps maintenance crews are fixing glitches. I wonder how far this will go, how deep people are going to sink away. Before long reality will be a thing of the past. My place will be its final stronghold. I must admit I'm scared. How will I know what's still real around me, especially as this technology will be perfected and no doubt will become all-pervasive? In what kind of world will my daughter grow up? Will she give in or be stubborn like her mom? Or am I simply being old-fashioned?

Will Stefanie bear with me…or drop me at one point and replace me with a patch that suits her preferences?

END

FRANK ROGER was born in 1957 in Ghent, Belgium. His first story appeared in 1975. Today he has a few hundred short stories to his credit, published in about 40 languages. A story collection in English, *The Burning Woman and Other Stories*, was published by Evertype in 2012.

Apart from fiction, he also produces collages and graphic work in a surrealist and satirical tradition.

Find out more about his work at www.frankroger.be

IN THE BEGINNING WAS THE MICROCHIP

Erin Lale

First published in *The Science Fiction Store Club Newsletter* in 1996.

Beta Universe

ONCE UPON A TIMELINE, in the Beta Universe, there was an Earth very similar to our Earth. Humanity had an advanced technological society, at least in most places, and a firm disbelief in UFO's, ESP, and the honesty of politicians. Except for a few intrepid explorers in the fledgling space program, humans were confined to their world, and lived every day with the knowledge that their many governments might get mad at each other and destroy all intelligent life in the universe.

The greatest social division was not between rich and poor, but between those who walked in the sunlight under the trees and those who spent their lives at computer terminals, eyes closed, hands at rest, uplinked with desktop models or with the overwhelmingly powerful artificial intelligences of the world's great libraries and corporations. Of the latter people, there was one named Myi. Myi was a thief. She was not any ordinary thief, stealing into second-story windows in the middle of the night or hiding frozen chickens in her bra. Myi was a thief of ideas.

She was good at her work, untraceable, undetectable, unarrestable. And she was obsessed.

In the virtual reality which represented cyberspace, she approached the Mountain. Invisible as a particle of dust, she attempted the Mountain once again. The Mountain repelled her; she could not scale its height nor dig under its depths, neither bore through it nor seep into it. As always, eventually she had to back away.

She opened her eyes on a dimly lit, perfectly square room, littered with packing boxes. She was hungry. She plugged into the wall socket, recharging the implants that allowed her to uplink with her computer, and through it to sift through the wireless network of other computers, public, private, corporate, government, and military. She had drained her batteries almost to the null point this time, and still she could not crack the Mountain.

She yawned and stretched as she stood at the power outlet. The recently installed food replicator in her arm would kick in with a jolt of glucose as soon as her batteries reached minimal charge. She talked out loud to herself as she charged up, a habit she cultivated so that she would not lose the skill of audible speech.

"I could run a power cord from that outlet so I can operate on house power while I'm online. But then I'd be drawing power from a particular place and uplinking from a particular place at the same time, and that would make me easier to catch. I've got to keep everything separate as a security measure." She had been tracked to her home after her last attempt at the Mountain, as close as she had ever come to getting caught. No one had made her personal identifier; they were just tracking signal, so as long as she stayed away from her own interfaces and access points, no one could connect her with herself. This rented room would do until she finished the job and the big payday came.

"I didn't know what I was getting myself into." She had taken on this task for money, but now she was in it for pride. She had never failed, and she never would.

"What are they using? What's so different about the Mountain? I'm not going to give up! I'm going to get that information somehow."

Glucose and inspiration struck at the same moment, and Myi was giddy. "Of course," she muttered. "Of course."

When she was done recharging, she uplinked again and steered clear of the Mountain. She went looking for data on the Mountain's owner. Where did he live? What brand of uplink implants did he buy? How secure was his house? And then she did something she had never done in her life. She went outside.

Myi didn't just leave her room and go into the corridor, ride the elevator to the subway and on to a shopping center or implant clinic or repair shop, as she had done a thousand times. She rode to a subway stop in an old section of the city, climbed a staircase, broke open an ancient wooden door, and emerged in sunlight.

She knew she wouldn't survive in it for very long. Those who lived on the surface developed resistance to ultraviolet rays by a process called a "natural tan" over the course of their lives, starting in infancy. Myi's skin was mushroom-white, translucent to her veins. She darted into the shade of a building and oriented herself to her surroundings, working from old maps she had copied to internal memory. She squinted into the light and plotted her safest course along the street, keeping close to buildings and the protective shade they offered. She followed her course to a corner and turned onto a narrow lane where she could walk down the middle of the street.

Hours of walking found her sweating and bone-weary, but the intradermal replicator kept her from becoming dehydrated or going into caloric deficit. Several times she passed people on the street, dark-skinned and unafraid of sunlight, strong, open-eyed and easy-stepping. They stared at her but did not challenge her right to be in their world. She became aware of minutiae: the smell of an old hydrocarbon-based fuel; pain in her feet; the way the wind dried her sweat and pushed her lanky hair into her eyes; the far-away sound of a child's laughter.

Finally she saw it: The shape that haunted her dreams. It was the Mountain, made real. It was a physical representation of all that had ever challenged her. It was an ordinary bubble-home on an ordinary street. Its occupant was Chairman of the Union of Nations Executive Council.

The bubble-home in front of her was mostly opaque, with clear sections only along the curve that faced the waterfront and was inaccessible from the street. There were no doors. If the occupants wanted to leave their home, they went down, to the subway and the underground city, not out to the aboveground old city.

She went to the spot she had found out backed onto the Chairman's office. She leaned against the curve of the bubble and pressed her face into its plastic surface. She reached out with all the power her uplink implants could muster and pushed her mind through the wall. She found the desk and the computer, and briefly uplinked with it. There was the Mountain, as impregnable a fortress as it had ever been. She waited.

Myi waited for hours. Her left calf cramped; she ignored it. The fierce sun beat down through the industry-ravaged atmosphere and blistered her vulnerable skin. She ignored it. The intradermal waste recycler that went along with the food replicator reached its maximum load and her bladder began to fill. She ignored that too.

Finally he came. The Chairman sat down at his desk and reached out with his mind to uplink with the Mountain. Myi intercepted him.

Myi was unprepared for what happened. Could not be prepared, for no one had ever uplinked with another person before. Waves of confusion washed over her as the Chairman realized something was wrong. Then panic; an attempt to sever the link; a wild explosion of colors and harmonies.

Myi got what she was after. She had not cracked the Mountain, but she had gotten the information anyway. Proud and satisfied, Myi tried to sever the uplink. And could not.

Myi backed out of range and still the uplink was there. There was no computer at the other end that could be turned off, the usual last resort if a severance signal didn't work. Myi turned and ran.

She ran down the middle of the street, heedless of the sun. She stopped blocks away, panting and weak. Still uplinked.

You can't run from me, Thief.

She tried to disconnect herself from her own implants, a gesture as futile as trying to rip out her mitochondria.

Forget your money troubles, Thief. I can provide you more than you've ever dreamed.

"I've heard that before," Myi responded, speaking her thoughts aloud out of habit. "What do you want?"

"One world government. But you mean, what do I want from you. Can't you access me?"

She started down the street once more, but distance did not dim the signal. She was at a loss to understand how this could be happening. It was impossible to uplink more than a few feet away unless you had a satellite-booster implant. Of course, the Chairman must have one.

Oh, very well, the Chairman sighed in her mind, sounding impatient. *I see great potential in what you've done, Thief. I see a world where no one is alone, or deprived of the beauty of art or mathematics. No one, even those who walk under the sun. No one need ever die alone and far from help. No one need ever die in war; when all are one, war will be obsolete. No lies, no secrets, no war, no deprivation, no loneliness, everything and everyone in community together. Do you see what a grand vision I have, Thief?*

"Chairman, I've never been one for grand visions. All I know is, I suppose we've got to work together to get out of this."

Out? Why would I want out? Why would you? Thief, listen to me. I have many followers. I have many enemies, too. If you go out and uplink with thousands of my followers, create a community of mind overwhelmingly strong and united in purpose, and then uplink with one of my enemies, how long do you suppose he could keep his own ideals?

"That's disgusting!"

No, it's paradise. Work with me, Thief. All your needs will be met, all your whims indulged. You need never want for anything again. And in a thousand years your thoughts and mine will live on, immortal, in the collective memory of the unified mind we will create. You will never die!

"How do you know? You're nuts. That'll never work."

Then you've got nothing to lose. Name your fee. I'll centuple it, a million times!

"Seriously?"

You're part of my mind now. You can see that I'm telling you the truth.

"Seems to me the people in your paradise would give up a lot of personal freedom in your world without secrets and lies."

A small price to pay to end warfare and economic competition between nations and individuals forever. Besides, you'll be rich.

"Right. Rich. Okay, Mr. Chairman. You've got yourself a deal."

END

ERIN LALE is the Acquisitions Editor at Eternal Press and Damnation Books. Her writing and publishing career began in 1985. She has an extensive list of published nonfiction, fiction, poetry, etc. In the print era, she was the editor and publisher of *Berserkrgangr Magazine* and owned The Science Fiction Store, and she publishes the shared world *Time Yarns*. Over the years, she has worked as a farmer, custom fabric dyer, and alarm dispatcher, invented technical processes in wireless communications technology, competed in martial arts tournaments, conducted drum circles, taught Russian in a university, developed new varieties of flowers, programmed user interfaces on UNIX mainframes, directed the art film *Rain Dance*, sang in a folk-rock band, and became the world's most prominent contemporary sunprint artist. She has won awards for costuming and recipes and The Double Ruby Award from the National Forensic League. She served on the Southern Nevada Adult Mental Health Advisory Board, was the founding Chairman of City Lights Artists' Co-op in Henderson, Nevada, is a leader in her faith community, and twice ran for public office.

PIE

Patrick Loveland

THE SPOOKY HOODED BASTARD'S eyes shifted down and reflected neon Chinese calligraphy from a puddle on the narrow Hong Kong market street's empty walkway, giving them a haunting glow.

Arjun realized the syndicate reaper must've been wearing AR lenses since naked eyes wouldn't have looked that way. And this reaper liked to play the part, didn't he? Black-on-black boots, pants, gloves, and big, puffy hooded jacket over a dark-skinned head and a thick black scarf over his face too. Those creepy eyes were the only thing Arjun could make out in the depths of the draped, puffy hood.

Arjun was sitting where the reaper had laid him out — with a surprising amount of ease considering the reaper's average size and slight form — and his legs were near the standing reaper's. He debated kicking the reaper's legs out from under him and running, but after the walloping the bastard had given Arjun already, he doubted his ability to execute.

Then he remembered the Triad thugs the reaper had used to clear the market of patrons and shop owners — the latter forced to close and lock their storefronts and not come out under pain of death — and decided he'd be dead before he could run to the next intersection.

<<*Bring me the children,*>> the reaper said in Cantonese. Arjun had been in Hong Kong long enough to pick up a decent amount of the dialect, but if he had understood it or not, the way the reaper said "children" would still have given him the same chill. Arjun watched Triads wheel two large cases from a white lorry that was parked nearby.

The dark purplish cases resembled comically large luggage hard cases on four wheels. Arjun noticed some block letters stencil-sprayed on the sides of the cases that read "PIE" in construction orange.

<<*How are they?*>> the reaper asked.

A Triad inspected the cases and said, <<Tired and anxious.>> <<*Let's make it easier on them, then.*>>

The reaper took out a small semi-auto pistol with an integrated suppressor. He chambered the first round and fired two rounds down into Arjun's right leg. Arjun cried out and clutched it.

The reaper re-holstered the pistol and walked back to the cases. The Triad who had checked the cases stepped back and lowered his gaze, seemingly as disturbed by the reaper's appearance as Arjun had been. The reaper pressed some buttons, and the cases popped open a bit at each vertical seam with hissing escaping air.

As the cases came apart, what Arjun saw stretching and rising from them hastened him to his feet. He desperately limped away from the reaper and his monsters.

IT'S COLD AND DARK here, Daddy, Boy said in his mind — *Daddy doesn't have to hear with meat ears.* Boy looked over at Girl, her pink skinclothes reflecting what little light this boring place had as she stretched and yawned. She agreed it was cold and said she wanted to go back to sleep.

Boy felt pinches in his neck, then warmth — Daddy was letting them see things the pretty way. With a pulse and beep, the dark place swirled with color and turned soft. Boy looked over at girl and could see a yellow bow on her smooth pink head now, which made him smile.

Cascading pinpricks of light coalesced into glowing flowers, butterflies, snails, birds, bunnies, and kittens all around. Boy could see the warm sun among huge, fluffy clouds.

Daddy told them to look at a gingerbread man who was running away from them in a funny, stumble-y way.

That gingerbread man is full of cake and candy! If you catch him, you can have it! Daddy said.

Boy became excited — *Oh! Is he like a piñata?* Boy and Girl looked at each other, ever so excited now.

Yes! Exactly that! Go get him — get all that cake and all that candy!

Boy and Girl rose up and bounded after the gingerbread man, feeling so happy now out in the sun with all the cute and happy things. Gingerbread man wasn't very good at running, though, and Boy and Girl were almost sad when they caught him so fast — that is, until they opened him up and got their yummy prizes.

A QUAIL EGG BURST at the center of a *siu mai* dumpling in Naoko's mouth, the intense yolk mixing with the minced pork and chopped shrimp just right. Naoko loved Hong Kong dim sum, and it made up most of her diet on these little meet-and-greet field trips — she could get it in Osaka, but it wasn't the same.

She slurped some of the tea — mostly to cleanse her palate, as she preferred Japanese tea — and went for the largest *cha siu bao* pork bun on its plate, snagging its plumpness with her personal stainless steel chopsticks. The metal utensils were black with bright pink blossoms appearing to swirl around the top third of their lengths.

Naoko moaned and hummed sing-song noises of approval as she chewed, not worried about being rude — her sounds were drowned out in the cacophony of the busy establishment. What wasn't lost on her in the din were snippets of conversation about her appearance, nationality, and/or mixed heritage.

It probably didn't help that she was wearing a T-shirt with cut off sleeves and her Second Skin tats were so new on the market. Slowly animating abstract graffiti in all major written languages covered her hands, arms, upper chest, back, and neck up to her jawline, and all with a subtle glow effect.

If they knew what other bleeding-edge tech she'd had installed *under* her skin, they would be even more confused and worried, she had thought.

Her dark green faded pompadour and pink eye shadow seemed to be another topic of discussion, taking it into territories of sexuality.

She did her best to ignore all the talk about herself as the "weirdo," "dyke," "gangster" girl, — and possible high-end, niche prostitute — and filled her mouth with a big hunk of crispy rice flour shrimp roll.

An obvious fellow Yakuza with long, straight hair squeezed his way as politely as possible from the door to her table. He tried to act cool as he asked in Japanese, <<Is your name Naoko *'Alexeyev'*?>>

She nodded and gestured for him to sit across from her with her chopsticks and he did.

<<What kind of name is Alexeyev?>>

"You speak English? I doubt many of these fine folks do. They strike me as old school mainlanders mostly."

"I do, yes," he said.

"Father was Russian and Chinese — mother was Zainichi Korean Japanese."

"I see. And...why is your hair so... <<boyish>>?"

"You're pretty forward. Are you asking me if I like men or women? Might as well join the discussion..." she said and nodded toward a group gossiping men at a nearby table who'd been at the core of the sexuality debate aimed at her. "I never decided — didn't see a need to."

He scrunched his face a bit and asked, "Okay... Why is it so short like that, though? Longer for women is better..."

"Ah, you're a neo-traditionalist..." Naoko closed her chopsticks at the center of a fist as she said, <<Let me show you.>>

Without leaving her seat, Naoko kicked one of his wooden chair's front legs, snapping it, and he collapsed down onto the table, trying to hold himself up as the chair teetered under his weight. With one swift motion, Naoko leaned forward, gathered his long hair into her free hand, and yanked his head down onto the table as she pushed the sharp steel chopsticks against his throat.

Some of the other patrons feigned shock but didn't seem that shocked, truth be told. Most didn't even look over. Naoko decided they found her more interesting when it wasn't as obvious how dangerous she was.

Naoko leaned in close and said, <<See? Your hair is a tactical weakness. Also, you're very rude. You haven't stated your name, affiliation, or purpose here, and I have been patient, I would say.>>

<<I apologize! My name is Kuwabara Takehiko! I was sent for you!>>

<<By who, Kuwabara? Who are you with?>>

<<Inagawa-Ikka! We need your help with a murder!>>

Naoko let go of Kuwabara's hair and pulled back her chopsticks, using her other hand to return them to eating position. She dipped them in the hot teapot to sanitize them, then replaced its top and snagged another cha siu bao bun and dug in. With a half-full mouth, she asked, "Murder? Aren't you boys mostly into running local porn game arcades?"

Kuwabara tried to look natural holding himself up on the three remaining chair legs.

"W-we were taking protection from Indian tailor…" Kuwabara looked around the room for listeners before lowering his voice and saying, "and he was also feeding news on the…*locals* — the ones we don't deal with already."

Naoko said, "I'm not police. I don't solve murders. I fix things."

"That is what we need. This no ordinary murder — this method was… <<unnecessary>>."

"I was in town for a meeting — not my normal duties. Why should I — ?"

Kuwabara interrupted, "This is for you," and took something from a pocket in his suit jacket, lowered his head, and offered it to her with both hands — by balancing and sliding on his elbows.

Naoko took the item — a small tea bowl. It had been broken at some point and repaired in the *Kintsukuroi* method—the pieces were rejoined with gold dust in the resin to call attention to the repair.

"Takeda-sama said it means — "

"I *know* what it means," Naoko snapped back. "Takeda gave you this — Takeda himself?"

Kuwabara nodded and bowed as much as he could while holding the table.

Naoko carefully pocketed the small bowl in a thigh pocket on her satin cargo pants. Then she dipped her chopsticks in the hot tea bowl again before securing them in a slender black case and tucking them in the other thigh pocket.

Naoko said, <<You should have given me the bowl first.>>

NAOKO HAD SEEN MANY grisly things in her career, but this was near the worst. The Indian tailor had been taken apart, then the limbs and viscera had been spread and draped around the shopping street, partially eaten, and…played with. The last part bothered her most, and as she studied a life-sized animated plastic stand of a popular Chinese singer with the tailor's large intestine wrapped around its neck like a feather boa, she shuddered a bit. The singer continuously smiled and winked in a loop, the boa blood smeared across her mouth area, giving it a macabre feel.

Local police had allowed them into the cordon, a favor to a local Triad group that Inagawa-Ikka had dealings with, Kuwabara had explained. He had driven them here along with two of his underlings, a buzzed headed thug named Murata and another named Higuchi who had messy hair, a translucent eye patch with a Jolly Roger on it, and something wispy resembling sideburns on the sides of his face.

Higuchi sneered, <<I did not know there was this much blood in a human body.>>

Kuwabara said, <<I have seen bad things…but this… There is no honor in this…>>

Naoko said, <<Whatever did this has no use for honor.>>

<<'What'? Don't you mean who?>> Murata asked.

<<'Who' implies a person did this — a human. Seems like human is becoming a fuzzy term, though, so I guess both work…>>

"What do you mean? Wait — not important. May I ask…?"

Naoko looked at Kuwabara, curious why he had switched to English again.

"What does the tea bowl mean?"

Naoko sighed and said, "I guess I was already pretty hard on you — I'll let your continued rudeness slide…" Kuwabara couldn't help rubbing the marks on his neck left by Naoko's chopsticks as she said this. "Someone called in a marker…an old, big one. Even with how awful and shameful this is, I don't understand why it was called in myself. That one was reserved for…"

She trailed off as she noticed a police car light glint off of something on the powered hinge system on one of the closed shop accordion shutters.

Naoko walked toward the closed shop exterior and looked closer. The glinting object changed some, and she knew she was right — it was a camera. It was the size of a marble and secured in the workings of the security shutters. Its auto-focus and exposure were making its aperture change in size and move very slightly as she approached. She couldn't see a microphone but didn't want to take chances, so she acted like she had decided the camera was nothing important, turned around and walked back the Kuwabara.

Naoko lowered her voice and said, "Does one of your boys have scanning equipment handy? I thought I'd seen something promising on Murata's belt under his jacket."

"Yes, for confidentiality sweeps during important meetings — why?" he started the look around nervously.

"Stop — just look at me." He did. "There's a camera behind me. I think this was a setup to see who would come looking. I say we look for them instead, right?" Kuwabara nodded. "Okay, go to Murata and turn him away from where my back is facing then have him zero any camera signals in the area that aren't official. Scrub all the frequencies — "

Kuwabara frowned and said, "'Zero?' 'Scrub?'"

She sighed and said, <<Look for location, search through...>>

He nodded his understanding and crossed to Murata, turning him away from the camera as she had said. Murata fought his obvious curiosity, and from what Naoko could tell from his blocked movements, he had started searching upon request.

Naoko strolled around casually, trying to give the impression she was still just trying to make sense of the messy scene. In her peripheral vision, she noticed Murata nod to Kuwabara and then to her.

<<Okay, time to go,>> Naoko said to Higuchi, who was poking what looked like part of a lung with a stick from one of many ornamental trees that lined the shopping street. He looked at her and flicked the stick down into a dried blood puddle then joined her.

They left the cordon and got back in the car before saying anything else, then caught Higuchi up. He was confused and angered but ready for what he knew Naoko was planning.

Naoko asked, <<Do you have another pistol?>>

Kuwabara said, <<You don't?>>

<<I had one for use during my stay, but I was supposed to leave a little after you came to find me, so I had already turned it back in. I don't travel with firearms on me — imagine that.>>

Higuchi opened a compartment in the console and produced a large revolver for her, as well as a few quick loads that she tucked into her cargo pant pockets.

<<Thanks. Okay, let's follow that signal, shall we?>>

Kuwabara drove while Murata kept on the intercepted signal and watched a small video screen that showed the feed from the camera back at the murder scene. As long as that feed was still live, they were in business.

So, of course, a few blocks away and with an unyielding signal source, the live feed cut out and they were blind.

<<Pull over and stop,>> Naoko said and looked all around as Kuwabara did as she said. There was nothing visible, and she almost decided to move on, but a white lorry parked down an alley to their left caught her attention — mostly because it didn't seem like it should, and there was no one in the cab. Nothing about it stood out, but she had learned to trust her instincts in her current employment and they were definitely talking to her now.

<<That's it — the lorry over there.>>

Kuwabara didn't want to question her, so he asked Murata, <<Seem possible?>>

Murata grunted in the affirmative as he switched his scanner off, set it on the dash, and took out his own weapon, chambering the first round with the slide. Higuchi took a machine pistol from under the front seat, loaded a magazine, and put it under his jacket.

Kuwabara asked, <<Should I be ready to drive?>>

Naoko tried to gauge how many thugs could be in the back of the lorry then said, <<No, come with us but leave the car locked and running.>>

Kuwabara took out a semi-automatic pistol of his own, chambered it, and engaged the parking brake. They all re-tucked their weapons and got out of the car, Kuwabara locking the car remotely.

The quartet entered the alley, Naoko and Kuwabara taking lead — one on each side of the lorry as they passed the empty cab — and Murata and Higuchi waited by the cab to watch the street behind them. Naoko and Kuwabara took their pistols back out and readied them as they reached the closed rear cargo doors.

Murata and Higuchi looked back at them, and they both nodded, so they slipped down the loading section's length and took up positions a bit behind Naoko and Kuwabara, guns readied.

Naoko gestured for Kuwabara to open the cargo section doors and aimed at their center. Kuwabara extended his hands but hesitated, then in one quick motion, threw the latch and swung them open and pulled his gun back to the ready.

Triad thugs inside the cargo box fired taser pistols into the quartet's chests, their prongs piercing just enough to make good contact before huge surges of electricity went through their bodies.

Before Naoko fully seized up, two things struck her — there was a creepy fucker with glowing, reflective eyes sitting in the cargo box between two weird cases near its rear, staring at her intently. And second, as smart as she thought she'd been, she'd had no reason to expect an actual trap, which she almost had time to be troubled by.

NAOKO CAME TO FROM being dropped into a puddle of now pouring rain. She blinked and tried to shake the thick treacle of forced unconsciousness out of her head as she watched the Triad thugs that had shocked them drop Kuwabara, Murata, and Higuchi down as well. They weren't bound in any way — which made her more nervous than she already was — but they had taken all their guns, of course.

She glanced around and saw that it was night already, and they were in a narrow alley in one of the poorer districts — one of many jagged, snaking alleys between densely packed high-rise low-rent apartment estates. These alleys were like a maze with few unblocked entrances/exits, due to their use in local crime and conspiracy. The local thugs were nowhere to be seen, though.

The alley was narrow enough that she could see the lorry had been parked a ways down at the mouth of the artificial slot canyon they were deposited in. Another set of Triads led by that creepy reaper — Naoko decided that's what he had to be, with that spooky getup — rolled those two large cases she'd seen before toward them.

Naoko had dealt with reapers before, but this one was especially strange — their origin was unclear, but their appearance and tactics had risen from certain Triad groups in Southeast Asia needing a way to instill terror at a level only supernatural implications could manage on a superstitious group who were their competitors. It was so effective, many teams had started using them as enforcers and Naoko had personally had to neutralize several in her time. But this one was something else. Something about his eyes and movement bothered her.

The reaper gestured for the thugs wheeling the cases to stop. Naoko noticed orange English letters on the side that said "PIE." The reaper approached the captive Yakuza and stood at their feet, examining them. He nodded as he decided something about Kuwabara, Murata, and Higuchi, then lingered on Naoko and narrowed his glinting eyes some as he sized her up.

<<*How are they?*>> the reaper hissed in Cantonese with a strong accent — Naoko decided it was Indonesian.

One thug checked the cases and said, <<Sad and confused.>>

Naoko watched the reaper tuck the tips of his fingers into his black puffy jacket and rub the palm up and down on the material like he was considering something. She could see the bulge of what had to be a pistol in that pocket, and she prepped herself for an attempt at a disarming move, but the reaper pulled his hand back out and said, <<*They have grown well and learned much — let's make it* fair *for once...*>>

The reaper turned away to walk to the cases.

<<What is this?>> Naoko asked in perfect Cantonese.

The reaper stopped, but only turned his head in his puffy hood so that she could see mouth movements in his face covering — which were also off.

<<*These unlucky boys are...*>> "collateral damage" <<*...but today you die, Naoko Alexeyev.*>>

Kuwabara, Murata, and Higuchi looked at each other, then Naoko, but she didn't take her eyes off the reaper as he walked to the big purple cases. The reaper keyed a few things into a panel on each case, and they popped a bit with a hiss, fully opened.

Naoko had never seen anything quite like what was in the cases — they had been human at one point, but now they were seamlessly fused with artificial extensions and enhancements. They each wore combination armor and bodysuits—one blue and the other pink — and big, round helmets that covered all of their features besides their jagged-toothed mouths. Their glowing eyes could be seen through translucent bubble on the faceplates above their mouths, and the helmets had many cables running to spheres of some sort on their backs that had thick plastic antennae sprouting from them.

Higuchi said, <<Are you serious?>> apparently unimpressed.

His expression changed when the creatures stretched and rose from the cases — they had to be eight or nine feet tall, and their artificial legs bent the wrong way and also had more joints than was natural. Their arms were also overlong and ended in curved foot-long talons of pattern-welded steel. It struck Naoko that they had been human at one time, but had been butchered and surgically fused with the most lethal parts of the US military's "Hüm" bipedal humanoid drone program. The *why* of that was something she would consider later, if she survived this day.

The blue and pink cyborg monsters hunched back down and looked at the reaper. From what Naoko could see of their faces, they looked miserable as they seemed to communicate wordlessly in some way. The reaper caressed their helmets, then pressed something on them, and their glowing eyes went mostly dark — it looked to Naoko like internal Augmented Reality goggles had come down over them, similar to modern combat helmets — and after a moment, the monsters smiled big. Ampules in their neck armor plunged something into their bloodstreams as well, and the cyborgs vibrated with excitement. They smiled even bigger, showing more of their decayed, broken natural teeth, and what looked to Naoko like translucent artificial canines and molars — all in a power-assisted jaw.

<<Oh… shit…>> Naoko muttered as she got to her feet. She couldn't remember the last time she'd actually been scared… but she was now.

The cyborgs stretched once more then started running toward the Yakuza, the blue one so excited that it tumbled as it ran, rolling then flowing back into running seamlessly.

The others were frozen in place, so Naoko grabbed Kuwabara and Higuchi by their jackets and pulled them stumbling to their feet as she started running down the alley.

Naoko looked back as she rounded the first intersection into another alley offshoot and caught a glimpse of the two abominations taking a screaming Murata apart with ease in a swirling mess of blood and other fluids. They started biting into him as Naoko ran around the corner and lost sight of them.

DADDY'S SO NICE, GIRL thought as she played with the bright, colorful piñata man and ate his juice-filled candy rope. She watched glowing butterflies flit about all around and thought, *We have so many friends to play chase with today.*

Boy laughed and hummed a happy song as he ate the cake from the piñata man's tummy and laughed at a cartoon puppy stumbling around near them.

Girl said, *We'll get too full — we should catch the others too now!*

KUWABARA KEPT SAYING, <<SHIT-shit-shit-shit...>>
as they all ran down the tight alley. He was in the rear as the pink
creature came around the corner, sprayed and laced with blood —
and teeth wet with it. She tumbled and rolled now too, the fresh kill
exciting her even more.

Kuwabara almost came apart in one slash of the pink cyborg's
talons, and his howl was cut short by the next. The blue monster
somersaulted around the corner and joined her.

Naoko knew they were dead if they didn't change the rules
somehow — as she ran, she looked up, and it hit her. She used her
own — comparatively modest — internal enhancements to help her
jump up to a bundle of phone, power, and TV cables that were rigged
in zig-zag patterns above all of these narrow stretches of the maze of
alleys. She swung up and climbed onto a dense stalk of the bundles,
then whipped one arm back down for Higuchi but he couldn't
comprehend why she had in the haze of fear and madness he was in.

<<GRAB IT!>> she yelled.

His head cleared enough to understand, and he grabbed her
arm. She used his momentum to swing him up onto the lattice of
crisscrossed cables, then climbed up the side of a vertical air duct. She
jumped for another, grabbed, and climbed, then up to the next and
the next.

Higuchi couldn't do the same things she could, and he had to
make do with scrambling up a thick pipe as the people in their
apartments closed metal security shutters all around, also dousing the
only light sources beside layered neon signs all around. At least she
had given him a chance, she thought.

The cyborgs didn't seem fazed by verticality or darkness and
used their unnaturally long limbs and agility to climb up the walls, air
conditioning units, and fire escapes with even less trouble than
Naoko. She was chilled by the reality that they seemed even faster this
way than running. They reached Higuchi with no obvious effort and
opened him up — the pink one pulled his right arm off and sucked
on the blood spurting from it and the severed brachial artery in his
exposed shoulder interior.

She considered breaking into one of the apartments and trying
to fight them in close quarters but quickly reconsidered when they
finished toying with Higuchi's bulk and cackled and giggled as they
eviscerated and strung his insides around the high alley walls.

Naoko kept climbing but knew she had as little hope of escaping them as she did fighting them hand-to-hand in a fair fight, even as skilled in multiple deadly martial arts as she was. She felt the tightness in her thigh pockets, registering for the first time since she came to — they had let her keep her chopsticks and the small bowl.

After consuming their fill of Higuchi, they seemed to be taking a rest before they would inevitably climb up after her. Naoko tried to master her fear as she saw the cyborgs' blood-smeared helmets and talons glistening in the dark below. Strings of indirect reflections from neon at far ends of the space between the buildings gave the blood-slick creatures a subtle, haunting glow in the dark as well.

Naoko turned her attention upward and climbed the air conditioners, ducts, and shuttered window frames with spider-like efficiency. As she climbed, she used a backup control system she'd had implanted to navigate her AR overlay—a metal bead in her tongue against the treated inner surfaces of her teeth. With adrenaline pumping and quick movements necessary it was difficult, but she was able to initiate a diagnostic on her body's implanted systems. AR self-check: glitchy but functional. Strength and endurance enhancements: functional and in use. Targeting assist: semi-functional. Stun field: non-functional — due to being shocked earlier she assumed — and possibly dangerous to her as well in all this rain. Sonic mid-to-high-frequency emitter: functional. *Better than nothing*, she thought.

She ascended to what would have been the roof of a conventional building, but in this part of Hong Kong, there was another level to these dense tenements: the rooftop slum. They ranged from shanty towns with corrugated metal walls and roofs to more complex, quality constructions. As Naoko hoisted herself up over the edge of one of these "houses." she saw this rooftop neighborhood was a combination of the two major styles. She heard shuffling and confusion down in the home she had just mounted. She could also smell chicken curry through the rain and rust. That made her hungry — hungry and mad.

Things weren't going Naoko's way today, and she much preferred when they did. She needed to change something else about this situation, and quick. She scanned the rooftop neighborhood, the pouring rain giving the whole jagged rectangle of makeshift abodes and gardens — and what looked like a bar — a shine that her AR overlay's filters had to adjust to. Dynamo-powered camping lanterns at varying levels of dimness were strung in several places, and candle-powered in others. Wet paths weaved between rows of buildings, and someone had patched into the building electrical and powered an old neon San Miguel Beer sign outside the DIY rooftop locals bar. There was her chance — but she needed to even up the teams first.

Naoko peaked back down over the corrugated metal roof edge and saw her pink and blue pursuers, still glistening and grinning as they ascended. She lined herself up with the pink — *female?* — monster in the lead. She sat down, then laid her back down onto the metal and raised her legs, tucking her knees toward her chest. She extended her arms and used her after-market heightened strength to clutch the metal roof, then dig her fingers in like claws with a chorus of tiny shrieks. She only had to wait a long moment.

As the pink monster clawed up over the edge, Naoko slammed her boots into its armored chest, sending it back off the shanty roof and down between the buildings. Naoko ripped her fingers out of the metal, rolled over, and heaved herself up into a run. Sounds of the pink one slamming into air conditioners and such down below were reassuring. She looked back in time to see the blue monster climbing onto the roof of another shanty home. More sounds of confusion and anger were heard from down in that home.

Naoko dropped to the roof surface and slid off it and down onto the roof slum walkway. She ran the tight maze from memory and neared the glowing sign outside the bar. As she passed it — ignoring a few sad sacks inside arguing about how many man-made chemicals were in the rain — she retrieved the chopstick case from her thigh pocket. She popped it open, took the utensils out, and gripped them both in her left hand. She tossed the case aside and slowed to a stop as she turned around.

The pink cyborg was dropping onto the walkway in the distance behind the blue one that was charging at Naoko. She decided this could go either way. She engaged her high-frequency emitter and warmed it up with a pulse — good to go.

As the blue monster neared the neon San Miguel Beer sign, Naoko raised her right hand and aimed it at the sign. Tiny surgically installed plugs filled her ears as she pulsed the emitter out on ultra-high. The neon sign vibrated, shuddering hard on the bar exterior. Naoko maxed the pulse level out and hit the sign again, just as the blue monster passed it.

The neon sign exploded into a brilliant cloud of colored light and showered the confused blue cyborg with glass. He staggered and ducked away from the blasting particles, covering his helmeted head as a child might in a sprinkler. Naoko bounded toward him, keeping the pink one's position in sight as she neared them both. As Blue lowered his arms to see and prepped a slash at her, Naoko dove into a roll. She rolled just under the slicing talons, then up into a half-crouch. She gripped the metal chopsticks tightly in her left hand, pressed her open right palm against them, and used all of her enhanced and natural strength to slam the sharp eating tools back into the armored but exposed ball of electronics on Blue's back.

The blue monster howled and shook, seeming to lose control of his artificial parts some as he tried to turn and face her. She side-stepped with him, raised the heel of her booted foot, and kicked the still half-exposed chopsticks in the rest of the way, causing Blue to jerk and spasm.

Naoko caught Pink still coming in fast in the corner of her overlay. She dug her enhanced fingers into the underarms of Blue and hefted him around toward his barreling companion, just as Pink struck.

It worked. Pink slashed down at an angle across Blue's armored throat and chest, her talons far too efficient at opening them up for Naoko's liking — but in this case, she approved. Pink's big smile finally drained from her face, in time with Blue's fluids, as she tried to understand what she had done. Naoko kicked Blue into Pink, Blue's weight causing Pink to collapse backward and down, his lifeless overlong arms tangling up with Pink's own. Naoko climbed onto the pile and used her tongue-on-teeth interface to direct all artificial strength to her upper-body.

Naoko's first punch broke Pinks helmet faceplate — and the still-natural parts of Naoko's left hand. Her second broke it further, along with her right hand. Three-four-five broke Pink's AR goggles — six and seven, what was left of her natural face. After that, Naoko counted in inches as she beat the human head inside the monster machine's helmet down to the brains, then those down into the rear of the braincase.

Naoko hadn't appreciated being made hungry and angry in the same evening.

After she finished, she just breathed heavily and held herself up atop the mess of blood, brains, and electronics. She heard shuffling near her and looked at it. A few old Chinese men were staring at her from the makeshift bar doorway, mouths hanging open. She ignored their dumbstruck horror and nodded toward a wheelbarrow filled with bricks that she'd just noticed past them at the doorway.

<<That spoken for?>>

The man that seemed like the barkeep shook his head.

THE REAPER HAD CUT his relay feed after Boy's vitals had drained and Girl's enhanced eyes could see her own head's contents. He figured Alexeyev was well out of the area by now. They'd have to reach the roof and clean up the rest of his failed children.

There was a creaking and thumping sound above in the high alley walls. The reaper took his pistol out and pressed its priming button.

A large AC unit dropped from above, crushing the reaper under its substantial weight. A moment later, the pink monster's body landed on a few of the Triads, killing two instantly and crippling a third.

Naoko swung down on a bundle of cables then dropped, rolled to the reaper's side, and grabbed his pistol. She rolled again, sprang up into a crouch, and fired fatal precision shots with her broken hands into the confused Triad thugs Pink's huge body had missed in a sweeping motion Takeda had taught her years before. She aimed at the crushed gangster under Pink and decided to let him suffer some.

The reaper was still alive, so she stepped back over to him, gun pointed down into his hood between those eerie eyes. She looked around for more thugs, and her eyes landed on the bright orange "PIE" stencil-sprayed onto the big cyborg cases.

<<Hey, reaper... Before I kill you, I'm curious—What's "P-I-E" stand for?>>

The reaper chuckled, his demeanor unsettling for someone who should've been moaning in agony. As he pulled his hood away, revealing *its* robotic head on articulated shocks with antennae and synthetic tendons and tubing, it hissed,

"Perception Is *Everything...*" and laughed as it pulled its jacket open—its torso was packed with plastic explosives.

Naoko took three steps and dove behind a dumpster just as the remote-controlled reaper exploded, decimating the lower outer sections of surrounding apartment buildings and almost flipping her cover over.

Pain from shrapnel that had caught her lower right leg throbbed, but she used it, hauling herself up to her feet and limping down the alley toward the lorry.

After she hot-hacked it and got away from this mess, she decided, she was going to find Takeda and make him tell her what this was about and, someday, she would find whoever had created those cyborgs and dummy reaper, and hurt them real bad.

Somewhere in there,she was going to squeeze in some more of Hong Kong's finest dim sum, though, no question about it.

END

PATRICK M. LOVELAND is a screenwriter and author from San Diego, California. He studied Experimental Filmmaking in San Francisco and worked as a projectionist and student small format film equipment manager before moving back to his hometown in the early 2000s. Patrick lives with his wife and young daughter.

SILENCING THE MACHINE
Tom Borthwick

Originally appeared in *Theme of Absence*, August 21 2015.

DAY 3 WITHOUT A recharge.

Sark sat on a makeshift bridge, dangling his legs inches above the flow of a small creek deep in the forest of Pennsylvania's Wilds. The cabin he'd found and decided to make his own loomed behind him, nestled in a plunging, compact valley as far from civilization as Sark could manage. The pines helped further shelter it from view. The oaks and maples were nearly bare.

Green paint peeled from the cabin's exterior and the whole place looked as weathered as the valley. The flat patches of earth in front of the deck seemed hectic — a junkyard of rust and withered leaves that wove through paling green grass decorated with metallic gray fallen branches. Each afternoon, before resting along the creek, Sark would venture out into the depths of the forest to gather wood for the fire. The hunters had left tools, at least, and the saw blade, though duller than he would like, did its job.

Soon he would have to rise and end his reverie. The day waned, and the pangs of hunger grew from a dull ache to a near-stinging throb. The batteries installed in his lower back and fused into his nervous system at the base of his spine tingled when drained too low. They'd been mildly tingling all day, and it would only get worse without the means to recharge out here. He could switch off the mechanism that warned him, but feeling hunger, feeling something normal, was as good as it was painful.

A wind rose, and Sark shivered. The large white propane tank attached to the cabin was empty, but he didn't need the heat, despite the autumn cold. He was able to start campfires or sear any food he caught with his electrical extrusion attachments at the base of his palms. Each use further drained his batteries, and that was fine with him. Food helped recharge slightly, but it wouldn't last forever and eventually his neural prosthetics wouldn't get the energy they needed to function, and he would shut down.

Ahead, the creek wound back and forth among the pines until it disappeared from view. A small island of sorts sat a few feet ahead of Sark. The creek split and the right of the fork formed a slow-moving, nearly stagnant pool where dead leaves mingled with a layer of scum. Before the fork, along the bank, Sark had placed a few bottles of beer to cool. He'd found them in the refrigerator, but without any electricity working out here, they were warm and likely skunked. Still, a chance to relax near the fire later and have a few beers sat well with him.

He knew he should get a move on. Using the heat sensors in his eyes, he'd gotten a squirrel earlier in the day, and so dinner was taken care of. Hunting drained his batteries deeply.

He'd charred the animal when he caught it and a weakness he hadn't ever felt before sunk into his flesh and bones — a consequence of not having recharged since the City. And so he lingered on the bridge. The megalopolis dragged from Philadelphia to New York City and was the center of the world. Every opportunity to live, thrive, succeed, and make a mark went through there. Nearly everybody had some kind of augmentation: brain chips for faster thought processing, muscular implants for speed and strength, specialized weaponry — the list was eternal. Early on in the days of mods, Sark had been ahead of the curve, one of the first adopters. It gave him an edge. And then…it was everybody. Without mods, no jobs, no status, no money. Even with mods, every week there was something newer, better, and necessary. It had been years since he'd seen his own eyes stare back at him in the mirror. They'd been blue.

Just reflecting reinforced the ache of total exhaustion. And so he lingered on the bridge.

He'd skinned the squirrel on a butcher's block in the kitchen and brought it out with him before he sat on the bridge. It awaited him on a cleared stump next to the fire pit. A leaf landed on Sark's arm, one of the few that had, until recently, remained on the trees. Maybe it was the last of them. He took it as a signal to get to work gathering wood for the fire.

Sark had stacked the wood he gathered next to the cabin. He stood and began the process of building a fire. He preferred to arrange the wood as a teepee rather than a log cabin, even though the teepee burned taller and was more conspicuous. The secluded area, however, kept the light unseen. The most practical advantage was that after the fire died down, the teepee would have coals piled in the center, keeping warmth longer. The coals of the log cabin would be spread out, and the heat would dissipate.

He placed one stick in the center, like a maypole, and carefully arranged kindling around its base in a circle, slowly adding bigger and bigger pieces in a layered circle around that. There were enough paper and small, flammable objects around the property that he opted to use those and a lighter he'd found rather than his attachments. It would've been easier to use his body, but the more natural way — if a lighter could be called natural—appealed to him.

After the initial spark, the refuse caught quickly, and the fire rose like a beacon before him. He sat down on a metallic fold-out chair he'd brought out here the first day after scavenging in the cabin. It wasn't comfortable, but that didn't matter. Watching the flames engulf the cone of sticks and logs brought a calm to Sark, not unlike the calm brought on by the sound of the creek nearby.

Dusk waned in the secluded valley, and the last fingers of light reached through the trees ahead of him. Nestled between two of the trees a few feet from the campfire was a makeshift cross. Whoever or whatever buried there had died a long time ago. The mound was not fresh, and moss grew from the base of the first tree, over the grave, and to the second tree.

He took in the rest of the valley as the natural light retreated. The long slope across the bridge, away from the cabin, was littered with debris. The shells near the campfire meant it was a shooting range for whoever used to come here. Sark had discovered a gun shed behind the cabin. It had long ago been broken into and emptied of weapons. They would've made hunting easier, but he was content spearing fish from the bridge or zapping squirrels. He was getting by on little and much of his day was spent gathering food, which was a welcome distraction from the encroachment of thought that idling brought upon him.

The last light of day was visible directly overhead, only slightly obstructed by empty branches. The sky was always gray here, typical of a Pennsylvania autumn, raining often. He didn't need to collect rainwater, as the creek seemed unpolluted and fresh. This deep in the Wild, the likelihood of a tainted creek was slim. The water was always crisp and cool and like nothing he'd ever tasted in the cities, where everybody ate and drank only because their bodies demanded it. Although he supposed he was doing the same thing.

Sark went to the creek, where he had placed the beer to cool. He averted his gaze so he wouldn't see his reflection in the ripples. He let his hands linger in the water and felt its ephemeral fingers intertwine with his own. The loud rush enticed him, and for a moment he contemplated going in. His attachments couldn't sustain prolonged immersion in water, though, so he thought better of it, fished out two bottles, and returned to the fire.

He sat and reached to the nearby stump and grabbed the squirrel he'd caught earlier. It had been lean even before he charred it, and so he knew it wouldn't satiate his hunger. He picked the meat from the bones and tried to ignore the taste. It had the texture of chicken, but tasted like gamey coal, if that were a flavor. Just as power plants used coal, he used this squirrel, so the comparison worked for him. A distant memory told him that the meat of squirrel was supposed to be dark, but he couldn't tell because he'd burned it black when he'd caught it.

After he had finished, the dull ache of hunger subsided slightly and the tingling with it. He cracked open a beer and relaxed and slid back in the chair. Flames danced higher and higher as he stared at them. In his youth, his father taught him how to build fires, how to hunt, and how to live in the way that few, if any, city-folk knew how. He remembered a trick his father always played with the flames: He would put copper in the center of the teepee, or log cabin, and when it blazed its brightest, he would subtly throw in a piece of rubber hose. The fire would turn blue and green and purple and a bright orange that made Sark think of the flames of the Sun. His father said it was magic, and despite his age, Sark still felt it was magic. It stood apart from the sorcery that the modern world imposed on everybody. The science and chemistry of such a small thing meant little to him in the face of all of the augmentation he and everybody else had gotten in the years since his childhood.

He stared at the campfire, and the rush of the nearby water lulled him to sleep. It seemed as though one thousand soft voices whispered into his ear. *Sleep*, they said over and over in a rush of breath carried by a rising wind.

He rose and went into the cabin. The place looked as though ransacked when he'd arrived. He'd done some cursory cleaning only so that a path existed from the front door to the bunk room and the kitchen. Whether or not the hunters had left the place in a hurry or others had come to scavenge, he didn't know. The unaugmented people of the Wilds likely scavenged to survive. They hunted for certain. Yesterday, he thought he'd heard a gunshot in the distance. The locals wouldn't be a threat unless he drained too low. The people out here rejected the new world — the augmentations to body and brain that pushed humanity through a new kind of guided evolution. He respected them for it. They lived and died the way his father had — normally. Not only did he respect them, but he also envied them. And so here he was, on their turf, living closer to their way.

As he crawled into a bunk, Sark disregarded the thought of leaving behind a note. It had occurred to him often to begin composing something over the past three days, but there was nothing to say and nobody to say it to. The world he left behind deserved to remain so, and it would not encroach here. One day somebody would stumble across his body, maybe after getting sick of civilization and augmentations and all that it meant to be post-human these days. But any Aug coming here would know why his body was here. The wires and batteries and tubes and generators mixed among the skeleton would give it away.

The bunks were uncomfortable, and he had trouble finding sleep, as he had each night previous. The sheets felt cool against his skin, not unlike the creek water. The tingling in his spine waxed and waned as he tossed and turned.

The muted roar of the creek called to him, and after staring idly at the ceiling for what felt like hours, he returned to the fire. Rather than the chair, he sat and leaned against the large tree next to the mound and the cross. The coals burned low and cast a dull light on the stones surrounding them. It didn't take long for him to feel sleep coming on. He regarded the mound between the great trees and wondered if, over time, a mound would come to cover him. He concentrated on the red and orange glow in front of him. The soft sound of water sliding over stones lulled him — he knew it was time and as he slipped into sleep, he hoped that when he woke, he could lean over the creek and see the reflection of his own, blue eyes staring back at him.

END

TOM BORTHWICK is an English teacher, adjunct professor, and MFA graduate of Wilkes University, where his mentor was author Kaylie Jones. Tom lives in Scranton, Pennsylvania, USA. His work has previously appeared in *Theme of Absence, Bewildering Stories*, and alongside Hugo and Nebula Award-winning authors in the previous iteration of *Altered States*.

HERMIT CRAB
Chris Reynolds

"DON'T WORRY, MY LOVE, I won't let you die again."

Peetr leaned down and gently closed her eyes. The Kariyn appeared serene, showing nothing of the fevers that had gripped her yesterday. The portable drive attached to her neck port was dark — Peetr had switched it off before the end, so that she wouldn't remember the final suffering.

Peetr kissed the drive before wrapping it in a small leather pouch that he tucked inside his jacket. He hefted his battered backpack and squinted at the sky. Gray upon gray upon gray.

The constant cloud cover they'd had for the past few days remained, but there was still enough of an impression of the sun to let him navigate. He pointed his antique watch at the dull glow and read the dial, finding the line halfway between the hour hand and the "12" position. It was always easier to travel north.

He took a handful of lopsided steps, accompanied by the wheeze of pistons. He paused to beat a fist against his thigh, but the dull clank of metal told him little. He felt for the strap connecting the prosthetic to his organic body and tightened it, wincing at the pain. He took a few more tentative steps, and it seemed that the mechanical leg would behave itself a little…for now. He limped on.

The rolling hills and scattered trees gave way to less hospitable country, with crumbling rock faces and towering mountains. Peetr felt the ground gently slope away from him.

Country like this would likely have a river, he mused, licking his dry lips. Snowmelt this far out should be safe, too.

He re-adjusted the straps on the backpack and briefly touched the hard lump of the leather pouch under his jacket. He narrowed his eyes and scanned the local area.

Patchy vegetation sprouted from the base of the cliffs. Peetr examined the collection of green and purple leaves, but he didn't recognize any. It was best to stay away from them in that case- the small chance of finding something edible wasn't worth the risk of finding a plant that stung, hosted parasites or was poisonous. Nonetheless, his stomach growled in protest as he walked away.

There was a break in the cliffs up ahead. The craggy surface swelled out and back in again and there was enough of a fold that it looked like he could enter. He glanced at the wan outline of the sun again, and traced his route. It was either through this rock outcropping or a bypass of unknown distance. He sighed and looked again at the fold. Even if it weren't a passage all the way through the mountain, it would likely hide a cave, with the attendant shelter to protect him from the coming night.

Of course, others might use that shelter as well.

He frowned and removed his backpack, unzipping the most accessible pouch on the outside of the bag removed the sole item. He grasped the pistol and checked it, lifting the improvised cloth cover from the power cell.

He tapped a button, and the power readout blinked amber at him. His grimace was involuntary — one half-charge, at best. Probably enough to kill a fox, but nowhere near enough juice to drop a bear. This far out, it was unlikely that the wildlife had encountered a weapon before, so he couldn't rely on them running on sight.

He carefully picked his way across rocky scree towards the rock fold, using both feet and his free hand. His mechanical leg slipped once or twice, but he was able to keep his balance on the other one. Once he was standing on relatively flat ground once more, he held the pistol close to his chest and calmed his breathing before he entered.

The fold in the cliff turned out to be substantial. Peetr estimated that it was at least fifteen meters wide at the mouth, and it was open to the sky at the mouth before the rock closed in again overhead. He stalked along the rust-browned floor, trying to keep his footfalls and the hiss of tired pistons to a minimum. The walls were smooth, the work of water over decades, covered in dark vertical stripes of condensation.

The cave in front of him grew dark, so he stood still and waited for his eyes to adjust before moving on. The sides closed in, leaving him nearly able to touch the rocky walls on either side. He swallowed hard and continued. He peered through the gloom until it eventually turned to true darkness, and he could barely see even his hands.

Peetr stopped and scrabbled in his pocket, feeling a pile of crinkled, empty wrappers. Finally, he found one that still had contents and pulled it out. He held the fresh glow stick in his hand, frowning, his eyes flicking up to the darkness before returning to the hard-won packet. He pocketed it again.

He moved slower now, taking two paces before pausing and listening. Left foot, right foot, halt. All clear. Left foot, right foot, halt.

He started to hear something, a distant and yet familiar sound. Good familiar, not bad familiar, he realized. As he moved forward again, he kept the same cautious pattern, just in case there was something else out there that he did have to worry about besides the sound.

He noticed the faint outline of rock wall again, and his heart leaped. He increased his pace as he started to make out the outline of his fingers wrapped around the pistol. The sound resolved itself into the burble of water. Peetr rounded the last bend and sighted it: cold, clear and moving. Perfect.

He put the pistol away and pulled out his water bottle. With a scraping metal sound, he exited the cave and moved to the water, blinking as his eyes adjusted once more. He crouched down by the running water to fill the bottle.

Movement. He froze. Through the corner of his eye, Peetr picked out the source of the movement, and very slowly turned his head to look.

It was a robot. Clad in dull gray and humanoid in size and shape, the bullet-headed bot was swiveling slowly at the waist. The primal part of Peetr's brain immediately sought the best escape route. His leg tensed in response, and he heard the grind and rattle as the gears locked up. He looked at his leg and then back at the robot. He swore quietly under his breath. Out here, there was nowhere else he was going to get parts. He breathed once, long and slow, and tried to relax a little.

He narrowed his eyes and picked out further details. It was battered and scratched, and holding a device that he guessed was a rifle. This far from any Station, it was most likely abandoned. If it was still functioning, it was either still fresh or a long-endurance model. Peetr estimated that he was probably still outside the likely sensor range. Probably.

He dipped his bottle into the water, trying to keep an eye on the 'bot while he did so. He didn't want to lose it in a moment of inattention. He took a long swig from the bottle, filled it again and replaced it in his pocket. He pulled out a screwdriver and worked his knee joint enough that he could move again. There was another grinding sound as the teeth came free, and he stood up.

Peetr carefully selected a concealed approach to the machine. He crouched as low as his leg would let him and slowly closed the distance, trying to approach it from behind. He hoped that it wasn't omnidirectional.

The hackles on his neck rose as he got closer. He could feel his heart rate increasing well beyond what Peetr expected for this sort of exercise, and tried to calm his breathing. He knew by sight that it was still around fifty meters away, but that primal part of his brain felt like he could practically reach out and touch it. It was definitely a security bot of some kind, and it was much larger than he was.

The robot was swiveling still, and it reached the end of its arc before it began swiveling back towards him again. Peetr identified a hiding place and loped awkwardly forward to it as quietly as he could before lying down behind a rock. He thought about its rotation speed and estimated how long it would be until the machine wasn't looking his way any more, counting under his breath. He swallowed and peeked over the boulder.

The bot was standing next to a few scraps of what looked like cloth. Peetr peered at them and realized that they were actually a body. Whether it was the last victim of the machine or the charge it failed to protect, he didn't know. What he did know was that the dead human's bulging bag could contain any of a range of treasures. His stomach grumbled again.

He still wasn't sure what this machine was capable of. He didn't bother getting his pistol back out of his backpack. There was no way the bot would fear it, and he'd probably not even further scratch its battered paintwork if it came to a shooting fight. His only hope was to get close enough to find an access hatch and hack at its circuits until it deactivated.

Peetr reached down and grabbed a small stone. He cocked his arm and hurled it. As the stone hit the rock, a *cak-cak* sound shattered the calm evening air. The machine swiveled rapidly to lock onto the disturbance, tracking the stone as it tumbled downslope with more *cak-cak-cak*. It stepped off, broad metal feet crunching on the gravel and stone.

Peetr hid behind his rock as the robot stalked down the slope. He greedily eyed the smooth action of its joints. This thing is practically fresh, he thought.

The machine halted, and a thunderous *Crack!* startled Peetr along with a momentary flash of brilliant white. Where the rock had previously been tumbling, a handful of gravel pattered to the ground. Peetr froze, his skin crawling.

He swallowed and asked himself if a new leg was really worth the risk. *It's not a new leg; it's a working leg.* The justification sounded hollow. His hand touched the hard lump in his pocket once more, and he looked down.

"For you, my love… I must persist." He whispered it like a small prayer. His mind scattered, seeking an excuse to run and an excuse to go on. We won't make it to the next friendly station without a working leg.

The robot returned to its previous position and resumed scanning. Peetr quietly removed his backpack and rummaged in it for useful items, attempting to concoct a plan with them. Try wrapping it in the reflective sheet to blind it? No, it would just shoot through it before he got near. Try to trip it with a rope line? No, it would detect the rope and its path-finding subroutines would simply avoid it. The screwdriver might be useful in getting into the bot's circuits, but he had to make it there first.

Soon, he was staring at the pitiful mound of survival equipment that amounted to the entirety of his possessions. He scratched his chin for a moment and then realized that he had one more possession that wasn't amongst the rest. He searched in his pocket and pulled out his last remaining glow stick.

He looked up at the hazy glow of the setting sun through the clouds. It was sinking low, nearer the horizon with each passing minute. He would wait and use the night. Peetr packed away the remainder of his gear and laid down behind the rock, his chin on his hands.

A moment later, he felt Kariyn drape herself across his back, her presence like a warm blanket. She ran her fingers along the back of his arms, absent-mindedly. She leaned down and whispered in his ear: "My darling, don't we have work to do?"

Peetr's eyes snapped awake again, and he shivered. He looked around, seeing nothing but darkness, and wondered how long he had been asleep for. There was no moon visible to try to tell the time. He waited for his eyes to adjust as he tried to wipe the sleep effects from his face.

The sky had cleared a little, allowing a faint glint of starlight to shine through. He rolled carefully out from behind the rock, half fearing that the robot was no longer there... but the machine was standing on its designated spot, exactly as it had before. He hid behind the rock again.

He got to work, pulling the small stick out of the packet enough to cut holes in the end of the plastic with his knife. He carefully bent the stick, wincing at the crack of the small plastic bubble inside breaking and carefully swirled it to get the reaction happening. A fluorescent blue glow emanated from the packet.

Peetr slowed his breathing, cocked his arm and hurled the stick high, well over the head of the robot. He heard the whir of motors as the machine followed the small blue light. The glowstick spun, end over end, throwing glowing liquid onto the rocks in small splashes. The robot rapidly swung from one glowing patch to another, unable to lock onto any one target.

Peetr stood up and padded forward as quietly as he could, coming around behind the robot. He prayed again that it wasn't omnidirectional as he crab-walked along the slope and stepped over a rock on the pathway, keeping his eyes on the machine. His robotic leg wasn't so nimble, and it kicked the rock over.

The robot spun around in an instant, and Peetr dropped to the ground, adopting a feet-first slide. The stone behind where he had been standing exploded, showering him with rock chips. His momentum carried him towards the machine, his arms and legs scrabbling for purchase. Another explosion sounded, and clouds of dust obscured his vision.

Peetr came to rest on his back, practically toe-to-toe with the robot, but its expressionless face revealed nothing about where its attention was focused.

He had frozen for a moment before he saw the barrel of the weapon start to depress towards him, and then he kicked out at the robot's leg. The machine fell forward, its elbow landing squarely on Peetr's chest. He felt something give way amidst a blossom of pain, and his vision momentarily went white.

He squeezed his eyes open to see the robot struggling to stand up. Every movement of its elbow in his shattered chest sent a fresh wave of agony through him. He punched at it, his fist ringing off the metal armor. He barely felt the skinned knuckles he received as a result.

He yelled and hit out again at the machine, but only succeeded in destabilizing it once more. The totality of its weight came down on him. He grappled with the head for a moment, trying to work himself free.

He suddenly realized that if the robot did stand up, it would be clear enough to shoot him. Tears streamed freely down his face at the pain, and he tried not to cough. He clung onto the machine.

It tried again to stand, and Peetr saw a reflection of the starlight shine from its casing. He saw the outline of a hatch. He didn't know what was behind it, but he gritted his teeth and brought his screwdriver to bear. The machine tried to throw him off again, but Peetr worked the panel edge until it came free. He peered inside, hoping for some sort of deactivation switch.

Inside, he saw the silvered contacts of the data port. He didn't have a diagnostic computer that he could attach and send it into maintenance mode. Hell, he didn't even have a virus on a portable...

His eyes went wide as he realized. Portable drive.

He reached, awkwardly, into his jacket pocket and pulled out the small leather pouch. The robot tried again to stand up, and this time it succeeded. Peetr clung to the machine with one arm and one good leg and clutched the pouch. It tried to shake him free, but instead, Peetr's weight caused it to sway and nearly fall over again. It stood straighter and emitted a screeching, powerful sound that seemed to pierce all the way through Peetr's skull.

He screamed and pulled the drive from the leather pouch. He hugged the machine's neck tightly. His vision focused until all he could see was the data port. He carefully guided the drive into the port, and then pushed it home.

Nothing happened.

He swore and turned it over to insert it the correct way. The Robot took advantage of his distraction and threw him off with one arm. Peetr thudded into the rock, his head bouncing off the hard surface. His vision swam.

The robot advanced on him: smooth, rapid and precise. It tilted slightly until the weapon pointed at Peetr's head. He looked at where its eyes should be, but he was distracted by the portable drive still attached to the data port in its neck. He looked at it and mouthed a kiss.

"Farewell, Kariyn, my love." He closed his eyes.

The robot stood there, frozen. The rifle in its hands was pointed at Peetr's head still, but it did not fire. Lights blinked across its CPU. The data drives clicked. After a long moment, it straightened and looked around as though for the first time. It extended its arms, flexing and examining the fingers on one hand. It took note of the starry sky and clouds, of the river and the rocks.

"WHAT IS THIS STRANGE NEW BODY YOU HAVE GIVEN ME, MY LOVE." The harsh metallic voice spoke the words without any intonation.

There was no reply.

"MY DARLING."

The Robot noticed the body lying at its feet.

"PEETR."

It kneeled, discarding the weapon. The robot's hands fluttered over Peetr, as if not sure they could touch him. The robot watched carefully for a moment and observed the tiny rise and fall of his chest. The onboard sensors told it that he was alive, but not for long.

Kariyn's tortured cry of anguish resounded within her new electronic brain, but the robot body couldn't process the sound and remained silent. She rapidly started deleting everything she could from this new body, making enough room to transfer the majority of her personality and memories from the portable drive. She cleared the device and disconnected it from her neck, kneeling down and feeling for the data port at Peetr's. She found it and pulled the skin back from the contacts before she inserted the drive, fervently hoping that there was enough power left in his brain to activate the device. She shook him gently, wiping gravel and dust from his face.

He opened his eyes a little and looked at her. His brow furrowed in confusion for a moment, but then he smiled. Kariyn stroked his cheek with one gray metal hand.

"THE DRIVE, MY DARLING, THE DRIVE. USE THE DRIVE."

His brow furrowed again, but then his eyes went glassy. The lights on the portable drive flickered and flared for a moment. Then they died.

Kariyn disconnected the drive and looked at it. She placed it back into the leather pouch and then stripped his jacket off. She held the pouch up for a moment before placing it away in one of the pockets, then hefted the bag of gear and collected the robot's rifle. She consulted the rudimentary onboard navigational suite and chose a direction.

"DON'T WORRY, MY DARLING, I WON'T LET YOU DIE AGAIN."

END

CHRIS REYNOLDS is an eclectic writer, writing horror, sci-fi, fantasy, crime, literary fiction, and even some comedy. He is supported by a loving wife and two walking distractions (his kids) who live in Canberra, Australia, and he also manages to perform services in exchange for currency. If you'd like to give him a (virtual) hug, please find him on Facebook.

SPEAK NOW

Thomas Olges

I CAN TELL THAT Campbellsville is unincorporated because of all the piano bars. It's not that they're unheard of in corporate sectors, of course — it's just that the licensing fees make running a bar (let alone performing or volunteering as an instrument) prohibitively expensive. In corporate towns, piano bars are rare; when you find them, they're typically sleek, ultra-modern, and obviously well-funded.

Here, though, it's a different story. I get off the rail on Campbellsville's main drag, and there are at least a half-dozen bars within a one-block radius offering live piano. It's discouraging, initially — more bars means more places to look for leads on the Dawson girl— but I don't have time to waste being discouraged. There's a wad of old money burning a hole in my pocket, and a huge payday waiting for me once I've brought her back.

I pick the second bar on my side of the street, partially because I like the look of it and partially because it would feel lazy to just go into the first one. It's a brick building, at least a hundred years old, and the entire outside has been decked out to look like a twentieth century joint. The main door is made of some kind of heavy wood, and there's a dark green awning over it to keep rain off of waiting patrons. The front of the place is almost entirely windows, but they've been heavily tinted so that there's no hint of what's going on inside. Most surprisingly, there are no LED displays on the outside of the building at all — not even adscreens — just a single old-school neon light proclaiming "Live Piano" in a muted silver-blue.

Barbara would have called this place a dinosaur bar.

I push through the front door, where I'm stopped by a thick little bouncer who's at least five inches shorter than I and fifty pounds heavier. He's dressed simply: jeans, a black t-shirt, and dark sunglasses, but I can see the tiny nub of a receiver poking out from behind the curve of his left ear. He might just be hooked into communication with the rest of the building's security, but he might also be wired with heads-up targeting assistance or aggression enhancers. There are a distressing number of fried former mercenaries who end up working private security, and they take a lot of military-grade hardware and pent-up hostility with them when they leave their old lives behind.

Still, this one looks far more bored than dangerous. He gives me a casual once-over, checks my pistol with a measured disinterest, then tosses an almost imperceptible nod over his shoulder. "Show's tonight." He produces a hand-held card-reader and inclines it lazily toward me. "Cover's fifteen."

I charge the cover to my business account and offer the bouncer what I hope is a friendly smile. It's a very low price — less than half what you'd pay for live piano in an incorporated town — but this isn't information I feel like sharing. At best, he simply wouldn't be interested, at worst, he'd get insulted and break my jaw.

Maybe I'll tell him on my way out, after I get my gun back.

I'm as impressed by the inside of the bar as I was by the outside. The whole place is retro: red vinyl booths, real wood floors and tabletops, and honest-to-god waitresses and bartenders instead of self-service terminals. Clouds of actual smoke even rise over some of the tables, instead of the faux puffs of water vapor put off by electronic cigarettes.

The house is about three-quarters full, and I give the patrons a quick scan. Not one of them, as far as I can see, is wearing a scrap of new-fabric. Instead, they're dressed in a medley of twentieth century outfits: here a table of mid-century beatniks, there a booth full of eighties power yuppies. I can't identify all of them (history and pop culture are not my strong suits), but I see enough to feel a hell of a lot better about my own choice of attire. When I'm investigating, I like to wear a plain shirt and tie under a battered beige raincoat. In the corporate sector, it helps me stand out; customers feel better hiring a dick if it's clear that he understands how to build a cohesive brand.

Here, though, my outfit should do just the opposite — for once in my life, I'll look like I came to the party dressed appropriately.

I move to the bar and slide onto a stool. The bartender is a pretty girl with close-cropped black hair, wearing a dark dress with too many buttons that I would have sworn was the outfit of a maid or a governess. She's clearly in a better mood than the bouncer, because she immediately greets me with a wide, toothy grin. "Nice outfit."

I offer her a self-effacing little shrug. "I knew if I wore this coat long enough it'd come back into style."

She grunts out a little laugh and arches one thin, black eyebrow. "You look pretty good for a guy who's pushing two hundred. What's a man your age drink?"

"A place like this," I venture, "has *got* to have something locally produced."

"Got a couple of throwback beers on tap, if that's what you're looking for. Nothing but good, old-fashioned alcohol." She leans forward over the bar and narrows her eyes. "You looking to score tonight?"

I grin, and shift my eyes, and try my damnedest to actually look sheepish. Truth be told, it isn't the FDA-mandated sexual depressants in corporate booze that I'm so worried about — it's the frequent addition of unlisted euphorics. Tonight, I need to stay sharp. "Let's just say I'm trying to keep my options open." I nod noncommittally toward the bar. "Give me whichever one you think is the best."

She moves toward the taps, and I give the place a closer inspection. There's a smallish wooden stage against one wall, lit by a little row of spotlights. Tonight's pianist is setting up just to the left of the stage, connecting wires and typing furiously on the keyboard of his computer. He's a squat man, probably only an inch or two over five feet, with a shiny bald head and round spectacles. He pulls on a pair of headphones while I watch, then resumes his manic typing. He cocks his head to the side for a moment, then gives himself a curt little nod.

"That's Will." I turn my attention back to the bar and see that the bartender has returned with my beer. "He's been our pianist off and on for the past six months. Best I've ever seen."

I fish my company card out of my pocket and hand it over, nodding at the stage. "He looks…focused. He always play the same piano?"

"Oh, yeah. Girl named Carrie. They're an act, like. You want me to open a tab?"

I screw my face up as if I'm considering it, then shake my head. "Nah." I lean in, raise my eyebrows. "Might want to leave here pretty quick."

The bartender laughs again, and it's so low and warm and throaty that I double her tip for it. I've always been a sucker for a pretty face — and Papa Dawson will be paying for my expenses, anyway.

I find an empty corner table and take a seat. My view of the stage isn't great, but my view of Will is unobstructed. I take a closer look at his rig, aping casual interest over the rim of my beer. His gear is mismatched: a pair of clashing-label monitors, three slate gray processors running in parallel, and a physical keyboard instead of the newer projected ones. These are all marks of professionalism among serious pianists — the corporate hobbyists might use slick pre-fabricated rigs, but dedicated artists have specific demands that are seldom met right out of the box. Though I can't attest to it myself, I've also heard that projected keyboards give you a one or two nanosecond delay in data processing, making real virtuoso piano shows a technical impossibility.

As I watch, he pulls a thin gray neural interface glove onto his right hand, then extends his arm at about shoulder height and holds it steady. He starts making a series of tiny movements with his gloved hand: first raising one finger, then another, then angling his wrist in one direction or another. After each gesture, he furiously punches a few buttons on his keyboard, occasionally shaking his head or nodding based on the degree to which the results of his motions please him.

Then, with no real warning or change in demeanor, Will types in a command that kills the house lights. A single spot comes up on the bar's small stage, and the audience chokes up a stilted smattering of surprised applause. I feel my shoulder muscles clench, and a nervous quiver works its way through my stomach. I pour a little local beer on it.

Will's piano takes the stage, seeming to materialize out of some hidden back room. She's dressed like a twentieth century actress: a white cocktail dress with a halter top and a long pleated skirt, big sparkly earrings, and curly blonde hair in a short, rounded cut. I can't quite remember the name of the woman she's impersonating — Mary something — but the audience goes nuts. People hoot, and cheer and one table's worth of men in gray suits and hats actually stand to applaud. Carrie gives the room a broad smile and a curtsy.

And then the show starts. Music kicks in first: some ancient classical piece with a light feel and a moderate tempo. Carrie begins an elaborate ballet routine, mincing and pirouetting around the stage in a way that smacks of years of training. As she turns, I can just make out the black plastic of the piano's receiver attached to her seventh cervical vertebra. It's almost but not entirely concealed by the strap of her dress, and noticing it makes me feel a little guilty. Like I'm stealing a glance up her skirt or something.

For the first minute or so of the act, there's no piano work at all. Just Carrie, ballet dancing around the stage to that old classical piece, and Will holding his gloved hand completely level. When he finally starts playing, his first key is subtle enough that I have a hard time catching it. He lifts one finger of his right hand, the spotlight brightens, and the tempo of the music shifts down — but Carrie adjusts her tempo and keeps dancing. It's only when she dances a little closer to my side of the stage that I notice the patch of gooseflesh on her bare left arm — Will has overridden her skin's temperature receptors and made her cold.

After that, Will begins to play faster. Each movement of his hand is accompanied by an alteration in the music and a change in the stage's lighting, as well as some physiological change in Carrie. Red spotlights and increased musical tempo indicate a rise in Carrie's body temperature — evidenced by the sweat that begins to pour off of her when Will hits that key. Other keys numb one or both of her arms: their physiological impacts are obvious, and they're always accompanied by discordant minor key whining noises and flat amber spotlights. Occasionally, Will cuts the overhead spot and leaves only a small ring of stage lights burning; judging from the corresponding changes in the way Carrie moves, I'm pretty sure he's left her temporarily blinded.

Shortly into the act, the stage is flooded with a deep red ambiance, and a nearly inaudible bass droning kicks up below the music. Carrie's movements lose some of their precision; though her dance continues, there's a loose new fluidity at odds with the structure of the routine. I wonder what Will is subjecting her to: pain, euphoria, sexual stimulation, or all three. From her face — lips pursed, brow wrinkled, eyes half-shut — there's no way to be sure.

Through it all, though, Carrie keeps dancing. When Will numbs one of her arms, she works around it. When he blinds her, she restricts her movements to a smaller portion of the stage. When the tempo spikes or dips with her body temperature, her adjustment to the new rhythm is almost automatic. I find myself rooting for her dancing, hoping with an unexpected earnestness that she'll keep her feet and maintain the order of her routine.

I can see why this act is so popular. Most corporate piano acts are just glorified strip shows. A hot piano dances around to music while the pianist gradually increases her level of stimulation. Eventually, she peels off her clothes and has a screaming orgasm center stage. The really classy ones use elaborate lighting and costumes. In the corporate sectors, the whole affair has become lewd and predictable: technically intricate pornography with higher production values and a higher ticket price.

Not that I'm trying to claim that Carrie doesn't turn me on. Will has done some serious meddling with her internal thermostat, and when she isn't shivering convulsively, she's pouring sweat. The dress she's wearing is soaked, paper mache-molded to the curves of her hips and breasts. Under the glare of the spot, the damp white fabric is virtually transparent, hinting at (if not actually revealing) her nipples and the cleft of her buttocks. Her expression is an alluring admixture of arousal and disorientation: eyes vacant and wistful, lips just parted, tongue barely visible.

Actually, her expression reminds me a little bit of Barbara, and I find it difficult to focus on her face for long. My hand strays nervously to the base of my neck, where my muscles have tightened noticeably.

After about five minutes of dancing, it's becoming clear that Carrie can't keep up. Will is hitting keys rapidly, and the spotlight changes overhead are approaching the speed of a strobe. Carrie's movements have become loose and erratic, with little resemblance to the ordered dancing that started her show. I realize now that the bass droning has been increasing in volume and tempo, and that its corresponding impact on Carrie's physiology must have been strengthening this whole time. She's panting now, visibly, and I think I can just make out the strained reverberations of her moaning over the persistent notes of the music. She sets a foot down wrong and stumbles forward, drunkenly, nearly spilling over the edge of the stage into the first row of tables. There is an audible gasp from the crowd, although it sounds more appreciative than concerned.

Then, very suddenly, the show draws to a close. Carrie corrects her near fall, dances crookedly toward the center of the stage, and launches into a series of wobbly pirouettes. Out of the corner of my eye, I notice Will clench his right fist, and the music cuts out in a sudden burst of discordant static. The central spot shuts off, while all of the accompanying effect lights turn on at once. I can only imagine what Carrie must be experiencing right now: blindness, numbness, freezing cold and blazing heat…exquisite pain and terrible pleasure. She must be close to disassociation now, and that thought sends a sudden jolt of familiar fear racing through me.

Carrie drops to her knees on the floor, belting out a keening wail that only just sounds human. She clenches her fists at her side, arches her back until she's nearly bent double, and starts to moan. It's long and low and deep, a sound from the bottom of the ocean, and hearing it draws me effortlessly erect. The sound of Carrie reaching orgasm is strangely reassuring; it reminds me that this is an established act and one that's not so very different from others I've seen before. Will isn't going to just fracture his partner's psyche on stage.

Carrie's moaning subsides, and the house lights come back up. The audience begins to applaud emphatically, and Will stands from his computers to take a bow. A couple of black-clad gentlemen appear from backstage, taking Carrie by her arms and helping her stand. She attempts some approximation of a curtsy, and the audience breaks into cheers.

I let out a breath I hadn't realized I was holding, and drag a shaking hand across my brow. Will flashes the audience an indeterminate hand signal, indicating some number of minutes (twenty? forty?) until the next show. I watch him return to his frantic button pressing, nursing my beer and giving my erection a moment to wilt.

When I feel suitably composed, I make my way to Will's table. As I go, I reach down to my wrist and toggle on the camera on my phone. Wrist phones were terribly unpopular (Barbara made me hide it when we were out together); most people went straight from headsets to internal communications software. I still have mine, though, because they were installed with 180-degree cameras. The cameras were famously difficult to aim and took terrible blocked video. For my purposes, however, an unfocused, wide-angle shot of everything in the vicinity couldn't be more useful.

I try to make sure my arm is pointed vaguely at Will, clearing my throat to get his attention. He turns part of the way toward me, giving my outfit a glance that's barely cursory, then turns his eyes back to his monitors. "The next show isn't for another 40 minutes. I don't give autographs, and Carrie won't talk to you."

There's something endearing about the pianist's gruffness; he reminds me of a character in a movie. I hold my right hand up plaintively. "I assure you, I'm not here for an autograph. I'm looking for a girl."

This time, Will doesn't even bother looking at me. "I'm a pianist, not a pimp."

"No, you misunderstand." I reach into my jacket, pull out a glossy high-resolution print of Sharon Dawson's face. "There's a girl who I think ran away to Campbellsville, and I was hoping you could help me find her."

Will keeps his eyes locked on the computer screen. "This town is unincorporated. I'm breaking no federal laws by performing here. I'm under no legal obligation to assist in any criminal investigation or testify in any civil… "

The pianist's gruffness is rapidly losing its charm, and I cut him off. "You continue to misunderstand me. The Dawson girl *eloped* to this town. Given the quality of your gear, I was hoping you might know a place in town where a person could get fitted with a wedding ring."

Will turns toward me this time, and behind the flat glare of his glasses, I can see that his eyes have narrowed. "Look. You obviously weren't listening. I'm a pianist. This town is unincorporated. What I'm doing is totally legal, and I'm under no obligation to assist in any criminal investigation…"

While he's launching into his spiel, I fish my wallet from my jacket pocket and start pulling out old bills. They're all twenties and fifties, pressed before the currency went digital and the feds started really scrutinizing what people did with their money. It isn't strictly legal tender, but it's wildly popular in unincorporated towns and on the black market. The sight of it locks Will's lips, and his eyes soften with sudden interest.

"Like I keep saying," I deliberately count off two hundred dollars' worth of old bills, "you misunderstand me. I'm not a cop, and I'm not a suit, and I'm not here to bust anybody. I'm just looking for a girl who eloped, and to do that I need to find out who might have made her a ring." I wave the money significantly in his direction. "Do you think you can help me?"

Will licks his lips, glances significantly down at the phone on my wrist. "Does that thing give you any kind of audio fidelity? Or do you need to jot this down on a piece of paper?"

I grin and hold my wrist up in front of his face.

WITHIN A HALF-HOUR, I'm hopping off the rail again, this time on the outskirts of town. There's a maze of low-rent tenement housing on Campbellsville's south side, a cheap alternative for employees of the nearby towns who can't afford apartments with corporate price tags. According to Will, the best installer in Campbellsville works out of one of those tenements — and he's most likely the man Sharon Dawson went to see. If I'm lucky, I'll be able to track her down before daybreak.

If I'm *very* lucky, I'll get to her before she goes under the knife.

Campbellsville's slums aren't even nice by slum standards. The tenements are all relatively recent: mid-century numbers, mass-produced to meet commuter demand with little or no attention paid to aesthetics or comfort. Square gray buildings, featureless and drab, squatting like massive toads in the corpse-white glare of budget-friendly fluorescent streetlights.

Still, commuter slums aren't the worst places in the world. The residents are usually far too strung-out or paranoid to bother passers-by, and there are never enough young people to support actual street gangs. This part of town might be ugly as hell, but it should be safe.

At least, that's what I keep telling myself.

My phone's nav-system takes me almost immediately from the rail station into a series of tenement alleys: charming little "streets" no more than three meters wide with names like "1A" and "3C." On either side, the complex walls rise sheer and featureless into the night, presumably meeting the sky somewhere beyond the hazy glow of the irregularly spaced overhead lights. Moving from faceless gray alleyway to faceless gray alleyway becomes a little nauseating, so I keep my eyes glued to the two-dimensional overhead view on my phone's screen. The map has about the same level of detail as the territory, anyway — it's just better lit.

I'm paying so much attention to my progress on-screen that I barely realize I've arrived; I have to stare at the blinking blue dot in front of me for a few seconds before I think to look up. When I do peel my eyes away from my phone, I immediately wish that I hadn't.

It appears that I've been had.

The address to which I've been directed belongs to a derelict building. It's the last tenement on the block, situated at the terminal end of an alley formed by two other complexes that face outward in opposite directions. A few sad steps lead up from street level to a sagging steel door, but a cursory examination verifies that the entrance has been welded shut. If the best installer in Campbellsville really works out of this tenement block, he certainly doesn't go in through the front door.

I peer around, looking without any real hope for another way in, but don't even see so much as a window. My search is made more difficult by the fact that the derelict tenement's overhead lights have gone dead, so the shadows at this end of the alley are thicker and more persistent than they have been so far. I curse a little, under my breath, and give the sealed metal door a useless shove. I'm beginning to suspect that I've flushed a large chunk of bribe money down the toilet.

Movement catches my eye, and I realize that I'm no longer alone. A figure is making its way toward me, walking slowly and a bit unsteadily down the alley. It's a man — I can make out a thick tuft of matted brown beard — but he's dressed in so many layers of clothing that it's hard to say much more than that. Identification is further complicated by the fact that he's wearing an adjacket; as soon as I turn toward him, the thing blazes to life. Ultra-bright colors swim across its surface, hawking mouthwash or breath spray or energy drink or something.

I don't know if I've ever been this happy to run into a homeless person. If there really is an installer in this neighborhood (the eternal optimist in me wants to believe that there is), this guy might know where to find him. Granted, I might have to cough up some more bribe money to make him talk, but his price will probably be pretty low. "Say, buddy," I begin, turning on my panoptic camera and starting in his direction, "I wonder if you could give me a hand."

He keeps walking unevenly toward me, hands thrust in his jacket pockets, giving no obvious sign that he understands me. He's probably a total burnout; still, all I need him to do is give me directions. "I'm looking for an address," I tell him, my hand slipping into my jacket pocket to liberate a couple of old bills.

I'm close to him now, close enough that his adjacket's sensors have done peripheral scans of my biometrics. Its surface switches to a hyper-color display for my favorite restaurant, complete with a discount code redeemable for 15% off my total order (within the next 48 hours). This is one of the classier adjackets I've seen; I'm surprised that this guy would be wearing it here in the middle of nowhere. I'm sure the ad firm that's renting him is monitoring how many peripherals he scans, and I can't imagine they'll be too keen on paying him to approach one or two people a night in some tenement's back alley.

I catch a glimpse of his eyes, vacant and glassy and just visible below the ragged rim of his stocking cap. There's a familiar distance in his gaze: the inky deep-sea glaze of disassociation. I'm reminded suddenly of Barbara. Of the way the sunset made a streaky halo of her hair. The way the rushing air whipped it around her head. The sound of the wind whistling past her. The feel of it.

His knife is out and moving so fast I can barely back away. It's a junkie's knife, one of those neo-ceramic jobs that's fiendishly sharp but notoriously brittle. The blade still catches my left arm just below the elbow, cutting cleanly through jacket, shirt, and skin. It's a shallow cut, but it bleeds freely, and I feel the warmth and moisture against my flesh before I even become aware of the pain.

When the pain does come, it's sharp and bracing. It brings with it a sudden clarity, and I realize I've been misreading the whole situation. Will didn't just take my bribe money and send me on a wild goose chase — he took my bribe money and sent me out here to be killed. On the plus side, that means that he probably knows where Sharon Dawson went to get her wedding ring.

The homeless man is closing in for another swing, but I'm ready for this one and scramble out of range. Between the general woodenness of his movements and the blank stare of disassociation, I can only assume that the man in front of me is a marionette. Somewhere beneath his fancy adjacket, around lumbar vertebra number two or three, a puppeteer's rig must have been wired into his nervous system. Now he's being driven by a third-party, comfortably off-site and quite removed from any threat.

Marionettes are clumsy and slow, but they're dangerously counter-intuitive. They're almost impossible to beat in a physical confrontation because their drivers don't have to pay any attention to their pain receptors. They don't feel pity, they don't listen to reason, and they can't be bribed. They usually only stop when they die — no big deal to the driver because most of them are random junkies or homeless people. In a town this small, the installer probably has a deal with the morgue to buy back any salvaged hardware with no questions asked.

My options are limited. I take another step backward, only to kick an ankle against the steps to the sealed tenement door. I slip my pistol out of my jacket and level it at the marionette. He doesn't flinch, of course — his driver isn't afraid of getting shot — but pulls back his knife arm and prepares for another swing. I don't give him the chance. I drop my aim by 10 degrees or so and fire off a round.

My gun is old — an early twenty-first century design, squat and black and business-like — and it was manufactured at a time before wireless connections to heads-up displays and internal targeting assistance were anything other than a dream of science fiction. Still, at this range, it's impossible for me to miss. The bullet hits the marionette squarely in his kneecap, which collapses sideways and dumps him unceremoniously onto the pavement.

Marionettes are hard to discourage, but they're also notoriously bad at improvising. This one fails to let go of his knife to catch himself, and crashes hard to the ground. The blade shatters into a dozen or so pieces in the process, and the escaping shards shred the homeless man's hand. For a moment, he merely spasms weakly against the ground, his driver either unsure of how to right him or incapable of doing so.

I move to his side quickly, flipping him over and planting one foot on his good hand. The marionette is still struggling, of course (he'll keep struggling until his body dies or his driver gets bored), but from his current position his efforts are futile. His adjacket has noticed my injury and is now helpfully displaying the addresses and numbers of local clinics.

Inspiration strikes me, and a smile crosses my lips. "Hey," I call out, nodding uncertainly toward the marionette's glazed eyes. "Is anybody watching me from in there? Can you work this poor bastard's vocal cords?"

The marionette's eyes do a few lazy rolls in their sockets, and his Adam's apple bobs spastically up and down. I'm on the verge of writing off his vocal abilities when the driver makes him reply. Words begin scraping out of him, each one wrenching free of his lips with a rusted screen door rasp. "Fuck...you...dick."

I chuckle and hold my wrist out so that my phone is in the marionette's field of vision, gesturing toward it with the barrel of my pistol. "I shot this whole attack with a panoptic camera. I have your shitty little-botched assassination saved. I can take it public."

The marionette does something wriggling and unwholesome, and I wonder if his driver is trying to make him shrug. "Un...in...corpora...ted," he wheezes.

I shake my head. "I'm not talking about the corporate police or the feds. I'm talking about the ad company that rents out your marionette." I tap one foot against the homeless man's adjacket. "I have you on film, using a piece of corporate property in an attempt to commit murder. If I release this, the advertisers are going to come down on you for damaging their trade dress. They'll hunt you down, and they'll make you pay. They've done it before."

This last part is at least half bullshit. I know that people have been sued for committing crimes while wearing adjackets, and I know that people have been convicted of crimes they've committed through marionettes. Still, it wouldn't surprise me to know that ad men would sue the hell out of anyone puppeteer-ing one of their properties.

Apparently, it wouldn't surprise the marionette's driver, either, because he's suddenly become very quiet. His eyes have very nearly focused on me, and the man on the ground below me has lapsed into what I can't help but think of as a pensive silence. I imagine a group of engineers sitting around a bank of monitors in a van, frantically searching legal databases for precedent on adjackets and intellectual property law.

Better to not give them too much research time. "Look," I say, "I only came to town to find a girl." I pull out the glossy picture of Sharon Dawson and hold it in front of the marionette's eyes. "She eloped here. If you can tell me where to find her, I'll delete this video and pretend this little attack never happened." I gesture broadly around me, to the tenements and the alleyway and the spreading pool of blood beneath the marionette's body. "I don't give a damn about any of this. I'm only in town to find Sharon Dawson."

There's a long pause, and for a moment I worry that the marionette's driver has decided to call my bluff. Finally, the homeless man's lips part and he begins to rasp out halting directions.

I LEAVE THE MARIONETTE on the pavement without so much as a backward glance. A part of me feels guilty for not calling an ambulance, but I don't want to run afoul of hospital security. His adjacket will put me at the scene of the attack; when he can't pay for his medical treatment they might just send collections after me. Better to leave him to his driver; he'll likely receive some back-alley stitch-job and be released back into the wild with no questions asked.

If the marionette's driver is to be believed, Sharon Dawson has been married for a little over eighteen hours. Apparently, she and her fiancé arranged the meeting before they arrived; they were in Campbellsville for less than three hours before going into surgery. They should be recuperating in a tiny motel just north of the tenements.

My phone tells me that it's less than two kilometers on foot, so I hoof it instead of bothering with a cab or the rail. On my way, I tear away the cut sleeve of my jacket and give my cut a cursory examination. It's as long as my pinkie finger but very shallow, and some combination of dried blood and ruined shirt fibers has already done a fine job of sealing it shut. I tie my damaged jacket sleeve around my arm, just in case — I don't want to take the chance of re-opening it.

Eighteen hours. She'll still be woozy from the surgery; in all likelihood, she and her new husband will be easing into married life. Even the little things will seem like revelations to her, now: eating a meal together, sharing a shower, conversing through walls. It hasn't been long enough yet for someone to have gotten hurt.

It *can't* have been long enough for that.

I REMEMBER HOW BIG the sunset looked. How it seemed to spread across the horizon: spilled juice, tinting the deep scarlet of fresh blood as it soaked into the hillside. The sunset was the only thing that stayed still; birds and windows and errant strands of hair kept vanishing out of sight.

MY NECK TENSES UP, and I massage it numbly with the cool fingers of my left hand.

The neighborhood doesn't change much as I approach Dawson's hotel. The tenements become less dense, replaced here and there with a vacant lot or abandoned building. There's an occasional stunted tree or twisted shrub. The lights become more frequent and more powerful: still cheap fluorescents, but the bulbs are higher-wattage. I move my gaze from one pool of cold light to another, eagerly chasing out the dull glow of remembered sunset.

The average marriage lasts for just over nine days. Some have lasted much longer — up to two months — but most of them are finished within two weeks. Young people's average times are disturbingly spiky; they beat the nine-day span pretty regularly but sometimes come up way short. Regardless of how long they last, marriages always end in disassociation for one or both spouses. The Dawson girl's clock is ticking, has been now for almost a whole day.

The hotel looks just like another tenement building: squat, gray, and rectangular. It has more windows than the other buildings, though, and a modestly sized flat-panel display over the front entrance proclaims the place's vacancies and clean rooms. I shoulder my way through the doors, noting with some relief the absence of any private security guards.

That'll make things simpler.

I stride up to the front counter, where a gaunt, shaven boy of about twenty is staring vacantly off into the lobby. Judging from the peculiar mix of distance and focus in his eyes, I'd say he's watching video through his internal communications feed. I snap my fingers to get his attention and give him my broadest smile.

He blinks twice, sluggishly, joining me in the lobby with all the urgency of a dead fish surfacing in its bowl. His mouth jerks into something resembling a smile. "Do you need a room?"

I pull the picture of Sharon Dawson out of my jacket and lay it down on the counter, garnishing it with 100 dollars in old currency. "This girl checked in this morning. Her name is Dawson, and she's honeymooning. I need a key to her room."

The kid behind the counter glances down at the money, then up at the bloody fabric tied around my left arm. His eyes drop back to the money and linger, though he doesn't move to fetch me a key. His lips quiver, but he remains silent.

I draw my pistol, casually, and rest it against the counter. My finger is off the trigger, and the barrel isn't aimed at anything in particular, but it conveys a sense of urgency nonetheless. "I need a key to this girl's room," I repeat. This time, the kid scurries off.

Sharon Dawson is honeymooning in room 512. I take the elevator; it gives me a chance to catch my breath and collect myself. I've looked better — my run-in with the marionette left my jacket half-ruined and bloodstained, and my shirt is rumpled and un-tucked after all the unexpected physical activity. I try to make myself presentable, using the dull metal of the elevator as an impromptu mirror. I've holstered my gun again in the hope that I can make it through the night without having to use it.

My optimism is one of the things that made Barbara fall in love with me.

There's a "Do-Not-Disturb" sign on the door to Dawson's hotel room; I ignore it and unlock the door's magnetic lock. The door itself only opens about 15 centimeters before it's stopped by an old-fashioned chain bolt. Sighing, I back up for a running start and give the door a solid blow with my shoulder. Part of the chain breaks and the door shudders open before me.

It's dark in Dawson's room; the only light is the second-hand fluorescence filtering in through the curtained window. I can hear a low rustling sound from what I assume is the direction of the bed, so I know at least one of the newlyweds is home. I close the door behind me, making certain that I hear the muted click of the mag-lock catching, then flick on the lights.

The overheads are a bright piss-yellow, and they snap on to an audible hiss from whoever's on the bed. I see with some satisfaction that it's Sharon Dawson, only half-risen from a reclining position since I broke into her hotel room a moment ago. She's a slight girl with short black hair, dressed only in a black bra and raggedly cut-off gray sweat pants. She's gaping owlishly at the overhead lights, looking very young and very vulnerable.

And very married. She's wearing a comically oversized white neck brace, the nearest thing they had to her size in whatever back-alley clinic married her this morning. Her new wedding ring is presumably hidden beneath it. It probably looks more or less the same as Carrie's piano rig from tonight's show; the first piano keys were just modified wedding rings, anyway. The difference between Dawson's piece and Carrie's, however, is that wedding rings both receive *and* transmit. Now that they're wed, Sharon and her husband are constantly exchanging sensory stimuli via direct neural link. The feed is constant, unfiltered, and permanent.

'Til death do they part.

Sharon has pulled herself mostly upright, blinking at me in owlish indignation. She pulls a sentence together with great effort as if each word is made of lead. "What…what are you doing here?"

I glance around the room before answering. The bed occupies the bulk of it, the opposite wall dominated by a massive flat-panel monitor. Two closed doors take up most of the wall to my left, one presumably leading to the bathroom and one concealing a closet. I don't see any immediate sign of Sharon's husband, although that isn't surprising. Newlyweds are strongly encouraged to ease into their lives together; the sensory feedback caused by direct contact can be difficult for the unaccustomed to handle.

I level my gaze at Sharon, force my lips into a smile that I know won't spread to the rest of my face. "Your father sent me, Sharon. He wants me to bring you home."

At the mention of her father, Sharon tries to rise from her bed. The effort is too much for her, of course, and she collapses back into a fully supine position. She wisely decides to funnel her energy into speaking. "Fuck him," she spits. "And fuck you. I'm married, and there's nothing he can do about it."

I sigh. "I wish you hadn't done this, Sharon. Don't you know how dangerous it is?"

She lets out a brittle little laugh. "You sound just like him. I knew the risks. But I wanted to be with Jesse. *With* him, with him. I *love* him."

As she talks, she idly slides her left arm back and forth over the smooth fabric of the bedspread. I can only imagine how amazing it must feel to be Jesse right now, basking in the second-degree contact between Sharon's skin and the sheets beneath it. By this point in their marriage, the most mundane activities still hold wonders. They probably haven't even held each other yet. Or made love. Or marveled at the baffling array of their sleeping partners' dreams.

"It can't last, Sharon. You know that. Marriage ends in disassociation. Period. You do this at the risk of your sanity. Your identity. Your life."

Sharon sighs explosively. "So *what*? I'll be with him as long as it lasts. And that will be better than living alone for the next 80 years." Her lips split into a broad grin, and I realize that she's smiling at something her husband is saying. "'Tis better to have loved and lost," she says, steadying the tone of her voice to indicate that she's quoting him.

I'm not quite ready to give up arguing. "It's not all like this. Within a few days, one or both of you will lose sight of what you're doing. You won't be able to keep up with all the sensory input, and some part of you will snap." I try to remember statistics, or examples, or anecdotes. All I can remember is the size of the sunset, spreading like a stain against the sky.

"You'll go waltzing off a balcony, just to see what it feels like." I shrug, swallow hard. "Or Jesse will push you for the same reason."

Sharon groans, and there's an edgy whine to it that threatens to turn into a scream. "Why should you even care what happens to us?" She snorts. "You don't know us. You don't know *anything*."

My left hand goes to the back of my neck, rubs woodenly at my scars. "Eight days," I tell her, "just shy of the new national average. I know plenty."

There's a sound behind one of the nearby doors: the dry scraping of metal or plastic on porcelain. Jesse's in the bathroom, then. I draw my pistol again, shaking my head. "I don't care what happens to you. I don't care…" I let the sentence trail off, realizing that it was already finished. "Your father, on the other hand, cares about you very much. And he's paying me to save you from yourself."

I'm reaching for the bathroom doorknob when an idea strikes me. I turn around, fishing a card from inside my jacket, and stride back to Sharon's bedside. I drop it on the bedspread next to her, gesturing down with the barrel of my pistol. Barbara always said I tended toward melodrama. "You're going to want that." I turn on my heel and start back toward the bathroom.

Behind me, Sharon is struggling to comprehend what's going on. Between the sight of the pistol, the recent surgery, and her current state of sensory overload, though, she's having trouble coping. All she can manage to do is stutter out a short series of broken questions. "What are you...? Why would...? Who...?" Finally, she manages to complete one: "Whose card is this?"

I stop at the bathroom door, my right index finger resting lightly on the trigger guard.

"My divorce counselor."

END

THOMAS OLGES makes his home in Louisville, Kentucky, the land of bourbon and horse racing — though he lacks the stomach for alcohol and the skills for serious handicapping. He earns his living educating the children of the commonwealth, a profession which forces him to both question his sobriety and lament his inability to gamble.

THE DEVIL'S HAT

Gary B. Phillips

Previously published in *Interstellar Fiction*, October 2012.

I know not with what weapons World War III will be fought, but World War IV will be fought with sticks and stones. — Albert Einstein

ORELLI WEAVED THROUGH THE homeless that littered the alley. The bright lights from the city streets lit up their eyes with neon-colored halos as they pulled on his coat and begged for credits. They were pariahs, adorned with scars, unable to connect in a world that lusted after technology. He swallowed and felt a mixture of disgust and envy.

He thumbed the wad of crisp bills in his pocket as he pushed past them and into the widening alley. The sky above was dead, threatening to release a torrent of water and cleanse the things that rotted in the city.

Orelli approached the end of the alley, where two men stood waiting for no one.

"What's a rounder doin' here?" the taller man asked.

Orelli let the insult slide. "I need drugs."

Drugs were plentiful, cheap, and coded with precision. It wasn't about who had the largest selection, lowest prices, or best mods. It was about who put on the best show. Dealers took on bizarre personas to please their clients. The two men standing in front of Orelli looked straight out of a mid-twentieth century comedy routine: One tall, the other short and round.

The tall one studied Orelli's face. "You're shifting."

"I am."

"We don't deal with shifters here. Like you got something to hide."

"I do."

"Did anyone see your face coming over?" the round one asked.

"I shifted after I passed anyone."

"Lemme see," the round man said, peering at him.

Orelli's face glitched and reconfigured itself. Soft eyes that waded behind a hook nose and loose jowls, a replica of the round man's face. It was a good illusion, not perfect with anti-shift webs installed on every corner, but better than anyone else could do.

"Impressive," the tall man said. "What's a man with your skill doin' talkin' to me? Don't you have gophers for this kind of thing?"

A nervous spasm wound its way up Orelli's spine. He shook it off. "I do my own business."

The round man pushed a stubby finger past Orelli's projected hook nose until it rested upon the real thing. He giggled, a high-pitched whinny and his belly shook. "I like 'im."

The tall one cocked an eyebrow at his partner. "Guess I like you too. We got black Voranil, reds, wash, any synth you want."

"None of that," Orelli said. "I need mushrooms."

"I can upload you some psilocin."

Orelli had already tried synthetic psilocin. It was no good, even if he didn't have a chemical balancer installed. The code itself wasn't bad, even quite clever as it self-modified per user, but it was too predictable. Not dangerous enough to protect him.

"I gave it my own special modification," the round man said, his red cheeks beaming with pride.

"That 'little something special' makes you an idiot. *Baka.* If you were a real hacker you wouldn't be pushing drugs; you'd be working for me. The government frowns on snubs like you tampering with their code. I'm looking for the real thing. Fly agaric."

The round man scoffed. "Now the rounder's talkin' funny. Makin' up words."

The tall man stepped into the light. His jaw came to a fine point, an exclamation to every word he spoke, as did his eyes that swam below a weighty crop of chestnut hair. A jagged scar ran from his temple down to his mouth. "Oh, it's real. But nobody would be caught dead with it."

"That means you know someone that has it." Orelli pulled the wad of bills from his pocket. "One hundred bucks," he said.

"Old America paper? Lemme see that," the round man said, his soft eyes turning hungry.

"Back off Cos," said the tall one. He grasped the bills with his long fingers.

The round man stood on the tips of his toes to see the money. They studied the bill and Orelli could almost see the neurons firing, sending electric signals to a chipset that transmitted out to the darknet. The tall man stood motionless, and Orelli saw his ping hit the net, asking to verify the serial number and looking for a buyer.

Orelli intercepted the ping and sent an anonymous reply with the credits, effectively buying back his own money. The tall man was none the wiser. It would have been a brilliant scam if Orelli needed the money.

The tall man looked up and smiled. "It's real. Found a buyer, too."

"I hope you got a good deal," Orelli said.

"Eight million."

A small price to pay. One of Orelli's couriers was already dispatched to pick up the cash. It would be back in his possession soon enough.

"You religious?" the tall man asked.

"Not if I don't have to be."

"You are now."

"Did I just get you eight million credits so you could tell me to find God?" Orelli asked.

The round man laughed again, his belly heaving.

"There's a shrine at the base of Mount Tsukuba, been there for centuries. You'll find a *Miko* there that can help you."

Orelli smiled and hoped she was more than just a Miko. He didn't have time for women and wasn't interested in what they were after, but he never turned down professional companionship.

"Thank you," Orelli said with a bow.

"I'll send word ahead for you. Show her your real face," the tall man said.

They returned his bow, and the tall man pocketed the cash. The round one opened an umbrella to block the rain that started falling from the black sky.

Orelli walked back the way he came, fingering the single bill that remained in his pocket. He dropped it at the beggar's feet as he passed him.

FATHER LET THE WATER rush over him. The valve shut off and he stepped out of the shower and wrapped a towel around himself. Smokie was already in the common room, eyes closed, mouthing a silent prayer. The room was pale green under the fluorescent lights, a cross placed above each doorway serving as the only decorations. A tangle of cables hung down from the ceiling.

Father donned a black cassock. "We need no armor," Father said, placing a simple gold cross around his neck. "God will provide for us."

"Amen," said Smokie.

Father scratched at the base of his skull, where the soft bald flesh met the thin silicone port. He grabbed one of the cables and plugged it into the port. Their partnership was simple and efficient, they worked quickly and split the pay down the middle.

A translucent screen appeared in his field of vision with the darknet boot sequence. He checked his messages, ignored the spam, and checked for an update on their mark. His dislike of technology only matched his distaste for who he had become.

Smokie grabbed a scattergun and a couple of pistols. Father never understood why he came so prepared, their fight was not on Earth but in the darknet.

"You see the message?" Smokie asked. "He was spotted in the Roppongi district. A homeless man reported him."

"Doesn't sound very promising."

"The man says he gave him American cash. A twenty dollar bill."

Father smiled. "That sounds like our man."

"You're too happy about it. Friends and fiends, we're all cut from the same cloth."

"I taught you that. Don't forget it," Father said. "The bounty increased again. Killing for God pays well. I can almost retire once we finish this. If you were to," Father searched for the right words. "Not make it, I could retire sooner." He smiled. "Of course, I pray that doesn't happen."

"If it is God's will, I accept it," Smokie said.

Back in his room, Father removed a twin pair of Bowie knives from their place on the wall. They were made from Damascus steel, striated with nanowires. He had paid handsomely for them, called them a gift from God. It was the only gift he could remember receiving in as many years.

A FLAT RED WARNING popped into Orelli's field of vision. Someone had called him in, the fat dealer, he guessed. He didn't blame him. Resisting that kind of money was hard. He hopped on his bike and dropped into the Roppongi district net for a quick data dump. He placed a few bombs disguised as bread crumbs for anyone on his trail. Any snub snooping the darknet for him would take the bait and find himself dead on the other end of the line. Killing an avatar in the darknet was as effective as killing the man himself. Every darknet connection linked directly to the brain, sending and receiving data. A well-coded signal is all it took.

Orelli had designed the best security systems out there, and yet even they couldn't keep him safe. He needed a way to short circuit the connection to the darknet without killing himself. Fly agaric, that small red mushroom, was his last hope.

He disconnected and returned to the old protocol where it was safe, a meaningless stream of text and unused code. The old protocols had been abandoned by the public a couple of hundred years prior when politicians passed laws that made criminals out of its users. The darknet rose after that. A seedy, unkempt place for pushers and those looking for a push. Orelli contributed to making it a virtual world that didn't just mirror the real world, but improved upon it. Some people lived their whole lives in the darknet, never bothering to come up for air.

He headed west, speeding across two districts and out of the city. The glowing skyscrapers winked out of view, like stars dying in the morning sunlight, as he crested a hill. The moon sat fat and high in the sky with a single cloud stretching over it like a ragged wound.

He felt probes at the edge of his mind, in the darknet. They took the bait, and Orelli figured them for a couple of thugs looking for easy money. He left more "beacons" in his wake but knew they would only buy him a few extra minutes.

FATHER LUMBERED THROUGH THE puddles, his broad shoulders touching the walls of the narrow alley. Thin rivulets of water poured from the pipes nestled in the brick, filling the cracks in the cobblestone and flowing like rivers searching for the ocean. Two men shared a single umbrella at the end of the alley.

"You two dealers?" Father said.

"Who's asking?" the taller man asked.

"I'm an easygoing fellow. Never liked trouble much. That's why I joined the priesthood." He laughed, a thick sound like a wet cough.

"Men of God don't need what I sell," the tall one said.

"I need information."

"You and everyone else tonight," the round one said and then covered his mouth.

Father smiled.

"I—I don't know nothin'," the round one said with a whimper.

The tall man drew a pistol from his jacket. "Maybe you should get goin'. Try prayin' for what you need."

Father returned the gesture by drawing the twin blades from their sheaths.

"Funny how you guys traded bibles for bullets to spread your message," the round man said.

"Ain't no bullets here. Just a thin strip of Damascus steel that would love to meet your bones. I'm looking for a man. His name is Orelli. The CEO of SigmaCorp. I have it on good faith from the vagabond back there that he spent considerable time talkin' to you. Made a trade."

The tall man stepped out from under the umbrella. He spoke from the side of his mouth that was untouched by the scar drawn across his face. "What's he to you?"

Father ignored the question. "He would've been shifting. I don't know what he wanted from you, drugs or information but," his voice trailed off, then softened a bit. "He needs saving."

The tall one chuckled, a thin, nervous sound. "Saving. I know what that means."

"Did he buy from you?"

"A lot of people coming through here buy from me."

"But not many of them bother shifting, do they?"

Father raised one of the blades and pressed the tip across the tall man's long face, letting it slide into and trace the crevices of his wound. The short man dropped the umbrella and drew his weapon as well. He pushed the barrel into Father's cheek. "Get that outta his face. My brother, he's a nice guy, won't shoot you. But I got no problem fillin' that position." The round man tightened his grip, and the gun shook in his fat, nervous hands.

The blade cut through the air in a flash of silver, and the gun and hand that held it fell to the ground with a clatter. A thick spurt of blood followed and washed into the cobblestone. The round man's scream echoed into the alley before another glint of steel silenced him.

Father grabbed the tall man's throat with his other hand and brought the blade's twin to his neck.

"Tell me," Father said, his lip curling. "Or I'll finish what someone else started." He pressed the knife into the man's scar until blood streamed out of it.

"My brother — " the man said, choking a sob. "You — "

Father flexed his arm, choking the words from the man's throat.

"Where did Orelli go?"

ORELLI HEARD A SMALL tone and a flat screen entered his field of vision. Jean's face smiled back at him.

"Hello, Jean," he said.

"Sorry to bother you on your vacation, sir."

"No worries."

"We got hacked again."

Orelli let his bike coast to a less life-threatening speed. "Details?"

"They got a lot before I realized it. I don't know how, none of our security programs saw them. I noticed when I walked past one of the servers and saw the data access light thrashing."

"Listen closely, Jean. In six hours I want you to kill the connections. All of them. Cut the wires. Make sure every node goes down."

"What? I...I don't understand. That will destroy half of dark... "

"Just do it. Grab the data stick from my office safe. It should have a current backup on it. Keep it on you; I don't care where you have to store it. Just keep it safe. Evacuate everyone and then get out once it's all shut down."

Orelli felt another firewall go down in the darknet. They were out of the city and on his trail.

"We've been livin' on borrowed time friend. That time is up. It was a pleasure working with you. Be proud of what we accomplished.

I'll transfer credits to your account. It'll be enough, consider it your severance. Take care of yourself, Jean. I'll send you a secure message when I can."

Orelli cut the signal.

The war had finally caught up with him.

He stopped his bike on the side of the highway and removed his helmet. He pulled a penknife from his pocket and adjusted the side view mirror until he could see the ear. He coded a quick calculation in his head, a beautiful golden-ratio arc, compiled it and downloaded it to the knife. The knife's blade changed into a hawkbill blade. He looped the hook of the blade around the back of his ear and slid it forward, cutting through the cartilage without resistance. Blood spilled out and ran down his shoulder, but he continued in a smooth motion until the ear fell to the ground.

The little red chip that sat on the bundle of nerves at the peak of his spine did its job, blocking any pain signals traveling to the brain. The red chip worked in tandem with a blue one, the chemical balancer, that would eliminate the desired effects of the mushrooms. Those chips would have to go, but he couldn't remove them himself.

He reached into the wound and grasped the metallic circlet in his ear canal. The first cut severed most of the connectors, but he wanted to guarantee no hope of being found. He tore it out and tossed it into the pine trees nestled at the edge of the road.

THE PAVED ROAD ENDED in a patch of dirt, and Orelli felt the bike shudder under him. He sent a new compile to the bike and the tires compensated for the uneven terrain with proper tread. The road curved and hugged the base of the Mount Tsukuba. Two red columns rose from the ground ahead, a gate that guarded the entrance to the shrine. Orelli parked and removed the shift that hid his face from the world. His skin was taut around his gaunt face, eyes sunken into dark sockets. He ran a hand over what remained of his hair and made his way up the crumbling stone steps.

A Miko waited outside the hall of worship. She wore a white *haori* embroidered with flowers, and a red skirt tied with a bow. In her hand, she carried bells that rang clear in the night. She was beautiful, milky skin with honey lips and two black eyes like inkwells that told the story of every man that had worshiped at her altar. She was bald, much to Orelli's delight. A temple priestess and sacred whore.

"Have you come to pray to the spirits?" she asked him.

"Nothing that pious I'm afraid. I was sent here by a man in the Roppongi district."

"Follow me," she said.

He felt another probe in the darknet. They were here. He followed her around the edge of the temple and across a stone bridge overlooking a small pond.

"You are not spiritual?" she asked.

"I was. But that was long ago. Before the war."

"The war changed us all," she said.

They entered a garden filled with maiden lilies and Himalayan blue poppies. Spruce trees lined the path. She knelt by one of them and picked the mushrooms that grew around it. They had tall stems with large red caps spotted with white. When she finished gathering them, they returned to a small room near the hall of worship.

He watched her steady hands cut the mushrooms into strips and place them in a pot already boiling with milk. "Fly agaric isn't like other mushrooms. It's a deliriant, not a psychoactive," she said. She slid the pot back onto the fireplace crane and pushed the arm until the pot settled over the fire. "It has been used for thousands of years by shamans and holy men seeking spiritual awakening. Its use can be traced from Siberia to Native American tribes, to the soma mentioned in India's sacred texts. Even early Christians used it to draw closer to God."

"And the rest of us?" Orelli asked.

"It was also used by warriors. They called it the devil's hat. The Zulu people ingested it before battle, believing it made them impervious to pain. Gave them a holy purpose. The same is said of the Norse warriors and their berserks."

"I need something else from you." It was a clumsy interruption, but he was out of time.

"I know," she said.

"I can guide you, but I need a pair of steady hands."

She put down the cutting knife. "Let me get something a bit gentler than this."

"Please," he said with a laugh.

She slipped out of the room and came back a moment later with a small box. Inside were scalpels, retractors, and other medical instruments.

"At the beginning of the war, I was stationed at a medical camp outside of Israel," she said.

"What made you become—?"

"A prostitute?"

She walked behind him and lifted his shirt off. Her fingers moved up his spine. "Is this the right location?"

"Yes," he said.

She rubbed her thumb across her lipstick and pressed it against the top of his neck, leaving a faint line. "I saw people do terrible things to each other. Both in the name of progress and God. Hold still," she said, pushing his head down. "I'm going to take out the chemical balancer first and then inject you with a local anesthetic. Then I'll remove the pain inhibitor." He felt the cold steel of the scalpel against his neck as it slid across and opened him up. She worked in silence, and he listened to the sound of the instruments clinking against each other. He felt each cut — still painless — as she worked deeper into his neck and heard a thick pop in his ears as she cut into the tendon. "Any pain?"

"Nothing."

He felt her breathe a small sigh of relief on the nape of his neck. When she finished, she washed his neck and returned to the boiling pot and stirred the tea. She poured it into a cup and handed it to him.

"I know who you are. And I believe you have pure intentions," she said.

He thanked her and drank the tea, feeling the warmth travel down his throat and bloom, expanding in his stomach like a flower opening to the sun.

"Tell me why you came here," she said. "What are you running from?"

"There are men who blame me for this war. Because of the technology I helped create. They believe that I value progress above human life. They blame me for those who have died. They wish me dead and... They are close."

FATHER SAT AT THE base of the rocks wiping the blades of his knives across his cassock. He spat on them and wiped them down, repeating the process like a ritual. Smokie sat a few feet away puffing on a cigarette. They were both connected to a small gray cube that balanced on a rock between them. An antenna extended from it, blinking green in a staccato pattern, confirming the sending and receiving of data.

Father hated being connected to the cube. He hated the cold, numb feeling of a fresh surge of data flowing into his neck. It felt wrong, like he was giving his body as a sacrifice to some strange gray god that spoke in ones and zeros. It was the most efficient way for them to hack into a local darknet, find their mark, and then drop their avatars there.

Father smelled his mark among the sweet scent of the spruce trees. He sat and watched Smokie's eyes roll back as he searched for Orelli in the net.

It was Orelli's control over all things code that had allowed him to elude them up to this point. Orelli was always prepared with a new trick or piece of code. Always able to hack and recompile the world around him, like a child stacking building blocks one moment and destroying them in a tantrum the next.

Father was glad that Smokie volunteered to go into the darknet without him. He preferred to be out in the woods, where the playing field was even. There was nothing to control in nature, no inputs or jacks. God was the only hacker out here.

ORELLI'S HAND TWITCHED, AND he felt something watching him. A ball of fear nestled itself into his stomach. The walls shimmered and danced as the drug took hold. The wooden floor shifted colors until it was a cold black void as if he were standing in space. The sound of the Miko's bells turned into the growl of a beast that watched him from the darkness, lurking in the black halls of the shrine.

He hopped into the shrine's darknet, a perfect virtual representation of the shrine itself, and found that things were no better there. Just as he had hoped, the drug was leaking out of his mind and into the darknet. The walls shifted and tore themselves apart, putting themselves back together incorrectly. Beyond the walls, the shrine floated in the vastness of space.

An alarm triggered. They were here with him now. He tried to pinpoint their location, but the shifting walls made it impossible. He steadied himself and followed the ever changing hallways, trusting his instincts in the maze. He journeyed through the shrine's labyrinthine darknet and found himself outside an altar room. A priest stood near lit candles and burning incense, gripping a scattergun and watching the walls explode and rearrange themselves at non-Euclidean angles. His brow was furrowed with deep worry as if he might never be sane again.

The priest saw him. "Wh...what are you doing? he asked.

Orelli took another step closer.

The priest raised his gun. "Don't come closer. I..." He looked down at the gun and then back to Orelli and shook his head as if remembering his mission. He pulled the trigger.

Orelli heard the boom of the scattergun and flinched as a shower of bullets pierced him. He looked down to see a fresh hole in his chest, but instead of blood, liquid polygons crawled out of his chest. The polygons shimmered and fell to the ground in a heap. It slithered along the floor, growing as it moved toward the priest.

He fired another shot, but the bullets never found their target. The shimmering snake wound itself up the priest's leg and pulled the priest into the floor with a sickening snap. Orelli disconnected from the net and touched his hands to his chest but found no hole there.

The monster growled in his ear, close enough to strike.

FATHER SAT ON THE hard ground, optimizing the code in the little gray machine, trying to parse the torrent of bad data that threatened to overwhelm the box. Smokie's body spasmed, and Father scrambled across the ground to him. He yanked the cable from the back of Smokie's head, but it was too late. Smokie's eyes had taken on the glossy stare that all corpses possessed. Father performed last rites and pulled the cable from his head.

In the distance, a bell chimed.

ORELLI OPENED HIS EYES and could not move. He felt ropes cutting into his wrists and legs, binding him.

"Relax," the Miko said from over his shoulder. "You're doing just fine."

"What did you do?" Orelli asked.

"You two are cut from the same cloth, even if you do not yet realize it," she said.

He lifted his head, straining to look toward her voice. Father was bound next to him, nude and bleeding. The Miko pulled a knot of wires from the back of Father's head and cut them.

"Is this God's will?" Orelli asked.

Father did not respond, but the Miko did. "This is for what I saw in Israel. For my friends... My husband." Her voice trailed off. "This war will not end with men like him chasing you." She turned to look at Orelli. "And they will not stop."

She was right. He felt no rush of adrenaline, no anger. Only guilt. He stopped struggling and bowed his head. Relief. His empire, crushed. There would be no more running. It would all be over soon.

THE WARM GLOW OF pink morning sunlight woke him. He rubbed his eyes and felt rested for the first time in as long as he could remember. The flesh around his eyes was perforated. Scarred. The connection to the darknet was gone. He felt the back of his neck and his arms and found more scars as proof.

Outside, the sky lightened as the sun peaked over the blue ocean. His toes dug into the cold clumps of sand on the beach. He took a deep breath and the salty ocean air licked at his nose and lips. Tears stung at the edges of his eyes.

There were a few tents nearby, and a group of men and women worked together, pushing boats out into the water. Another group sat around a campfire cooking a meal. They were all shirtless, adorned with the same scars. He scanned the crowds looking for a familiar face, friend or foe.

A man excused himself from the campfire and walked toward Orelli

"We wondered how long it would be before you woke up," he said.

"Where am I?" Orelli asked.

"A small fishing village. You were brought here a few days ago."

"Why?"

"To live your life," the man said. "We have everything you need here. We will not judge you."

"It's the life of an outcast."

"Some men choose their fate; others have it thrust upon them."

"Did you choose this?"

The man ignored the question and beckoned Orelli away from the beach.

"We're a few days walk from Toyko. You and I both know what that city holds for men like us." He touched the scar at the base of his neck as they walked down a dirt path. "We've seen them in the streets, suckling at the tit of a city that ignores them."

Orelli stopped at a small clump of red topped mushrooms growing on a fallen tree. He let his fingers touch one. "I chose my own fate," he said.

END

GARY B. PHILLIPS lives in Arizona and writes horror, science-fiction, and fantasy. His fiction has appeared in *Stories in the Ether*, *Interstellar Fiction*, *Lacuna: A Journal of Historical Fiction*, *Daily Science Fiction*, and the *Another 100 Horrors* anthology. He is currently working on a YA Horror novel.

LIMITLESS

Matthew X. Gomez

TOM STOOD IN THE alleyway, leaning against the brick wall, cigarette dangling from his bottom lip. A back door opened, forcing him to squint against the sudden bright, a cloud of perfume assaulting his nose.

"I didn't think you'd come."

Tom smiled at Shari. A long coat hung to her knees, but he saw she was still wearing her working shoes, six inches of stiletto with clear heels and rhinestones. Tom remembered the last time he'd seen her, storming out of his apartment and cursing up a storm. She'd been wearing a lot less then.

He plucked the cigarette out of his mouth and dropped it to the ground, grinding it out under the heel of his boot. "You sounded worried. I figured if you were calling me, you didn't have too many other options."

Shari nodded. Her eyes kept darting up and down the alley, her arms held close to her body. "I've got to get back to work soon. I've only got about five minutes."

Tom shrugged. "You called me, remember? So, what's going on?"

"One of the other dancers, Milan, hasn't shown up for the past couple of days."

Tom scratched at the stubble on his chin. "Yeah?"

"Yeah. She hasn't called in either, and I'm worried, okay? It's not like her not to show."

"Is the club looking into it?"

Shari raised an eyebrow. "What the fuck do you think? No, they aren't looking into it. As far they're concerned she's a no-show. Probably found work at some other club."

"But?"

Shari tilted her head and squinted at Tom. "Look, Milan's all right. Not like most of the girls who work here. She and I would hang out sometimes outside of work. She's only a kid, nineteen or so. She's been working hard, sending money home, that kind of thing. She's not the kind to up and leave and not say anything."

"I'm guessing you haven't called the cops?"

Shari laughed, an ugly harsh sound full of derision and spite. "Yeah, I'm sure a stripper calling them about another missing stripper will get launched right to the top of their priorities. They'll probably tell me she ran away with a customer."

"And that's not what you think."

"Damn straight."

"Anything else you can tell me?"

"She had a couple of regulars, but one guy really seemed to spook her. She'd laugh and call him the Mad Scientist, but I think there was something about the guy that set off her asshole alarm. He never did anything that broke club rules, though, so what are you going to do?" She pulled a thin phone out of her case, her thumb flying through the screens. Tom blinked, and there was a picture of Milan and her address superimposed on his vision.

"Any chance of a picture of the regular she was worried about?"

"Nope, sorry," Shari replied.

The back door banged opened, and a hulking guy in a too-tight black T-shirt and black slacks leaned out into the alley. "You're on next, Shari. Boss doesn't like you girls conducting personal business when you're supposed to be working, remember?"

"Yeah, I got it, Hank. Tom here was just leaving, weren't you Tom?"

Tom looked the big man up and down. His upper body was massive, with arms thicker than Shari's thighs. His legs were like spindles.

Tom worked his tongue into the side of his mouth. Every nerve told him to walk away. Tell Shari to fuck off and find someone else to do her dirty work. There was no angle here for him, no profit in it.

But.

He remembered Shari curled up in the crook of his arm. He remembered her crying when he came home, shot and bleeding. Again. He remembered her laugh the one time he brought her flowers.

And somewhere out there was a girl. Might be dead already. Probably was. But might not. And she'd be scared, and maybe hurting, and needing help.

And here Tom was, thinking about money. Like a wage slave. Fuck that noise.

"I'll call when I find something," he said, turning to walk away.

"Tom?" Shari's voice echoed off of the bleak, neon-soaked walls of the alley. "Be careful, okay?"

Tom looked over his shoulder. Shari stood in the doorway, still hugging her arms around herself, chewing her bottom lip a bit like she did when she was nervous.

Tom tried to think of something witty to say, but the words died before they hit his lips. "Yeah."

TOM'S HEAD-UP DISPLAY POPULATED a street map, leading him to Milan's apartment. It wasn't a far walk from the club, meaning it was in a bad part of town. Tom wasn't worried. Ten years out and he could still affect a military stride, head up and alert. Unlike most folk out on the street, he didn't carry a gun, not least because if he were caught carrying, he'd be spending a long time staring out from the inside of a cell.

Trash lay scattered outside the apartment building, and Tom breathed hard through his mouth, keeping the stench at bay. A few of the locals were hanging around the entrance, and they all gave Tom the hard eye from where they slouched. The unblinking eye of a rusting security camera captured the street outside. Tom wondered who was watching the feed, if anyone.

"What are you doing here, borgie?" one of them called out.

Tom tried smiling, but the way they all flinched back told him it didn't come across as friendly as he would have liked.

"Came to see a friend, heard she was sick."

"Huh. Your friend got a name? We look out for each other here. Don't need no trouble, borgie."

Tom took a deep breath, pushed away the anger he felt at the epithet. "Goes by the name Milan. Short girl," he held his flesh and blood hand up to just under his chest, "purple hair. Tits out to here." He cupped his hands generously out from his body.

"Oh, you must mean Willa," one of the slouchers said, getting a kick from one of his compatriots for volunteering information.

"Yeah, I must," Tom replied. The slouchers spread out, circling around Tom. His mouth went dry, and he felt sweat running down the center of his back. He stayed relaxed, though, nice and loose like he'd been taught. Metal gleamed in the hand of one of the slouchers, and Tom caught sight of a club in another's hand.

"Are you sure this is how you want this to go down?"

"Yeah, I'm...."

The sloucher never got to finish his sentence as Tom's left arm, the all chrome and titanium lacing one, crashed into his chin, sending him sprawling backward.

One of the slouchers swung his metal bat, but Tom saw it coming and slipped under the blow. His foot lashed out, catching one of the attackers on the side of the knee. He went down with an audible crack. The guy with the knife came in, hard and fast. Tom closed up, and the knife snapped off at the hilt, shattering against his metal arm. Tom reached out, grabbed the sloucher by the back of his head and drove his forehead into the sloucher's nose, smashing it against the side of his face.

"All done?" Tom asked, picking up the pipe from off the ground.

The slouchers slinked off, half-dragging their wounded with them. Tom felt his meat hand start to shake and forced himself to take a few deep breaths. He thought it strange that he always acted the same in combat. Nice and easy during it, but close to a panic attack after. He forced his breathing to slow down, felt his heart rate approach something close to normal. Only then did he head up the steps to the building, flipping the pipe into the nearby alley.

The lobby inside was much like the facade, cracked, peeling plaster, and trash piled up. A bundle of old blankets shifted in the corner, and a pair of eyes blinked owlishly at Tom.

"You run that trash off, mister?"

Tom looked back at the street. "Yeah, I guess."

A dry chuckle turned into a cough. "Guess that makes you the trash man, huh?"

"Something like that. Hey, do you know a girl named Mill— sorry, Willa."

"Why? You a boyfriend or somethin'?"

"Or something." Tom crouched down before the blankets and tried hard to block out the rank stench. The person inside was younger than he thought, artificially aged by the toxic atmosphere and shitty living conditions. "I'm a friend of a friend."

"Well you don't look like no cop, and I don't think any heavy would have stopped at beating that scum out there. Haven't seen Willa in a couple of days, more's the pity. She's real easy on the eyes."

"Yeah. Anyone come by recently that don't quite fit in?"

"What's it worth?"

Tom reached into his pants pocket, pulled out a half packet of cigarettes. He placed one between the lips of the blanket lady, then extended his left index finger. A small blue flame ignited the end.

"You're a saint, you are," the blanket lady said.

"Hardly," Tom replied, a genuine smile crossing his face.

"Yeah, three men came by in the last couple of days. Two big guys trying hard to look like they were slumming. The guy with them was a skinny little thing. Slicked back hair, and a nice suit. Looked like he was afraid to touch anything. Don't know if they have anything to do with Miss Willa, but they did head upstairs around the time she stopped coming down."

"This place have a back entrance?"

"Sure does, freight elevator heads down to the basement, and there's a back alley there. Some people use it to take their trash out and such."

Tom placed the rest of the cigarettes on the blanket. "Thanks."

"Don't mention it. You seem like a nice young man."

Tom stifled a laugh and took stock of his options. A bit of tattered paper plastered on the elevator declared it out of order, and Tom couldn't see where the freight elevator was. Deciding not to bother the blanket lady any further, he located the stairs and made his way up. Six stories later and with legs burning, he faced the door to Willa's apartment. His hand rested on the doorknob and pushed lightly, the door opening with the whine of rusted hinges. The door frame was warped and bent, and the chain lock had been forced out of the wall. Someone had come in without an invitation.

The one-bedroom apartment inside was nice, if sparse. The furniture was all cheap particle board, what was left of it anyway. Tom noted the tell-tale signs of a struggle, overturned furniture, strewn clothes, and cheap takeout containers on the floor. The wall mounted television sported a nasty crack running vertically through the screen. He didn't see any blood.

Checking the small refrigerator in the equally small kitchen, Tom noted few if any spoiled items. So not gone for long then. A pack of cigarettes, half-opened and left on the counter, made their way into his jacket. A faded framed head-shot confirmed he had the right apartment. A quick search didn't reveal anything, and Tom stood in the middle of the apartment scratching his chin.

Then he remembered the camera outside.

Concentrating, he brought his internal directory up into his field of vision. A series of deliberate eye movements selected the number he wanted, and the call was placed.

"Hey there, bro. What's going on?" For a change, Sunny's face didn't pop up in his field of vision. Usually, she liked to have conversations face to face.

"Hey, Sunny. Need a bit of a favor."

Sunny let out a loud sigh. "Yeah, of course, you do. Get shot again?"

"What? No, it's not like that at all."

"Okay, so what is it? Hey, stop that, I'm on a call here."

"Bad time?"

"No, it's .... I said stop it." Sunny broke off, and Tom could hear what sounded like giggling. "Sorry, okay. So what do you need?"

"I'm looking into something and have hit a dead end. I wanted to know if you could help out." Tom gave the address of the building. "There's a camera out front, so I want to know who came in that didn't fit. Should have been about seventy-two hours ago or so. Somewhere in that time frame?"

"Seventy-two hours? Yeah, give me a second. God, their protection is weak. Hey, stop that, I'm working here."

"Excuse me?" Tom couldn't help but smile a little.

"No, not you, it's .... Never mind. Yeah, got it. It's going to take a bit for me to cycle through this and get back to you, okay? You're not planning on dropping offline or anything like that are you?"

"Huh? No, nothing like that."

"I want a cut of what you're getting paid, too."

"Yeah, sure." Tom looked around the apartment one last time, sighed and left.

"Twenty percent?"

"Sounds good," Tom said, peering down the corridor. Empty.

"You're not arguing?"

"Nope."

Sunny opened her chat window and scowled at Tom, her synthetic green eyes narrowed to slits. "There's something you're not telling me."

"I'm not getting paid."

"What? Fuck! So who are you...? No. Nope. No. Uh-uh. Don't like it. You're doing this for Shari aren't you?"

Tom's smile disappeared. "Yeah. Kind of. Look, one of her coworkers stopped showing up at work. I agreed to look into it, okay?"

"That's it? You and Shari aren't getting back together? Just some stripper stopped showing up to work, and you decided to stick your nose in?"

Tom sighed. "Yeah, pretty much. Look, if you don't want to do it, I understand. I can find…."

"Fuck. That. Noise. You can't afford anyone half as good as me. If I find out that you are doing this to get Shari to drop her panties for you."

Tom snorted. "If I wanted that, I could go through a lot less hassle and get a drink on top of it."

Sunny sighed. "Yeah, fine, whatever. Go get a cup of coffee or something. I'll have something for you in a couple of hours."

TOM TINKED HIS METAL fingers against his third bottle of beer as he sat at the bar. The cheap particle board was pitted and stained, the air filled with smoke, and the jukebox played nothing but vintage Country & Western. Still, it had everything Tom wanted in a bar. Alcohol and the natives kept to themselves. A faint pinging told him Sunny was calling. A slight fuzzy feeling told him the beer was working.

"Got something for me?"

The bartender looked up, shook his head, and went back to cleaning and reading the news on his phone.

"That coffee looks a lot like a beer."

Tom coughed and shifted the bottle out of his view. "High-jack my image feed again?"

Sunny laughed. "Built my own backdoor into it last time you were here for service. This way when Mom asks how you are doing, I can tell her. Oh, which reminds me, you should call her."

Tom checked the time-stamp in the lower left of his vision. "Pretty sure she's asleep right now."

"Yeah, yeah." Sunny stifled a yawn. "That's what I'm going to be as soon as I'm done talking to you."

"You found the people I'm looking for?"

Sunny cracked a smile. "Did better than that. You've got incoming."

A series of three images floated in front of Tom, all rendered in two dimensions.

"Cheap ass security camera wasn't upgraded to three-dee. I cleaned up the resolution, managed to fill in some details, and ran a search to figure out who these guys are. Tom, I…I think you need to step away from his one."

"Who are they?" Tom's hand clenched around the beer bottle. The bartender edged further away.

"Okay, these two? Standard corporate security." The images focused on a man and a woman. They wore casual, nondescript clothing, and didn't seem to be armed.

"Yeah?"

"Yeah." The image zoomed in, capturing the detail of earpieces blinking steadily. "Bit of a giveaway they aren't natives. Nothing distinguishing about either of them otherwise. They might be doing heavy work, but they're collecting a wage-slave salary. You can tell from the way they're dressing. And their cheap-ass haircuts. Pretty sure their gear is strictly off the shelf. Pathetic." Sunny clicked her tongue in disapproval.

"Got it. And the other guy?"

"Yeah. Him." Sunny's voice dripped contempt over the connection, and her face screwed up like she smelled something foul. "Rufus Winkler." In Tom's view, a resume replaced his image. "He's like some bizarre mash-up of biologist and computer engineer. Got his start at Coven, Inc. Moved from there to Limitless Industries sometime last year."

Something about Limitless Industries seemed familiar to Tom, but he couldn't quite place it. "Wait, aren't they involved in wetware development?" Wetware involved biological models for computation instead of inorganic ones. Tom scratched the back of his neck where the scar was, where they'd placed the microcomputer running most of his subsystems.

"Bingo, big brother. Mr. Winkler — sorry, Dr. Winkler — seems to be something of an expert in the field. Limitless' public statements say they are still in early stages of developing something big but hope to have something released for trial within the next five years. Winkler is listed as one of the leads on the project. "

"What's he doing slumming in this part of town?"

"Good question." Sunny typed on her keyboard. "No idea. I see them going into the building but not out."

"There's a freight elevator that only exits out the back."

"Why didn't you say so? Crap, no camera back there. Wait, give me a moment. All right, yeah, I picked up another feed. Hold on a moment."

Tom sipped his beer as Sunny worked, the tip of her tongue poking between her lips.

"All right, got it."

A video image came up in Tom's sight. In it, he saw Winkler and the two security heavies escorting a young woman down the street. Her hands were in front of her, and she stumbled along. Tom felt his mouth go dry.

"Hey, you're going to have to pay for that," the bartender grumbled, pointing at Tom's hand. He didn't realize he'd shattered the bottle in his mechanical grip.

"Sorry," he mumbled. He produced a credstick, thumbed the amount over to the bartender along with a tip. He stood up and headed for the door.

"So that's it, right? All done? Time to call Shari and apologize you can't find her girl, right?"

"No." Tom pushed his flesh and blood hand against the door, stepped out into the world. A cold drizzle pattered off his coat and bare head.

"No? Come off it Tom, you don't owe this girl anything. And going up against Limitless by yourself? Are you nuts?"

Tom turned his collar up against the rain, started walking toward his apartment. "Are you saying you won't help?"

"What? Fine. Yes, I'll help. You've updated your will recently?"

"Yep, everything goes to Mom." He started a mental checklist of what he'd need.

"Oh. All right then. What do you want from me?"

"Get some sleep for starters. It's getting close to dawn, and I've got some prep work to do. Get me an address for Limitless, all right?"

"Yeah, sure. Don't do anything without me, all right?"

Tom smiled. "Sunny, if I didn't know better, I'd almost think you cared."

TOM SAT ON THE floor of his apartment, a disassembled handgun in front of him. He'd taken it apart, cleaned each piece, and was in the process of putting it back together again. They weren't his favorite kind of weapon, but Tom wasn't the sort to let personal feelings get in the way of practicality. A variety of other useful items were arrayed around him, waiting to be put in his satchel bag.

He'd muted his headphone, but a steady blinking message told him he had incoming from Sunny.

"What've you got?"

"Advice. Step away, Tom." Heavy bags were around her eyes, and a half-burned cigarette dangled from her bottom lip.

"Thought you quit?"

"What, the cigarette? Heh. Yeah. Except when I'm stressed. And guess what I am right now? Thank you very much for that, by the way."

"So what did you find out?" Tom busied his hands with putting the gun back together. He didn't need his eyes to tell him what piece went where.

"Rufus Winkler is officially dead as of two weeks ago."

"What? But...."

"Let me finish. Winkler was declared dead by Limitless. We obviously saw Winkler up and walking around on that video feed. Ergo, Winkler is still alive."

"Or?"

"Or he is a zombie or somebody stole his face and is wearing it, or someone cloned him, or…. Yeah, I get it. Anyway. Moving. On. Limitless confirmed his death, along with the death of two security personnel in a lab accident two weeks ago." Sunny took a long drag on her cigarette. Images flashed up in Tom's vision. Body bags being dragged from a smoking wreck of a building.

"Same personnel we saw last night on that feed?"

Sunny nodded.

"Looking pretty spry for dead people." Tom finished assembling the gun.

"I was thinking the same thing. So I did some digging. Did you know Winkler bought a warehouse in an industrial park six months ago? Or that there have been steady shipments to that warehouse? Last delivery happened last week. All of it paid for out of one of his own accounts."

Tom blinked. "How did Limitless not pick up on this?"

Sunny smiled and stubbed out her cigarette. "Winkler did a decent job covering his tracks. He used a false identity and a couple of shell companies to handle the purchases."

"And you found him."

Sunny's smile grew wider. "Damn straight I did."

"So he's out of bounds then. No corporate back-up. No one watching his back but these two goons, right?"

Sunny shook her head. "I have no idea. For all I know, this is Limitless' way of going black with his project. Plausible deniability. Fake the death, set Winkler somewhere up away from the main campus, let him do his thing. A lot of the shipments were high-end computer components, biological laboratory stuff. I have a bad feeling about this."

"You've got an address?"

Sunny glared at Tom through her emerald eyes. "You're still going?"

Tom smiled, finished loading the gun, and slipped it into his shoulder holster. "What do you think?"

TOM CROUCHED LOW AGAINST the wall in the industrial park, staring across at the warehouse Sunny had identified. A single van sat in the parking lot out front, but there was no other indication that anyone was home. A fine rain fell from the skies, trickling down the back of Tom's neck. The park had seen better days, the rusted shells of stripped cars dotting the asphalt. Rats as large as dogs scuttled through the dark, beady eyes watching Tom.

"Not too late to turn back," Sunny chimed in.

"Come on, don't you want to know what's inside?"

"Not if it means losing my favorite brother."

"Sunny, I'm your only brother."

"Picky, picky. Come on, if you're going to do this, we might as well get it over with. Oh, hey, I figured out where the security cameras are." A map superimposed itself in Tom's eyes. A red line from Tom's position squiggled its way to the warehouse. "Stick to this route, and you should be fine."

"Should be?"

Sunny smiled. "Shit happens, bro."

Tom made his way according to the map, keeping his movements slow and deliberate. He froze at one point, hugging a wall as a car drove by, then kept moving.

"Hold up, there's a camera coming up over the back door. You see it?" Sunny's voice crackled in his ear as the map disappeared from view.

"Yeah, I got it."

"Good." Tom waited as Sunny worked her magic on the other end. "All right, you're good to go. There's a RFID transmitter on the door. See it?"

"Yeah, I got it." Tom knelt by the back door and pulled his tool roll from the satchel he wore crosswise. It didn't take long to work the plastic cover off the box to expose the electronics underneath. It took even less time for Sunny to walk him through the next steps. The door gave a slight click, and Tom, gathering his tools, was in.

Tom blinked. The entire warehouse was bathed in a cool blue light, reminding him of an aquarium. At some point, Winkler had converted the entire space to a combination of a server farm and medical theater. Transparent plastic sheets ran from the ceiling to the ground, and the chill air raised goosebumps on his one flesh arm. Tom passed an empty, red-stained operating table behind the plastic sheets as he scanned the area, alert for any other presence, his gun held loose in his hand.

A figure, slightly built, came out from behind a bank of computer servers, carrying a tablet, his eyes fixed on it.

"Dr. Winkler?" Tom asked, keeping his gun down, hoping Winkler hadn't seen it yet.

"Oh, fuck! Protocol Seven!" Winkler backpedaled, feet getting tangled as he spun to get away. Instead, he sprawled on his face, the tablet cracking underneath him.

"Dr. Winkler, I have a few…." A bullet impacting near his feet interrupted Tom. He sprang back, taking cover behind a pylon. "Guess we can't talk about this, huh?" More gunshots replied.

Tom peered around the corner. A security guard Tom recognized from the security footage dragged on Winkler's arm, getting him to cover. The other crouched nearby, gun held steady with both hands. Tom swiveled his head back in time to avoid catching a bullet. Tom dug into his satchel, his hand closing over a cool metal cylinder. He lobbed it around the corner as he covered his head with his arms. The thunderous crash from the flash-bang made everything sound like it was underwater.

Tom went around the corner, gun firing. The security guard providing cover twitched and jerked as the bullets hit her. Tom slid to his knees to get behind a crate as her answering fire sliced through the air, a sharp pain hitting him in the shin. Cursing, he rolled, a line of bullet holes stitching up the side of the crate. Tom came up firing. The guard sprawled on her back, gasping like a landed fish. Tom limped over, pants clinging wetly to his leg. She tried to raise her gun. He pulled the trigger twice.

As he dropped the clip out of his pistol and slammed home the next one, he saw her still trying to raise her gun.

"Sorry about this," he said, then paused. One of the bullets had impacted her head, but instead of penetrating, it had formed a dent, the bullet still visible.

"What the…?" Tom stepped down hard on her wrist, pinning it to the ground.

The guard opened her mouth, but nothing came out. Tom leaned down, pulled off her sunglasses. Silver lines ran across her body, and her eyes were featureless lenses. Despite her wounds, she tried to move, to attack. Instead of blood, her wounds leaked a quicksilver fluid over the floor.

"What are you?" Tom raised his gun, hesitated for a moment, and put a final bullet through her eye.

Tom headed toward the back of the warehouse where he saw Winkler and the other security guard go. Passing a row of hospital beds, some still occupied by flat-lined occupants, he saw the security guard crouched behind an overturned desk, his pistol aimed at Tom. Tom didn't move fast enough into cover, the bullet spanging off his metal arm.

"Winkler? You want to talk now?"

"Limitless sent you, didn't they? They cut my funding, do you know that? I showed them demonstrable progress, and they cut my funding, and now they are sending you to kill me. Well, I was ready for you, wasn't I?"

Tom wrinkled his nose. "Limitless? Nope. This is a private matter. I'm looking for a girl named Milan. You remember her? Maybe you know her by her other name, Willa. Nice girl. Sweet girl. Never harmed a fly. Took her clothes off for money. Ring a bell?"

"You're here because of the stripper?" Winkler laughed, a high tittering noise that echoed off the walls. "It's too late, you know. The process is complete."

"Process? What process...?" Tom's sentence was choked off by the arm-like steel cable around his neck. As he tried to bring his gun around, a knife-hand strike hit the inside of his wrist, disarming him. He twisted his head down and tried to tuck his chin.

He felt the security guard twisting, trying to bring his head around. Tom stayed with it, even as his vision narrowed and a rushing sound filled his ears. He struck with his elbows, but his attacker swung with him, absorbing the blows and refusing to loosen his grip. Tom bent his knees, letting his whole body go slack. Feeling the arm around his neck loose, Tom pushed up explosively. His head cracked against his strangler's jaw. Pain exploded along the top of his head, but Tom kept his presence of mind to bend and throw his attacker to the ground. Scrambling for his gun, he brought it up, only for the security guard to tackle him, driving him back against a pylon and knocking his gun from his hand. Tom locked his arms around the guard, driving him down to the ground.

Tom lifted his metal arm. It was the hammer. The floor was the anvil. After Tom had finished, the guard's head was a shattered mess.

Leaning against the pylon, weak from exertion and blood loss, Tom half-expected to find Winkler gone, but he was still there, lying face down, a pool of dark red spreading out from his body. Standing over him, holding the other security guard's gun, was the girl Tom recognized from the picture. Only naked. Quicksilver lines ran across her limbs like circuitry.

"Willa?"

The girl looked up with the same camera lens eyes as the security guards. Tom bit back the bile and raised his gun.

"Wait."

Tom blinked. He kept his gun half-raised, but his finger was off the trigger. "Why?"

Willa blinked. "Because I want to explain."

Tom sniffed. "Winkler used a slave drive, right? Isn't that what he did to the security guards? Turned them into drones? Is that what he did to them? What he did to you? Is that Limitless' big development?" He shook his head, took a step closer. Tom blinked, and Willa pointed her gun at his head. He didn't remember seeing her move.

"No." Willa looked down at Winkler, then back at Tom. "Well. Yes. That is what he did to them. But not to me."

"Oh?"

"This body was dying." Willa tapped the side of her head. "Brain tumor. Couldn't afford the medical treatments. Doctor Winkler was a regular where I entertained. Told me he could cure me."

"He lied."

"Yes." Willa tilted her head to the side. "He needed a new subject. A test subject for uploading artificial intelligence into a meat body. The guards were experiments only. Not enough independence to be considered a success. No chance at learning." She paused looking down at the bodies. "The interface he used was crude, destroyed higher thinking. He modified it with me. Direct neural uplink of an artificial intelligence into an organic system."

Tom blinked hard. "He did that? He uploaded an AI directly into your body?"

Willa shook her head. "No. Not quite. Not enough space in the body to store the unit needed. He developed a nanite system, one designed to interface with the neural connections. It also eats cancer."

Tom snorted. "So he killed Willa."

"Aren't I Willa?"

Tom lowered his gun. "No. I'm not sure what you are, but you aren't Willa."

"So you'll try to kill me?"

Tom holstered his weapon. "I'm not that person. Other people might, though."

"Like Limitless?"

Tom breathed hard. He felt in his pockets, found the cigarettes he'd stashed there. He slipped one between his lips, lit it off his left index finger. "Yeah." The nicotine didn't make him feel any better.

Willa dropped the gun, the sound of it echoing across the concrete. "What should I do?"

Tom limped past her, toward the exit. "Put some clothes on. Try and start a new life." He stopped, looked her over, thinking, *what would a rogue AI trapped in a human body do, anyway?*

"Look, fine, you can come with me for a bit. I know some people. Maybe we can figure something out."

Willa placed her hand on Tom's shoulder, stood up on her toes to brush her lips against his. He tried hard not to think about how very naked she was.

"Thank you."

"For what?"

Willa tilted her head again. She didn't blink, the all-seeing lenses of her eyes taking everything in. "Is that not a proper way of saying, 'Thank you?' I still have some of Willa's memories and…"

"Yeah, yeah, okay. I still prefer money, though. Come on, see if you can find something to wear. I have a few calls to make." He looked down. "I need to get patched up. Again. Sunny's gonna throw a shit fit."

Goddamn, Tom thought, *how the fuck am I going to explain this to Shari?*

END

MATTHEW X. GOMEZ is a speculative fiction writer who lives in Maryland with his wife, two kids, and two cats. His work has appeared on the Dark Futures website, in *Phase 2* magazine, and in the *Midnight Abyss* anthology from Writers Carnival (2013). He can be found on Twitter @mxgomez78 and his assorted short fiction can be found at mxgomez.wordpress.com.

WHEN THE WORM TURNS
Tanja Cilia

CERISE SIGHED. SHE'D YET to get used to how her newly-implanted *haws* functioned. It was a weird sensation, feeling them moving horizontally. She wanted to rub her eyes to get rid of what was not quite an itch…but she knew that her fingernails would probably burst her eyeballs, and where would she be, then?

Her employers told her that the nictitating membrane was just the thing to stop her getting infections in the Orchard. She had done her research, and she knew that this particular body modification was as useful as it was important. But she resented it nonetheless. Oh, yes, she'd seen what happened to those who got something in their eye before the Operation happened. A corneal injury was not pleasant. If sepsis, or what passed for such, set in, they would be relegated to the Underfloors, losing several castes in the process.

The caterpillars they were harvesting were descended from Australian Lepidoptera. So sometimes, there was a throwback, and a couple of them developed one or two of those stinging hairs — fragile spines — which are really modified hairs anyway. This happened despite the careful genetic manipulation that was supposed to ensure it didn't happen. Because to err was human, still. Stung by the splendor, to wreck a quote from Browning…

Anyone whose skin came into contact with one of these urticating hairs developed a terribly itching, and burning skin irritation, and inflammation, and ugly papules. There was worse; if the hairs were of the venomous kind, there could even be anaphylactic shock. Safety gear was supposed to be worn at all times — but you know how it is, sometimes you need to scratch your nose, and a gloved hand just won't do. And of course, the bullies called you a sissy if they dared you to remove the gloves, and you didn't.

One of the newest Operators, who'd had a panic attack and felt that the face mask was "stifling" her, had inhaled a couple of hairs, and she nearly died when they traveled to her lungs. She still had breathing problems — Cerise could hear the slight wheeze when the girl was tired, nearing the end of the Shift. But she pretended not to notice and surreptitiously threw a couple of caterpillars into the girl's pail every so often. If the girl told anyone she wasn't feeling well, she'd have been demoted.

Cerise felt as if she'd been lumped with these — what had they called them back on Earth? Windscreen wipers — back in the day when vehicles did not have sensor-operated regulators for the Plexiglas.

Now she felt like an aardvark, which, according to the Acroasia history tapes in the library, closed its second eyelid when raiding termite nests to protect their eyes — or a woodpecker, which closed it when pecking at tree-trunks to prevent its eyes from popping out of its head because of the force. But she kept these thoughts to herself. Of course. It wouldn't do to show you were a swot, a nerd, or a geek. You'd get bullied. Or worse.

Coming so soon after the titanium knee replacements, which were supposed to aid mobility and give staying power when she had to stand or walk for long periods of time, Cerise assumed that the *palpebra tertia* insertion was almost a guarantee that the operation meant that she was destined to die here. She would never be able to walk properly again in Earth's atmosphere. To think what a good party trick it would have been, though, to look directly into the sun and not blink.

Cerise envisioned a bleak future spent in picking fluorescent grubs off cabbages, with maybe a sabbatical when the weighing machine counted a billion strynes. But this was the stuff of legend — no one had ever managed it yet. And she didn't like it one iota. But there was nothing she could do about it.

There were certain things androids could never do, despite the fact that their fine motor skills were much better than those of their predecessors. Even though their pincer grasp had been improved, the wastage rate was too much for the Company. They had reverted to hiring humans. Protein and trace minerals were an important source of nutrition in a rarefied atmosphere. The caterpillars, which looked like animated jelly-beans, were genetically modified and imbued with added vitamins and minerals.

Ironically, just like the prickly pears of the Mediterranean climate for which Cerise still yearned, the green grubs were the sweetest; the red ones the juiciest, and the orange ones the tartest. Colors had been introduced to make the caterpillars more attractive, and to differentiate the flavors. The Company had cornered the market.

Gourmet packs of worms were sold by the millions. They were packed during the last shift of the day, nestled in a bed of pollen-sprinkled beeswax, and wrapped in gold film, because of the proven added medicinal properties. Gold was not inert here, as it was back on Earth. Talk about different realities.

Funny how the things you took for granted could be stolen from you in a split second. Who would have told her that replying to an advert in the Situations Vacant columns would have had such dire consequences? *Work in a smoke-free environment. Employee benefits. Good Pay. Transport provided.* How could she know that most of those who had applied for the job would be drugged, abducted, and sent to work on Grenada III?

All her fellow Orchard operators had been like her, back on Earth. Single, no family, between jobs. No one would file a Missing Persons Report for them. Qualifications — or the lack of them — had had nothing to do with whether they were selected, or not.

Cerise thought their situation was reminiscent of that horror story, in which a young medical student tries to buy a human skeleton on the black market, and gets her own, delivered to her address after she has been seized by the body-snatchers who had run out of graves from where to filch cadavers. But at least they were still alive. For now.

None of the Operators could complain. They could not join a Union. The Common Good Law saw to that. Moreover, Cerise knew that the *haws* did their work well because she never had to rub her eyes because of the pollen here, as she had had to do on Earth, each springtime. However, she would gladly trade the previous discomfort, and more, with her air-foam bed and privileged status as Operator.

She picked a few more caterpillars off the cabbages and smiled. Oh, the irony of it all. Back on Earth, the larvae were treated as pests.

But on Grenada III, they were worth their weight in platinum (there was so much gold here that it was practically worthless). They had become a staple part of the diet and were exported to worlds beyond. Cerise often wondered what the reaction would be, if someone keyed in the wrong coordinates on the delivery disc, and a package found its way to Earth.

The fattest, most succulent grubs were set aside for the Bosses. But there was nothing Cerise liked better than to pluck a particularly luscious-looking one and crush its head between her thumb and index finger and then popping it into her mouth. Wasn't that the same as eating raw limpets and sea urchins? Didn't some people eat locusts or octopus, raw? Back on Earth, it was said that a tailor was entitled to his cabbage. She knew that the term referred to pilfering, rather than to Orchard Business. Wasn't there a book by Harold Robbins which had this premise as the downfall of a merchant? The absurdity of her situation called for a hefty dose of irony, did it not?

It was her way of thumbing her nose at the Company, a silent protest for having been exported like a factory component and stripped of her dignity as a human being.

In the mess, there had been gossip about how the Company was thinking of giving Orchard employees the *tapetum lucidum*, too. Were they trying to turn them into cats? Why on earth would they need yet another membrane in their eyes? What good would having reflective eyes be? And why should they be able to see well in semi-darkness? Did the Bosses intend to lower the level of light on the Orchard, yet again, to save on energy and power bills?

Cerise was made of stern stuff. She had developed her own mantra to get her through the humdrum repetitive work of endless days. She recalled the rhyme from her History Lessons, which was supposed to help children remember the names and order of British Monarchs;

> *Willie Willie Harry Stee;*
> *Harry Dick John Harry Three;*
> *One Two Three Neds, Richard Two;*
> *Harrys Four Five Six….then who?*
> *Edwards four five, Dick the bad;*
> *Harrys (twain), Ned Six (the lad);*
> *Mary, Bessie, James you ken,*

Then Charlie, Charlie, James again…
Will and Mary, Anna Gloria,
Georges four, Will four Victoria;
Edward seven next, and then,
Came George the Fifth in nineteen ten;
Ned the eighth soon abdicated,
Then George Six was coronated;
After which Elizabeth,
And that's all folks, until her death.

The piped muzak got on her nerves. She rarely talked to the other operators. She did not want to waste time, and in any case, their conversations were mostly a mixture of inane chatter, their own interpretations of what they would have seen on the videoscope the night before, and idle gossip. On their part, they thought she was stand-offish, if not downright weird.

But she had a Plan — as they used to say back on Earth, "there's an application for that!" Cerise was the ultimate Model Granger Operator. She meant to work her way up the ranks until she was no longer on the factory floor. The kitchen would do nicely.

Lunch on that particular day was crowder pea stew, corn-on-the-cob, and cucumber raita. Most of the Operators grimaced, but she cleaned her plate; not because she really wanted the food, though. She wanted to make a good impression on the Company, for she sensed there were CCTV cameras hidden unobtrusively here and there, which caught every movement the Operators made during Recreation Time and Eating Time.

She had practiced her deadpan expression to a T. It was perfect. Not one muscle twitched as she put her plate, glass, cutlery, and napkin in the Chute. On her way out of the Dining Hall, she bowed reverentially from the waist before the Company Logo; she knew this would make a further good impression on whoever was watching. Most of the Operators just gave the Logo a perfunctory nod.

Cerise bided her time. Operators came — and went, never to be seen again. Talking on the job, go figure friendships, was frowned upon. Each day was much like the one before it. *Follow the instructions, and you will be all right*. Walk, select, pluck, weigh, sort. Walk, select, pluck, weigh, sort. Walk, select, pluck, weigh, sort. Walk, select, pluck, weigh, sort. She hated being on the packing shift, where she just had to sit down…and she was not adding to her quota of plucked caterpillars.

The notice stuck to the door of her Cubicle caught Cerise unawares. *You have reached a billion strynes. You are cordially invited to attend Company Office at your earliest convenience.* It was an order, not an invitation, and Cerise hied off to the Administration Block.

Little did the Company know it, but this was the beginning of the end — for them.

Cerise was offered the choice of a Reversal Operation, with a view to working in an exalted position on Grenada II. She refused it, saying she did not want to face the knife — the laser — any more than she had to. It would, in reality, spoil her plans. That impressed the Administration, so when she for a transfer to the Kitchens, they did not refuse her request.

She wrought her revenge over five *dirths* — about two Earth years — by introducing certain elements into the food meant for the Administration, that left cumulative effects. Even when the illness was rife, the Medics could not pinpoint the cause. It would never have occurred to them to link the insanity, followed by suicide, to the most hardworking Kitchens worker ever.

And that is how Grenada III was claimed for Earth, and how I got to know my grandma's story.

END

TANJA CILIA is a freelance writer from the Mediterranean island nation of Malta.

BIOMORPH

Roy C. Booth

Originally appeared in serial form in *Phase 2* #'s 3–5, Dark Futures, 2014–2015.

DANGER.

THE SKIMMER'S CRACKED viewscreen flickered back to life once more.

Danger.

Randon Klooge installed the Entron-Imex Intrude Alert System in his skimmer to ensure that no undesirables could ever surprise him and endanger his life or his mission. Tonight it failed to protect both.

A massive hand of circuits and bio-engineered flesh plucked the broken, lifeless form off the control console and let it slump to the purple filament floor. Deftly, the same hand punched out the proper code-frequency on the viewscreen's communications system. The digital interface faded away, replaced by a seductively dressed woman in revealing robes placing a disk into what appeared to be a larger version of Klooge's intruder system, logo and all. After a pause, she asked, "Anything else?" with a sultry smile.

A low, chuckle-like grunt escaped from the thin lips of skimmer's lone live occupant.

"All right, then. The information has been transferred, as per requested. Stand by for further instructions. Dispose of the body as you see fit. Your account has been updated. The Enlightened One shall contact you personally, Labelos." The viewscreen returned to its blank, greenish state.

Labelos shook his scaly head in wonder. Pure breed humans, for some morbid reason, always fascinated him. So fragile, so illogical. The longer he intermingled with them, the more he subtly became like them. He almost found that ridiculous, nonfunctional raiment attractive on her, for example. It was bad enough he was developing a sense of humor. With that in mind, he smirked. It was humorous the way Klooge, in a stiff, robotic sort of way, tried to defend himself after the initial shock of Labelos bypassing his defenses. Labelos wished he'd savored the moment a bit longer before slamming the fool's head into the control console, thus snapping the neck in the process. Yes, he was developing a sense of humor, all right, a rather sick one, but a sense of humor nonetheless.

Labelos slowly emerged his three-meter frame out of the battered skimmer and scanned down the garbage-strewn alley. So far no one had noticed what was happening thanks to the holo-projector he had set up earlier. To the average passerby, the entire area looked like any other alley on Syferius VII: desolate and incredibly filthy.

Labelos went around to the passenger's side, opened the dull metallic door, and casually lifted Klooge's broken corpse out. From there he tossed it against the graffiti-smeared wall where it landed in a crumpled heap very similar to that of a child's rag doll. Pressing the silver stud on his left gauntlet brought the miniaturized laser cannon humming to life and soon two quick bursts reduced Klooge to a smoldering pile of ash. Labelos allowed a smile to pass on his thin lips: His second mission of the night was a resounding success.

Labelos slowly climbed back into the skimmer and flicked the ignition switch on, then released the mag brake. From there he proceeded down the narrow, cluttered streets until he entered the section of town appropriately known as the Thieves Quarters. Once a proud terrestrial spaceport in the days of the Frontier, this desolate place of gloom and despair only produced brigands and cutthroats now whereas in earlier times it was noted as the center of transportation of the most exquisite rare herbs and spices. That was quite some time before the Church of Enlightenment "purged" the area of "sin and corruption." Labelos smiled again. He now felt like he was coming home.

A moonbeam pierced the cloudy, multi-hued Syferian sky, illuminating the moldy deteriorating docks as it reflected off the rolling fog over the dark, brackish waters. Labelos took this as a good omen.

A shrill, ultrasonic scream emitted from the control console. The cracked viewscreen began to crackle to life once more. Labelos knew quite well the message was of the utmost importance for the ultra-high frequency used could only be heard with his technologically boosted senses. The Enlightened One was making contact.

"Greetings, Assassin Prime." The slow, methodical, almost inaudible voice of the scarlet-robed hooded figure always sent a chill down Labelos' spines. Rumor had it that the Enlightened One had all but utterly destroyed the former Assassin Prime in personal combat, a no mean feat for anyone to accomplish. The Enlightened One continued, "I trust your encounter with Ambassador Klooge proved entirely satisfactory on all facets?"

"Aye, O Great One. All has been done as your will dictates." Labelos made certain his diction was in strict accordance with the True Speech, even though it was excruciatingly painful to speak in his cybernetic throat.

"Splendid. I am transmitting the dossier over for download on your next victim. Eliminate this thorn in the High Church's side, and you will be richly rewarded. Failure will not be tolerated. I hereby bless thee in my name. Go forth and do glory to my name."

Labelos bowed his head and made the Church sign as the only thing he feared in the Eleven Known Inhabited Galaxies slowly flickered and faded away. He knew the dread price he would pay if he failed. Another cold sensation ran down his spines made him even more uncomfortable.

The skimmer slowly came to a stop once all of the data transferred from the Citadel of Enlightenment. Labelos set the mag brake and reclined as far back as he could in the plush velvet seats while thinking about his next contracted victim.

If the Enlightened One himself has personally contacted me, my new foe must be a very worthy adversary, indeed.

Perhaps this would be the challenge that Labelos so desperately yearned for. After all, dispatching Ambassador Klooge to whatever hell he believed in was mere child's play, as were his other dozen or contracted kills.

Labelos called up the dossier on the flickering, cracked viewscreen and scanned through the pages to see who or what he was up against. He expected to see some huge hulking brute or a well-known political foe of the High Church, something intriguing, something well worth his time and effort. Instead, he found pictures of a slightly stooped man of moderate height and medium build. At least in any physical sense, the humanoid appeared to be no threat to the Enlightened One or himself, nothing that would require one of his skill and power to dispose of. He checked the bio-scan records that were outdated by five full cycles: No evidence of any cybernetic enhancements or any DNA modifying. A pure breed human. And a born Terran citizen at that. Further data revealed an elevated intelligence score, a minor criminal history involving trespassing and petty larceny, and a series of registrations and permits for small arms weapons and various vehicle operations. Nothing appeared to be worth Labelos's time. Disappointment began to set in.

And then he saw how much the kill order paid.

Enough to buy a small moon outright.

Labelos clicked his tongue.

Now he was intrigued.

Labelos scanned further down and found his target's known address.

Garkov's Bar and Grille, The Point

The address was only a mere few blocks away on foot. Labelos allowed himself another smile. Slowly, he squeezed his enormous bulk out of the skimmer and began his preparations. He adjusted the power cells to his titanium electro-mace and then injected into his bull-like neck the specially treated saline solution to maintain his "psychological edge." The sudden surge of adrenalin and euphoria made the Biomorph shudder in the dim, smoky light.

Satisfied that the solution had worked as it should, Labelos placed a detonator under the skimmer's left front anti-gravity unit. Ever the professional, there would be little trace of anything to prove his presence save that of an unrecognizable shell of a scorched skimmer. The blame would eventually rest on one of the many freedom-oriented terrorist groups that opposed the High Church of Enlightenment; the High Church would see to that.

A red, streaked bolt of lightning scorched its way across the dark gaseous clouds high overhead. Another good omen as far as Labelos was concerned. Labelos trudged down the acid-rain soaked alley and when he rounded the corner, set off the detonator, never breaking stride after the resulting *fwa-whumph!*

After a few blocks, his destination came into full sight, an appropriate dead end. Garkov's Bar and Grille took up most of the bottom two levels of the Vieths Building, a living anachronism dedicated to an age long past, circa mid-20th century Sol III-Prime. Constructed mostly out of granite and other forms of stone from the quarries far to the west, the twelve story building rested precariously near a cliff's edge and seemed quite capable of tumbling down to the jagged sea-rocks over 300 meters below at any given moment. None of this greatly concerned Labelos, however, what interested him the most about the age lost relic and its gaudy neon lights was the apartment that jutted over the side of the building and the sea-rocks below. It was the so-called "Twelfth-and-a-Half Story," the home and office of William J. Flortz, the man he came to kill.

The walk over proved unremarkable.

Two roughly carved stone gargoyles greeted Labelos as he made his way to the establishment's entrance. They were uncanny statues nearly capable of having lives of their own, and if seen from the proper angle late at night, they did indeed seem to watch intently with cold gray eyes. For a moment he thought he saw one set of cold eyes dart his way but dismissed the entire notion as pure foolishness as he opened the door and made his way inside. Apparently, the saline solution's after effects were taking hold early or the dosage was off.

A trio of ludicrously dressed non-human individuals — perhaps skerns from Aletius II, they all looked alike to him from that system — greeted Labelos as he strode through the entryway. Apparently, they were the bouncers. All three wore ill-fitting baggy black suits with ridiculously over-sized bow ties, possibly another attempt at a touch of 'decor.' The attire did nothing to hide their long fore appendages and stubby, slug-like tails. One was balding and fat, another rail-thin with madly strewn curly hair, and the other had a shaggy black name that looked like someone put a bowl over his head when they cut his hair. All three had multiple small cuts and bruises on their faces and were now bickering senselessly with one another. Labelos ignored their manic antics and slipped past them as they started to push and shove one another. The whole brief incident annoyed Labelos somewhat, yet he could not pinpoint why. It was not his concern if this so-called Garkov insisted on hiring such incompetent staff.

The main bar area rollicked with a myriad of beings: bipeds and non-bipeds alike. Harlots, thieves, fishermen, and even a few well-known local politicians, all professional liars, chatted and caroused. Nonchalantly a few recognized him, yet made no outward sign that they knew him for it was political suicide to speak with a Biomorph in public, especially it could be the one who eliminated the competition during the last election race. A few individuals even thought he had appeared for them and slowly made their way to the nearest possible exit. Labelos ignored all of them and made his way to the nearest, and only, elevator unit.

It was out of order.

"Vildron's hooves," cursed Labelos under his breath.

Labelos quickly moved an eye to the side to see if he had gained any undue attention. A ruckus erupted behind Labelos as the three bouncers forcibly and loudly removed a drunken patron from his bar stool. The slovenly head bartender on duty even oversaw the sudden eviction. A glance in the opposite direction caught a young woman in a silver silicon-based dress that flashed sparkling lights all around her.

Good, a sex worker, he thought. *She can tell me what I need to know and will not be soon missed.*

Labelos blinked. Somehow her outfit interfered with his visual sensors, so he powered them down. Deftly, he pressed another silver stud on his left shoulder to initiate his personalized hologram projector, an implanted device composed of various micro-diodes and lenses throughout his coarse, steely hide. He merely copied the area in front of the elevator unit and deleted the prostitute from the scene. Even if he moved about without making too many sudden moves and the like, the hologram would remain as it should. The other patrons and staff would see him waiting by the elevator unit as long as nothing got in between the array or until he left the designated area and went about his further business.

Labelos strode over to her as she adjusted her hemline in a nearby private isolation alcove. By the time she noticed him looming over her, it was too late. Like a coiled Dralian snow viper, he struck out, pinning her lithe body against the shock absorbent, noise-proof duro-plastic wall while his right hand firmly clamped her by the throat. He made doubly sure the array remained unimpeded and only stood halfway into the alcove.

With a low, malicious hiss Labelos demanded information about the building, security, Flortz, and other mission vitals. She told him that there were two ways other than the elevator unit to get to the top level. The first consisted the use of an old wooden stairway that wound its way up to the "12 ½ Story." He ruled this out immediately as being a too direct approach leaving him in far too vulnerable position. His best course of action was to use the maintenance stairway behind the elevator unit. Labelos wondered why there wasn't a freight elevator, then realized the single elevator arrangement proved efficient enough since many of the floors above consisted only of offices and storage units, very few apartments. That, and since the closest system to Syferius VII was the Alterian System with its two binary stars; its space-faring inhabitants were much denser due to their far heavier gravity. Having only one industrial level elevator unit to handle such potential traffic now made a world of sense seeing how much space and power would be needed to operate safely and efficiently. And this ancient building could only take so much internal stress as it were.

She quickly answered his remaining questions and then, when satisfied with the results, he dealt with her the same way he fulfilled his first contract of the cycle concerning the assassination of a wealthy arms dealer from Narcos IV: He twisted her head 180 degrees and dropped her where she lay.

Labelos took his place by the elevator unit door and canceled the pre-programmed illusion he had set up earlier. He found the uncovered maintainer stairway entrance and proceeded to climb the long flight of stairs.

About three stories up he encountered an old blind man with dark glasses and a white sonar cane, groping along the wall until he reached the railing, grumbling about how elevator units were more reliable in his day.

On the fifth floor, Labelos encountered a food cart blocking the doorway. He pushed it out of the way with ease and continued on his way. Behind it was a pile of chicken feathers.

On the sixth floor, he had to sidestep a pool of skimmer transmission fluid and strangely began to start feeling uneasy about his mission. Were these just random encounters or something else?

Labelos did not meet anything unusual until he reached the ninth floor. There he found a righted crucifix with a figure of a man nailed to it. The small bronze relic intrigued Labelos for he had never seen one before, yet had heard rumors of such a thing existing amongst the Inner Planets. It sent a chill up his spines.

Finally, Labelos reached the top floor. As he tried to make his way to the roof, he discovered that the stairs leading beyond were blocked off by an electrified titanium gate. He could now either force his way through with his laser cannon or electro-mace and lose the element of surprise or go back down a few flights and go out onto the wooden spiral stairway snaking its way up to Flort'z office. Reluctantly, he started heading back down again.

The crucifix was missing on the ninth floor.

The wooden spiraling stairway proved to be a challenge for Labelos: A storm had now formed complete with raging winds and bursts of coin-sized hail. Soaking wet and mildly bruised, he made his way up to the office door. On the door was a small, tarnished nameplate that read: FLORTZ. Another one of the gargoyles he had encountered earlier rested above the door in a menacing manner with wings outstretched and fangs bared while its serpentine tail appeared to twitch in the flashing din of thunder and lightning.

Labelos inspected the door and discovered a milky-white screen of sensitive circuitry on the left side of the door. It was a Watch Corp. Palm Reader, no doubt only set to Flortz's unique specifications. Facial muscles twitched for a moment as the rage inside Labelos eventually abated. He could not break in without alerting his victim as was the case earlier with the stairway leading to the roof. Labelos savagely cursed under his breath as he tried to figure out his next plan of action.

"May I help you, sir?"

The cold sibilant voice seemed to be coming from all around Labelos.

"Wha..?" he rasped

"Mr. Flortz is gone for tea-time. May I assist you?"

Labelos then realized the voice was a self-programmed answering service most entrepreneurs set up to answer questions and the like while they were out on business, sort of a high-tech receptionist that didn't need a break every half an hour or so.

"Yes, when will Mr. Flortz be back?" he calmly asked.

"I do not know. He is rather unpredictable when it comes to tea-time. You'd best wait in the lobby for him to return."

Labelos thought he detected a mocking tone in the voice decided not to press the issue. "Thank you. I will see him later then." With that, Labelos turned around and made his way back down the lobby to wait for Flortz to show up. For about an hour he waited in the hallway only to be annoyed by the old blind man who wanted spare change, and the occasional smooth line from a con man or a prostitute to which Labelos only had to flash his four-inch steel fangs, which ensured his return to privacy in quite a hurry. Finally, a man who fitted the description of Flortz came in and dropped off a small parcel with the strange trio of bouncers and exchanged a few words of greeting with each as he made his way over to the elevator unit. To Labelos' surprise, the doors shut behind Flortz and then transported him to wherever he was going. The elevator unit became "out of order" again by the time Labelos got to it. That was when Labelos lost it. With a roar, he threw all caution aside and charged up the maintenance stairway. Labelos had been mocked, thwarted, used, and abused, in his mind, at least. Besides, it was about time he learned why Flortz was such threat to one so powerful as The Enlightened One. His savage, animal-like alien persona now took control. He was now the ultimate killing machine and nothing and no one was going to get in his way and survive to tell about it.

Labelos did not encounter a single living soul up the stairs and reached the wooden spiral staircase just as he caught a glimpse of Flortz entering his office. Labelos gazed over the railing. Below large waves rolled with tremendous force over the jagged rocks. Labelos was going to throw Flortz's broken corpse down there when he finally finished him off. Flortz had only a few more minutes to live before he would wind up down there.

The door shattered as a well-placed stroke from the electro-mace sent shards of debris flying in all directions. From the entry way, Labelos boomed a shout of primal rage as he advanced through the office's waiting room making short work out of the cloudy glass door that served as a partition to the outside world. Labelos was now face-to-face with the room's only occupant.

"In the name of The Enlightened Pone I, Labelos, Assassin Prime, hereby sentence thee to death!" Labelos' voice reverberated throughout the cubicle.

Seated behind a cluttered desk full of papers sat a slightly stooped man with his sleeves rolled up and a pen in hand. To the left of him was a coat rack with a long, tan coat in a style Labelos had never seen before. By that was a carved statuette of a black bird on a pedestal. Flortz had an equally odd brown hat on and wore glasses, another anachronism. With a faltering voice bordering on sheer terror, Flortz pushed back his glasses and replied, "Er...uhm...hi, what can I do for you? Heh... Heh..."

Labelos's only reply was a low, vicious hiss as he stepped closer from the entangled mass of armored circuits and coarse flesh.

"Er...could you ah, say, tell me what all of this is about?"

"The Enlightened One says you must die."

"Heh...oh...yeah. The Enlightened One. He still isn't sore about that run in on Quorp is he? I don't suppose we could...uh, say...discuss this in a more civilized manner like...er...rational sentient beings?"

"Die Terran scum!!!" roared the giant as he swung the electro-mace with all his might.

The devastating blow went unchecked though Flortz. The only proof of Labelos' handiwork was a desk reduced to splinters and a ghost-like wraith of Flortz hovering above it.

"How could...?" Labelos began to grope in total astonishment.

"Quite simply put Mr. Labelos, I have truly never been here in the first place."

The matter-of-fact voice came not from the wraith-like image hovering above the desk but from behind Labelos. Labelos quickly wheeled around to see Flortz standing by the door, placing his white sonar cane in the corner. He had been in disguise the entire time.

"Good night, Mr. Labelos. It has not been a pleasure knowing you. Have a nice trip."

As he spoke those prophetic words, Flortz yanked a seemingly innocent cord along the wall, thus activating the trap door poor Labelos had been standing on.

Labelos roared in anger as he dropped from the sky onto the jagged sea rocks far below. Flortz sighed and shook his head as the crashing surf slowly hid Labelos' battered, pulped form from view. "Sometimes they just never learn," he wearily muttered as he closed the trap door and dispersed his holographic doppelganger with a hand gesture. Making sure that the portal was secure, Flortz then turned and picked up the unscathed communicator lying on the floor. With communicator in hand, he stepped outside to the edge of the foreboding elements, turning it on.

"Yeah, Garkov, it's me. First of all, you can tell the ambassador that he can now leave the planet safely. Yes, all clear. Second, you can remove the other android I cooked up from isolation booth 6-B.

Right, the jammers worked fine and also send up a cleaning crew. I'll be pulling another desk out of storage tomorrow. Thanks."

Deftly, he turned the communicator off and placed it in his coat pocket along with his dark glasses. He looked out over the raging spectacle that was taking place before him one last time, then stepped inside, shuttering the doors. It would be only a matter of time before he and the Enlightened One played the Game again.

END

ROY C. BOOTH hails from Bemidji, MN where he manages Roy's Comics & Games (est. 1992) with his wife and three sons. He is a published author, comedian, poet, journalist, essayist, optioned screenwriter, and internationally awarded playwright with 57 stage plays published (Samuel French, Heuer, et al) with 825+ productions worldwide in 30 countries in ten languages. He is also known for collaborations with R Thomas Riley, Brian Keene, Eric M. Heideman, William F. Wu, Axel Kohagen, and others (along with his panel presence on the regional convention circuit). His latest three novels, also from Indie Authors Press, *Blood of Nyx*, *Raiders of the Seventh Planet,* and *MacGuffin,* have been recently added to his Amazon Author Page along with another hundred or so existing titles – www.amazon.com/author/roycbooth

See his entry on Wikipedia, his Facebook pages, and his various publishers' sites for more.

ELECTRIC LOVE
DJ Tyrer

FLASH FLEW WITH AMAZING speed above the virtual British landscape. Black ground merged with black sky, only the red lines of the data-paths differentiating them. Icons seemed to whizz past her, each representing a system. Soon, nanoseconds really, the silver ninja would be saved within the memory of the 'board that her flesh fingers operated in unison with the relayed pulses of her brain-waves.

Back.

Cara Hinton's eyes snapped open. She jerked the hitcher-jack from her data-port and let it fall free. It took only a moment to shut the 'board down before she carefully, lovingly packed it away. It may only have been a Virgin T-12, but it was her bread and butter. Without her 'board and the information it gained her, she'd have nothing left to sell but her body. As it was, it barely kept her in the dingy flat she called home.

Cara Hinton aged 25; a competent, yet minor-league jacker, average height, short brown hair, blue eyes, and still good-looking despite her fall from grace. Corporate background, tenement future.

As usual, after the stress, mental exertion, and exhilaration of a 'run, she was damp with sweat. She peeled off the recyclable vended vest and shorts she wore when on the job like this and stepped into the tiny wet room with mould-stained walls.

She stepped out of the shower and, once she was dry, pulled her smotch back onto her wrist. It took two attempts before it understood the command she gave it; like most of the things she owned, it was old and knackered. As she dressed, she left a voice mail for her client, "I have what you want. Meet me at The Holistic Lounge in one hour."

A few minutes later, dressed in the cheap synthleather jacket and miniskirt she preferred for nightclub visits, she was ready to go. She picked up her driving chip and slotted it in one of her data-ports. She'd never learned to drive but the activesoft allowed her to drive the old Peugeot 108 she kept in one of the lock-ups in the undercroft of the building. She'd never trusted a self-driving car since breaking free. She slipped the data-chip into another 'port, where it would remain hidden till she was ready to hand it over.

She left, smiling.

THE HOLISTIC LOUNGE WAS a simjunkie dump that was the perfect place for clandestine meets — most of the clientele were off in some other reality, slumped about with simsense helmets on. With so much of the country without power, addicts who couldn't afford data-ports congregated in places like this for their fix. A few chipheads would be slotting or purchasing or renting chips — The Holistic Lounge had a thriving lending library. Baz, the twitchy booster-addict who was paid in vials to stand outside the club beneath its tacky neon sign, barely glanced at her as she went inside. She headed for the makeshift bar near the entrance that existed for those, like Cara, who were here for business, or perhaps, soaking up what passed for "atmosphere." The place was dingier than her flat. The only thing the place had going for it was size — it was located in what had once been something called, if the half-hidden signage was complete, Tesco.

Cara bought a clear liquid that purported to be vodka and sat on a table away from the bar. She didn't have long to wait. She'd met the man who'd hired her here once before with her fixer, Hawkeye. Some work was all online, some involved meeting up in the flesh. It was swings and roundabouts really; neither was any safer.

He entered the Lounge and sat down opposite her. She knew his name was Dr. John Harrison — despite the usual "Meneer Smit" alias, the communications he'd needed her to look at had dispelled any illusion of anonymity. He was younger than she was and the fact he hadn't spent the last three years living on his wits only emphasized his youth. With his sculpted features, sharp demi-casual suit and chromed data-ports, he was almost the stereotype of a junior exec and not the sort of figure usually seen around here.

"You've got it?" he asked, despite the message she'd left.

"Yes." She slipped the chip from its socket and dropped it into his outstretched hand.

He looked at it, then looked at her.

"Robert Huntingdon doesn't exist."

"Of course he does. We've been dating for over a year."

Her client was what he appeared to be, a junior exec with AstraGlaxo CE. He'd struck up an unvetted online romance with someone calling himself Robert Huntingdon with the naivety of someone who worked more with genes than computers. When communications had abruptly halted, he'd offered Cara ten thousand nuRand to locate Mr. Huntingdon.

"He doesn't exist," Cara restated. Even video chats were no guarantee someone existed — he wouldn't have been the first person to fall in love with a virtual representation. But, he wasn't. "Robert Huntingdon doesn't exist, but Marianne Wellesley does."

"Sorry?"

"She's a niece of the Duke of Wellington and would much rather be his nephew. One year ago, she received access to her trust fund and flew to Switzerland to undergo gender reassignment. Having created a new identity, Robert then settled in Strasbourg, secured a position with ETC and entered into a long-distance relationship with you."

Her client waved his hand as if to say all that was inconsequential; to him, it probably was. "But," he asked, "why break off contact?"

"It wasn't of Robert's own volition. Jupiter Corporation put a lot of effort into tracking Marianne Wellesley down. The Duke," she added, "is a board member." He nodded. "Robert was snatched a week ago and is currently awaiting reversal of the reassignment."

"But, why?"

Cara shrugged. Who could fathom the reasoning of the corporate elite? Was it pride, an unyielding morality or just a vindictive streak? Was Robert's crime rebelling against nature, renouncing his family or taking a job with a rival corporation? Having lost her mother as a child due to such intercorporate rivalry, Cara understood how far they took the security of their industrial secrets.

"You have to help me rescue him!"

She laughed. "That's going to cost a lot more — and, just what do you imagine you'll do? Get married and live happily ever after? They'll just come after him again. You'd have to disappear off their radar altogether."

"Could you help us do it? You could erase our data trails, help create new identities."

"That costs even more..."

"I have a sizable R & D budget; if I gave you the codes, you could spoof the system and drain the funds."

"Okay, I could do that. But, you and Robert would have to start over on the streets."

"You did it," he said. She must have looked worried, as he added, "You're clearly corporate, originally. You don't talk quite like the...street people."

"Then, believe me when I say, it's not easy."

"But, it is possible?"

She considered. If he had the skill-set she assumed he did; he could probably find work in a backstreet gene-clinic, while Robert clearly had decent computer skills and could work as a jacker like her, just so long as he didn't do anything to attract his family's attention.

"Maybe. If you're willing to give up the easy life and take a risk."

"I am. For Robert, I am."

"Okay, then let's see just how much credit we can embezzle..."

WITH THE CODES HER client had supplied, it was almost ridiculously easy for Flash to sleaze her way into the AstraGlaxo CE system and clean out his budget. Converting the corporate credits into nuRand, they had almost eight hundred thousand to play with.

Cara called Hawkeye and arranged a meet at The Holistic Lounge the next afternoon. Her client had wanted to take part in the rescue, like some sort of modern-day knight in shining armor, but she'd made it clear he'd only be a liability, and he'd agreed to be holed up in a squat run by a simjukie she knew while they retrieved Robert. She just hoped that Robert wouldn't prefer to go it alone.

Hawkeye was already waiting for her. Once, she would have stared at someone like Hawkeye — in places like Chelsea; they were conspicuous by their absence. His mother had had the misfortune to be pregnant with him when the Attenborough Loyalists had put a cocktail of abortifacients and sterilizing drugs in the Liverpool water supply; he'd made it to term, but while his body and head were those of a child, his metal limbs were full-size. One of his eyes was ringed in steel and obviously artificial, giving him his name. He spoke with a rich Irish accent that she was pretty certain was fake. Right now, he was hunched over a pint of Guinness, or more likely some knock-off stout.

Beside him were two razors. Cara recognized one as Miss Match. She liked to say her name was due to the one-shot mini-flamer hid in her left hand, but it really referred to her appearance. More machine than woman, no two parts of her matched, and most of her prosthetics were chromed rather than hidden under synthskin, giving her a peculiar look. From what Cara had heard, she'd lost her limbs to a tartan missile while patrolling the border of the DMZ. The other razor was almost as heavily chromed, but had a sleeker look to him, and twitched with the readiness of augmented reflexes.

"This is Bonzo," Hawkeye said, nodding at the male razor. Cara refrained from asking how he got the nickname.

"We'll be breaking an unwilling patient out of a Harley Street chopshop," she told them. She'd already given Hawkeye an outline of the mission but explained it now in great detail.

"Okay," said Match, "that's all well and good, but how do we actually get to Harley Street."

That, of course, was the problem. You didn't just stroll into the Secure Zone from the sprawl. However, AstraGlaxo CE had a solid presence in the area, and her client had been able to give her the codes to provide them with both a pass and an official corporate ambulance to ride in on. According to the manifest, they would be carrying organs harvested from the poor for sale to corporate clients.

"Sounds easy," said Match, her tone sarcastic.

"It is," said Cara. "Just as long as AstraGlaxo CE don't notice they've got a deserter before we get in and we don't attract any unwanted attention before we get out again."

"May the saints preserve us," said Hawkeye, taking a gulp of his drink.

THE AMBULANCE WAS PARKED where it was supposed to be, and as they approached the barrier on the edge of the Secure Zone, it swung open for them without a physical check, the vehicle broadcasting the correct code. Cara was driving, and Bonzo was riding shotgun. AstraGlaxo CE security would be more likely to be upgraded with wetware, but the corporations took their guards as they came. Hawkeye and Match were hidden in the back, being too distinctive. She guessed they were scanned as they passed through the barrier, but their pass stated there were two more guards in the back and that that shouldn't cause any problems. Hawkeye had even brought along a chill-box of what he assured her were pig organs, so any scan would even pick that up as confirmation of their story.

"We can have a fry up to celebrate," he'd joked as he slid the box into the back.

Cara had decided she'd rather stick to soyburgers.

From here, Cara let the ambulance do the driving. She hated smart vehicles — it was so easy for control of them to be jacked, but the last thing she wanted was to get lost or break a traffic law and attract attention. Even driving manually risked someone taking notice.

"Here we are," she said as they neared the rear gates of the clinic in which the data said Robert Huntingdon was awaiting reassignment reversal. As they approached them, she connected the hitcher-jack from her data-port to her 'board; the city street vanished, and she was outside the icon for the building's system, the wireless connection here better than a hardline from outside the Secure Zone.

She had inserted a patient delivery onto their rota earlier, so the gates should open automatically open to admit them. While in the system, Flash had also left herself a back door, allowing her to slip back inside the art deco hospital icon without any trouble.

Flash headed for the node controlling the building's security systems. She didn't doubt it would be well protected with countermeasures, but thanks to the codes John had supplied her with, she had a head start on spoofing the system into thinking she was legitimate. Moving quickly but cautiously, she did nothing to arouse suspicion while planting the viruses that would take down the cameras and other security protocols as they entered the yard; she had no desire to have their identities recorded.

Then, her eyes opened and she was back in her meat body as the gates swung open to admit them. The hitcher-jack was pulled free and her 'board shut down before they reached the loading bay, where two doctors and two nurses were waiting for them, expecting a patient. They headed for the back of the ambulance, opened the doors and immediately put their hands up as Match and Hawkeye pointed guns at them. Cara and Bonzo came round to join them.

"That's it, me lovelies," said Hawkeye. "You climb in here and let us tie you up, and you won't get hurt." He eyed up one of the nurses, who was Cara's size, and said, "First, take your uniform off."

The woman wasn't going to argue, but Cara told him, "Could you do that without leering so much?"

He grinned. "Hey, you've gotta find your kicks where you can."

"Sorry about this," she said to the nurse. "Unfortunately, I need your uniform and my colleague is a slob."

The nurse shrugged as if this happened to her all the time. Maybe it did; you heard stories about these clinics.

Hawkeye would stand guard over their prisoners and the ambulance while they went inside.

"Don't you dare touch those women," she told them as they walked inside.

"Would I?" he replied with faux decency.

"Yes, and that's why I'm telling you I'll shoot you if you do."

"Fine." The door slammed behind her. She was fairly confident he would behave professionally.

Looking through a window in the swing doors that led into the front lobby, Cara decided Match and Bonzo didn't look quite right compared to the unchromed uniformed guards there. However, with her in a nurse's uniform and pushing a gurney, she hoped they wouldn't arouse too much attention as they headed for the service elevator. At least there were no signs that the "security glitch" had got them worried; perhaps they hadn't even noticed it yet.

Cara pushed a button and a moment later the lift doors opened, and she wheeled the gurney inside, the others stepping in behind her.

They reached the tenth floor without incident. There were four bulky men in security uniforms and helmets standing outside the doors of Robert's suite. Jupiter was taking no chances.

As they drew near, one of the guards stepped forward, hand on holster, and told them to halt. "This is a restricted area."

"We're here to take Marianne down for surgery."

He frowned behind his visor. "I didn't receive notification."

She shrugged. "Scheduling isn't my department."

The medical files and surgery schedules were on a standalone system, meaning she hadn't been able to access them from outside the building and doing so once inside was too risky. Had the data on Robert not been on the Jupiter system, she wouldn't have been able to jack it, and the run would have been far harder, if not impossible.

The guard took out a 'pad and began to tap at it. He was diligent; that was unfortunate.

Cara stepped forward as if about to point to it, saying, "If you look there..."

The guard started to move, knowing to keep a distance, but, whether through politeness or having grown lax, he was slow and she able to jam the taser she'd slipped from her pocket into his throat. He stiffened.

Before his three companions could realize something was wrong, Match and Bonzo began to move. Bonzo moved with lightning speed and took two down before Match had even reached hers. He was drawing his pistol, but she caught his arm and snapped it. He yowled, then combat claws sprang from her knuckles, and she drove them into his throat, changing the yowl to a gurgle. She tossed him into the wall with casual ease, and he slumped to the floor, blood dribbling down his uniform.

Cara felt the bile rise in her throat as she let the guard she'd tasered drop. He was unconscious. She wondered if it might have been better to kill him, too, but she had qualms when it came to physical violence.

She stepped up to the door and pressed 0-0-0-0, to which she'd defaulted all security codes. There was a click and the door swung open.

Bonzo burst inside, almost faster than the eye could see, to check whether there was any more security.

"Clear," he called, and Cara went inside, while Match stood watch over the four unconscious guards.

Robert stared at them in confusion.

"John sent us," Cara told him. "We're going to get you out of here and take you to him."

"Really?"

"Really. Hop onto this gurney; we've got an ambulance waiting."

Robert looked wary, distrustful.

"We need to hurry," said Bonzo.

"He's right," said Cara. "They must know the security systems are down by now."

Robert still stood unmoving, confused and doubtful.

With a sigh, Cara jabbed the taser into his chest and, with Match's help, lifted him onto the gurney and strapped him in.

They were halfway to the service elevator when the front elevator disgorged a trio of guards, each armed with a Milkor N1 SMG, which they held casually. Cara guessed that having no response from the other guards, they had assumed the security glitch was affecting communications, without dreaming that a raid was underway.

Before the guards could raise their weapons, Match and Bonzo had opened fire with theirs. Match had a Magpul FAP-7 machine pistol, while Bonzo favored the chunky Milkor Mamba pistol, the first shot from which blew a chunk out of the wall and the second the head off one of the guards. That and Match's unaimed spray saw the two survivors throw themselves back into the lift with only a cursory burst that made a mess of the corridor ceiling.

As they ran for the service lift, Cara just hoped they wouldn't face a protracted fire-fight, as all she had was a tiny holdout pistol.

Match was out of the lift first, firing unaimed bursts. The waiting guards fired their own, before scuttling for cover; Cara heard at least one round ricochet off Match's chromed limbs.

Then, they were back at the ambulance, where Hawkeye was waiting with a shotgun in his hands. When a guard popped his face up at a window in loading bay doors, Hawkeye unloaded some shot into the reinforced glass, blowing it out and making the guard disappear for cover.

"We don't have long," he called to where Match and Bonzo were throwing out the bound medics from the back of the ambulance so that Cara could thrust the gurney carrying Robert in.

Still wearing the nurse's uniform, Cara jumped into the driver's seat and inserted a hitcher-jack from her data-port to the dashboard.

"I'll have to drive us out of here," she said as the others climbed in.

The gates, still accepting the ambulance as legitimate opened for them and she sped out onto the back street just as the guards dared to exit the building and open fire on them.

She put the siren on as the ambulance careened along the streets of the Secure Zone, nearly taking out a cycle courier and forcing a limo to take evasive action and almost crash into a building. There were sirens somewhere — if nothing else, her speeding was probably setting off alarms on the traffic grid.

She slowed as they neared the edge of the Secure Zone, praying their details weren't all over the system. The gates opened and, a moment later, they were exiting the Secure Zone. Someone, somewhere, she was certain, was going to be sacked for letting them go.

AT ONE POINT, CARA was certain she heard a helicopter, but the sound of rotors dissipated and nothing happened. It seemed as if they had made a clean getaway.

Once she was sure they weren't pursued, Cara called John on a cheap burn phone Hawkeye had set him up with. "Meet us at The Holistic Lounge in one hour."

Hawkeye dropped Cara and Robert off at an entrance to the Underplex; he'd drop the others off somewhere else, dispersal making it harder to track them. Doubtless, Hawkeye would strip the ambulance down for spares and destroy anything he couldn't sell, leaving no evidence for anyone trying to track them.

Unstrapped from the gurney, Robert was a little wobbly on his feet but seemed glad to be free and on his way to meet John.

"Follow me," said Cara, having paused to change back into her street clothes, and they entered what had once been the entrance to a tube station, but today hosted an impromptu marketplace. Ignoring the stalls, they headed down an escalator that hadn't had power in years and entered the Underplex.

The Underplex was the grandiose name for the network of disused tube stations, abandoned cellars and latter-day tunnels colonized by squatters, fixers, and outlaws. She hated the place — it was dirty and dangerous and even managed to make her flat seem salubrious.

They only made a short trip through its dank tunnels before returning to the surface where her car was parked. It was old and scratched enough that it could be safely left in an out-of-the-way corner without it being boosted.

"Get in," she said, opening the door for him.

"You drive *this*?" Robert asked. He'd probably only ever ridden in a smart car.

"Buckle up," she said with a grin and drove them over to The Holistic Lounge.

John was waiting for them. Robert ran to him, and they hugged. Cara gave them a moment, then joined them and said, "Well, my involvement is over. If you need my help in future, you'll have to find a way to pay for it." She almost apologized; it wasn't fair, but then life never was. "Take my advice. Use your skills to earn a living, but make sure you lay low. If you do anything to attract attention, they'll find you. Jupiter and AstraGlaxo CE will both be looking for you. ETC, too, if they realize who Robert was. I've erased as much data concerning you both as I can, but I can't guarantee copies don't exist offline or in more secure systems. I've also prepared the skeletons of new identities for you both — Robert has the skill to finish them off. Choose names they won't recognize — nothing." She smiled at Robert, "Connected to Sherwood Forest."

"Thank you," said Robert, hugging her.

"Yes, we're very grateful."

"Your payment was thanks enough," she said, although it wasn't entirely true. "Remember, you are new people now — avoid anything that hints of your life before." Then, she turned and headed for the exit. If all went well, she would never see or hear of them again. She hoped they would find happiness together on the streets; so few people did.

END

DJ TYRER is the person behind *Atlantean Publishing* and has been widely published in anthologies and magazines in the UK, USA and elsewhere, including *A Grimoire of Eldritch Inquests, Volume I* (Emby Press), *State of Horror: Illinois* (Charon Coin Press), *Steampunk Cthulhu* (Chaosium), *Tales of the Dark Arts* (Hazardous Press), *Cosmic Horror* (Dark Hall Press), and *Sorcery & Sanctity: A Homage to Arthur Machen* (Hieroglyphics Press), and in addition, has a novella available in paperback and on the Kindle, *The Yellow House* (Dunhams Manor).

DJ Tyrer's website is at djtyrer.blogspot.co.uk. The Atlantean Publishing website is at atlanteanpublishing.blogspot.co.uk/.

THE SMOKE IN DEATH'S EYE

Jorge Salgado-Reyes

PROLOGUE

LEDS RAKED THE BUILDINGS with their kaleidoscopic adverts while doorways and railings gouged out shadows of pitch. My soul craved the shadows. My pulse rose and fell in synchronicity with the dark hum of the Smoke.

The target leaned against a scarlet spinner. His eyes scanned the traffic above, waiting for his clients. A pusher of the worst kind, he sold 24-hour addiction to the net, the matrix, whatever you call that mutual illusion that we call cyberspace. Watching him was an issue in of itself because he'd hacked the local cams with his built-in wetware. But he possessed the knowledge that might take me to them.

Despite the poor lighting, streamed video from my TacScreen allowed me to see him as bright as day. ANA, my built-in AI, took full advantage of this augmentation. He stood at least 6 feet tall in his unfastened jump boots, skinny for his height. Retro style jeans and a denyl jacket cut off at the arms made up the gangsta look. A skull and cross-bones glowed fluorescent green highlighted the body art on his torso. He was a local hood of mixed race, his dyed blond hair cut in a Mohawk and long in the back, sat atop his head.

'ANA', I sub-vocalised, 'show me his wetware.'

'Sure thing Lobinho.' She caressed my old nickname with her soft girl-like voice, her accent a sexy Portuguese that only I heard. Artificial Neurological Analyser-what a mouthful-I called her ANA for short. ANA streamed the list of enhancements he'd done to himself. The quality of them was questionable. No doubt acquired in the black markets in Chinatown.

On reviewing the list, it seemed obvious that he would need to be overwhelmed before he could alert his brethren. ANA showed me his neural pain limiters and standard built-in firewalls; no surprises there. I activated my own little surprise: attack nanites designed to infiltrate his systems. These were a release and forget type, totally independent and once released they would make their way down to him. It gave me about an hour before I needed to make my move.

I gazed down at him while crouched on one of the balconies of the old No.1 Croydon building. My position overlooked the spinner landing pads. He stood with his back to me, about three floors down. He must have sensed something because he started to fidget and look around. Probably a heightened paranoia as a result of his way of life created a kind of sixth sense. That can happen, so I unlocked my gaze, and when I returned to him he looked less jumpy.

There was no way he could see me from that distance without artificial help as I had dressed in my standard black jumpsuit and military-grade jump boots. Its opaque material with dark, changing colours blended in with the shadowed landscape. My heavier coat made of the same material but cut into a retro style Mac had my blaster concealed within it. An anachronistic eight inches of Sheffield steel completed my weapons of choice.

In the interim, I accessed the same webcams he'd hooked into. I could see for quite a distance through those vistas, the swarm of people from a multitude of places all here in the Smoke. The buildings had grown into Arcologies in the mid-part of the 21st century and with them the number and types of ubiquitous CCTV. I looked up to catch a glimpse of the moon, but the hyper-tall buildings prevented it. I sighed and switched over to the Luna Vista views, a series of webcams dedicated to following the progress of the fledgling Luna City. The giant 'G' logo glowed on the surface of the moon, a testament to the power of the mega-corporation Google. They had a facility on the dark side of the moon that looked out on the cosmos. Right now, it was pointed at the centre of the Milky Way, at the giant singularity there. It made me think about all this—Source code. The source code is the language that the web is made of, what makes it do what it does. What if you could view the source code of the universe? What if the source code is dark matter? Can you see the source code in the fabric of space-time? Can you see it in between the molecules of the air that we breathe? Or in the sunbeam glinting on the wave breaking over the sand?

'If there is code at all, there's no reason to suppose the universe is open source. It would certainly be compiled, for efficiency, because after all, there are a lot of operations per second. And if there is code, it is not a thing in the universe; it would control the behaviour of dark matter along with everything else.' ANA answered my thoughts as if I had asked her opinion.

'But if there…'

'Lobinho, the TacKnights are almost ready,' ANA interrupted at the edge of my consciousness. I sighed again, my melancholy thoughts dismissed while I ran through a quick system check. My watch read 4 am, and my target would be at his lowest ebb. His trade died off, and he looked to quit for the night. He had a place in the same building I stood on but on the 3rd floor, which left his floor beneath the level of the water. I had already prepared a place for our little chat also on that same floor. The water and age of the building made it more secure by reducing the possibilities of being overheard. This whole building sat derelict now, ideal for what I had planned.

I made my way down the stairs, wanting to be in place before he made his own way there. As I went, I released my own network of insect cams along the route. They scurried away like little, black spiders, inbuilt with audio and day/night CCTV sensors. All feeds controlled and streamed to me by ANA.

Shadows danced across the floor as the arid aroma of stale urine wafted across the corridor. My plan depended on both tactical and strategic surprise. I waited in the doorway opposite the corridor leading to his suite, pretending to sleep. Most people relax when they are on their way home. That and the time of night meant I would take him unaware.

I checked my cams as he headed in my direction. As I waited, the seconds stretched out in front of me, each one seemed to last an infinity. My mouth felt dry and adrenaline began to pump its way into my system. I closed my eyes; my cams kept me informed of his progress. My heightened hearing picked up the sound of the door from the emergency stairs opening, the dull clang as it closed. His footsteps echoed toward me.

An old song popped into my head, a remake of La Roux's In For The Kill, as he passed me and turned into his corridor. I launched myself at him, my mind blank. Some instinct or small noise made him turn. His lips curled into a snarl.

I struck at his right ear as he drew his gun. My initial blow missed and hit his temple, but it was heavy enough that he stumbled. Blood thundered in my ears, and my vision narrowed; all I saw was the gun leveled at me.

Sliding forward, I stepped inside his guard and gripped his gun hand. My right hand sliced the air, almost of its own volition, toward his collarbone. His collarbone snapped. Metallic clattering echoed through the corridor as the gun fell to the floor between us. I knew the fight was over when he looked up at me. His face was pale as the moon, slack in disbelief. I felt my upper lip twitch in contempt and followed through. After hammering his ribs with a knee, I sidestepped, landing a phoenix-hammer punch to the left ear. He hit the ground in a limp heap, out cold.

The fight took thirty seconds from start to finish. Despite feeling an urgency to pull him out of the corridor, I took a moment to catch my breath and let the shakiness in my knees subside. As soon as my hands had stopped shaking, I picked up his feet and dragged him over to the room prepared earlier.

The room measured twenty by thirty feet, stripped bare of almost all furnishings, the walls a dirty pale brown with damp spots. There were no outer windows, and I expected this room had been an inner office before the floods and its abandonment. A single, dirty bulb hung from the middle of the ceiling, the room's only illumination.

I studied him as he regained consciousness. He sat in a plasteel chair. I had taped his head to the pillar behind him, legs and wrists manacled to the chair. His skin goose-bumped with cold as he started to struggle, his breath visible in the cold air of the unheated room. With white ringed eyes, he scanned the table where his clothes and property sat.

'Who are you? Why am I here?' he asked, licking his dry lips.

I allowed silence to echo across the room while going through his clothes, pocket by pocket, piling the contents on the table. I took my time and searched the inner lining of each garment, throwing them on the floor as I finished with each one.

Having finished, I turned my attention to the man that fate had sent my way. 'ANA,' I sub-vocalised, 'is he ready?'

'Si, Lobinho, he has tried to access the net already. I've blocked that, but it will take about five minutes to break through his firewall.

I am also keeping his pain levels down, so he has no idea his pain inhibitors are offline.' As she responded, ANA fed me his autonomous responses and interpreted them for me in a simple truth or lie overlay on his body. His emotional state of mind would be clear to me.

'I need to ask you a few questions, if you cooperate, no harm will come to you,' I informed him.

'Me no talk to pigs!' He made an attempt to spit in my direction, but his dry mouth made it impossible.

I couldn't be sure if he referred to the police or to the Professional Investigators Guild-PIGs for short. Either way, it made no difference to me. Curious. He spoke normal English at first, but now he spoke in street gutter dialect. His file indicated that he had never been to the Caribbean but thought it made him sound hard. Of course, I spoke street slang; I had to speak it to get about.

The overlay indicated that, while he appeared hostile, he was experiencing fear and confusion.

I continued, 'What's your name?'

Silence answered me. The file listed his name as Demetrez Brown, but his brethren called him 'Dem'.

'You know, I'm disappointed in you, Dem. I thought you would be harder to take down.'

His eyes widened when he realized I knew his identity.

ANA broke in: 'Lobinho, I have broken through and am downloading all his files. Encryption ice runs through some of the files, so we are going to need the key.'

'Okay,' I replied. 'Allow his pain through now.' I watched as he began to shudder.

'Dem, I have some questions. If you answer with the truth, we can forget all about tonight. If you lie ...well let's just say you won't enjoy it.'

'Fuck you, man. I ain't no grass.' Dem looked at me with some confidence. He thought he had protection.

'I thought that's what you would say.' I smiled at him. 'ANA, initiate interrogation program Alpha.'

Dem screamed as the program ran through his systems. It installed itself, feeding into the pain centers of his brain. The total effect of this intrusion-ware would create a hallucination his body would believe. His pupils dilated, every muscle in his body contracted and his body dripped sweat. Thirty seconds passed, and I knew he would not be able to hold on much longer.

'ANA, why hasn't he released the key yet?'

'Lobinho, he has a high threshold for pain. If he keeps this up, his wetware will leak.'

'Dem, give me the key, and all this will be over. Tell me what I need to know while you can still walk away without any permanent damage.'

Dem looked at me without answering, his teeth clenched. Every muscle of his face stood out. I knew then I had to go to phase two.

I drew Veracity, my eight-inch surgical steel blade. It had taken thirty-six hours to forge it, using ancient Japanese techniques now lost to all but the most dedicated. A weapon forged in fire and blood. Its simple elegance defined by the slight curvature of the primary edge with the distinctive wave pattern. A pity I now had to put it to a use that I did not approve of, an interrogation method thought to have died out but kept alive by the Dark Sensei.

I inhaled and pushed out three quick breaths before beginning the dance. Dem continued to scream while ANA monitored and adjusted the program to assist the dance. My blade caressed his flesh as his skin parted. After five minutes of slicing and dicing, I paused.

'How about it, Dem? Anything you want to tell me?'

Dem sobbed, his body covered in blood. It impressed me. So far he had withstood what so many others could not. ANA's program was the only thing preventing him from going into shock.

As my blade slid through skin and muscle tissue, his body tensed and quivered. Dem gritted his teeth and bucked while Veracity probed delicately into his nerve points. The dance progressed, leaving a pattern of blood over his skin, stripping away his resistance. The pattern of cuts appeared random, but appearances were deceptive. They created layers of pain which, as the dance continued, left the subject desiring to tell me what I wanted to hear. Of course, the danger lay in the subject telling me complete bullshit just to make the pain stop.

Flesh parted to the silken voyage of Veracity.

'Th-the code is zulo alpha three romeo,' Dem gasped and then convulsed. I lowered my hands, my arms red with blood up to my elbows.

'ANA what's going on with him?'

'I am analyzing,' ANA replied.

Intense disappointment flooded through me as I watched him die.

'ANA, please tell me that this wasn't all for nothing?'

'Can torture ever work?' she asked.

CHAPTER ONE

TENDRILS OF MIST DRIFTED across the windscreen, beckoning like ghosts. Antique street lights cast their jaundiced illumination on a dead and forgotten body curled in a pile of blown rubbish. The smell of rot and refuse wafted along with the fog. Typical night in the Smoke.

Piles of shipping containers loomed over the wharfs. I sat in the cockpit of my spinner perched inside one of these sea-cans, staring down toward the river walk with the camera in my hands. The small splashes of the river lapped against the piers dampened by mist. Spinners overflew our position, their engines resonating against the background of the night.

'Mr. Castillo, are you there?' Valentina asked.

'Yes,' I replied. 'Don't worry, we're not going anywhere.' That made it six times she had called me over the wire. Only fourteen years old, she tottered back and forth on her stripper heels, hips swaying to the unheard music of the night. The black denim mini-skirt only just covered her modesty. A matching denim jacket over a white bra-top left her abdomen visible to the night's predatory clients. My zoom lens picked up the goose bumps on her skin, caused by the chill in the air. Her beat included Woolwich Docks, a dirty little corner of the Smoke.

'Charlie three to Alpha one, Tango one is in sight and headed your way,' Kiya broke into my thoughts.

'Roger that. All units stand by.' I zoomed in on Tango One, our call sign for the target, Valentina's hebephiliac ex-boyfriend, ex-pimp, and soon, her ex-stalker. He came in on foot, his hairless head turning left and right, searching for watchers. He never looked above him. Weird how they never looked upwards. His ebony skin shone in the pale glow of reflected lights. Six foot four inches of muscle now turning to fat, he wore faded docker boots and dark clothing.

He paused on the corner, staring at her. I knew the type, and according to everything I'd heard from Valentina, he fit the profile of a textbook abuser. His lips curled up, showing his teeth, eyes gleamed like a hungry predator, Valentina his prey. He didn't know I watched him watching her, stalking the stalker!

My camera whirred and clicked on the edge of inaudible. I continued to take stills, my vehicle recorded the video. We needed this evidence - without it, he would walk. We had taken a chance using our own client as bait. The object of the exercise - to lure him out into the open and take clear photographs and video.

A friend of mine who worked at a refuge for abused women had referred Valentina to us. Valentina ran away from home and ended up in the Smoke, alone and vulnerable. Befriended by a pimp, she soon took drugs she couldn't pay for. It went downhill from there. Addicted to drugs and servicing the pimp and his friends, she soon had a place in his stable of young women, none of them over the age of sixteen. He beat them to keep them in line; what a cliche! She'd managed to run away from him and found herself in a woman's refuge.

The refuge's lawyer obtained an injunction preventing the pimp from continuing to abuse Valentina. This included going anywhere near her. Only hard evidence could guarantee permanent incarceration. An arrest without a warrant would see him freed on bail within a few hours.

'All units, close the circle and stand by,' I instructed my team. They acknowledged one by one.

'Control, you monitoring?' I asked.

'Alpha one from Control. I am receiving footage, stills, and transmissions from all call signs,' Eve, my office AI confirmed.

'Roger that. All units…'

'Castillo, I-I think he's here,' Valentina broke in.

'It's okay, Valentina. We know he's here. We are all around you. See that girl at the other lamp post? That's Lexi. Anything happens, you run to her. OK?'

Lexi leaned back, one stocking-clad leg rested on the pavement and the other on the lamp post. Tight fitting shorts encased her hips, a crimson and black basque emphasized her hourglass figure, drawing one's eyes upwards to her over-spilling breasts. She held the neon-lit handle of her umbrella; cigarette clasped in her fingers, acrid smoke curling from her lips before the wind whisked it away. A small crease puckered between her oriental eyes, the only sign of stress. She played the part well and she should because she made up the other half of my senior team.

Converted shipping containers where the call-girls took their clients lined the road. Each container had a bed, a shower and little else. Rented out hourly by the enterprising docks owner, they offered a sordid oasis of lust to those willing to pay.

'Okay,' Valentina said.

She held her index finger up to her left ear, head cocked in that manner that all non-professionals adopt when using a wire.

'Valentina, take your finger away from your ear and act natural,' I said. 'Remember, there's five of us and only one of him,' I reassured her.

Her hand jerked away, and she flushed, looking down. I smiled in the dark and scanned the surroundings. We waited for the pimp to make his move. We had enough now to detain him, but I wanted more. I wanted him to do something other than just watch Valentina. I figured if he threatened her, as he often did, that's enough for the judge to commit him to jail.

He had a history of violence towards women. Two years ago, he put one of his girls in the hospital with two broken ribs and multiple facial contusions. The girls refused to testify against him; a normal state of affairs. They often had nowhere else to go.

People often presumed that I led an exciting and glamorous life. In truth, my eyes drooped, and my senses faded away after several hours of watching the comings and goings of the girls, their clients, and their perverted pimps. Somehow you had to stay alert. Patience became one of the watchwords we lived by. Patience and a certain dark fetish for the night, the night and the darkness in men's soul.

Now I must deal with the darkness in this man's soul. How did it come to this? Men traded little girls for money to fulfill the lusts inside?

'All units, I'm moving in.' I exited the vehicle and picked my way to the ground keeping to the shadows. My team's whispered acknowledgment in my ear reminded me that my team surrounded me. The Thames on my left coiled like a giant serpent through the mist.

My boots left a soft pattern along the moist pathway. Valentina locked eyes with me, her knowing smile disturbed me in someone so young. Except for a small scar intersecting her left eyebrow, she had flawless skin. Large brown eyes set off an exquisite face framed by waist length brown hair.

'Hola Papi, You looking for someone?' she said with a wink.

I smiled back at her, 'Hey babes, that depends. What you offering?' Beyond her, in my peripheral vision, I could just make him out. His face hovered over his body in the shadow cast by the container.

I concentrated on her, smiling down at upturned face, my hand touching her hair, striving hard to ignore him.

'I do most things, ya know the usual stuff,' she breathed, her hand pressed against my chest--her musky fragrance made my head swim.

I couldn't see him anymore, I couldn't see anything except her eyes burning into mine, locked into a soul gaze.

'YOU CAN'T HAVE HER, YOU FUCKER!'

His shout my only warning, I shoved Valentina back and behind me. I pivoted to my right, muscle memory snapped my arms forward. My eyes registered a brown paper bag in his left hand. It blurred towards my abdomen. My own arm half blocked it. The pain hit sharp and sudden - knife, he had a knife in the bag. He shouted again, guttural, unintelligible. Adrenaline sang its way through my system, my knees trembled, my vision narrowed to a tunnel with his face in the middle. He punched again. I moved into it, my extended right hand slashed down and outward in a small half-circle. I gathered his knife-hand and moved it a few centimeters to my right. The blade still went in, but I didn't feel it.

My turn; I punched him with my left fist, swinging it like a hammer across his temple. I followed up with two quick strikes to his sternum. He staggered back off balance and slashed in front of him. The tip of his knife seared across the right side of my chest.

Blood soaked my upper body, I raised my leaden arms again. Despite efforts to control my breathing, I felt lightheaded from panting. I needed to finish the fight before the fight finished me.

He lunged from the ground, and the point of his knife gleamed a dark rusty brown, aiming for my gut. No time to block with my arms. I raised my knee, protecting my guts and groin. The blade penetrated my upper thigh, but the adrenaline in my system made the pain inconsequential. I struck him with my elbow full in the face, throwing him onto his back. The knife remained in my right leg.

He rose to his feet, holding his face; blood splatter running down his hands.

'Oh shit!' My hardest blow hadn't stopped him!

CHAPTER TWO

HE LUNGED AT ME. I hopped sideways, desperate to place some space between us. He gripped the knife protruding from my leg and twisted. I screamed; the pain ripped through me like a bolt of electricity, driving out all strategy, all thought. He knelt on me, pinning my legs, and yanked out the blade. He raised the ten inches of Sheffield steel over his head and thrust it downward, slicing through the air.

My wrists flew up and crossed over my chest, blocking the strike. The atavistic blade glistened a few inches from my face. My arms trembled under the strain. Although my elbows had locked, I couldn't hold him for long. I did the only thing left: I withdrew my left arm and released his knife to slide down my arm and into the ground. I twisted and delivered a vicious punch into his lower ribs.

A shout rang out. His weight left me. Lexi, Kiya, and Alex swarmed over him like coyotes over a bear. They struggled to contain him until Lexi punched him in the neck with her taser. The arc of electricity illuminated the scene.

'Arh shit' Kiya cradled his hands.

The pimp lay stunned, face up on the ground. Lexi kicked him over and cuffed his hands behind his back.

'Hey Boss, you looking a bit fucked up. Shall I call an ambulance?' Kiya stared down at me, his hands still held to his chest, a small smile played on his face.

'What do you think asswipe?' I managed to retort.

'Ambulance and the old bill are on their way and should be here momentarily. Alex is looking after Valentina,' Lexi said. She knelt down next to me and assessed my wounds.

'Kiya, bring the first aid...'

Tears dripping on my face woke me; Valentina cradled my head on her lap. Kiya and Alex stood looking worried, their faces morphed with their avatars. Lexi's green luminescent wings moved in pretty patterns in front of her, and a giant flying insect with a green cross on its side seemed about to land on her. The stars swirled across the sky, 'where's the rain?'

'Take a deep scan of the stab wounds on the upper torso. I want to know if it punctured the liver.'

'Yes, Doctor.' echoed in my mind — I came to again but this time in sharp focus. People in fluorescent coats with green crosses knelt around me; my head lay on no-one's lap. One had a tube in my arm, another had a hard metallic band around my upper leg. Pain blazed a trail through my veins, my vision edged red with the intensity of it.

The giant insect became the air ambulance, it's rear gaped open with strange looking instruments inside. Lexi's wings lay discarded on the ground; a pair of fluorescent wands.

'What's going on?' I managed.

'Hello, I'm Dr. Lau,' She went on. 'You have a deep stab wound to the upper leg that nicked the artery. Your colleague managed to prevent too much blood loss; otherwise, you might not be having this conversation. You also have a few slashes to the torso and one puncture wound above your liver. If it's punctured your liver, then it's off to hospital you go. Okay?'

'What's the stuff you're sticking in my arm?' I asked.

'That is just plasma to replace the blood loss'

'Doctor, that wound hasn't penetrated the liver.' The medic showed Dr. Lau a hand-held screen.

'Okay, glue it up and spray it then.' She went on to me, 'Do you have access to an auto-doc?'

'I have an iBed with an auto-doc program,' I replied.

'Hmm, okay, that will have to do. If it tells you to go to a hospital, then please do what it suggests.'

I DREAMED AGAIN; MY movements, slow and clumsy poured over me in opaque images. She smiled and waved goodbye at the door. I couldn't stop her. I turned over in my bed and smelled her scent on the pillow, the smell of our passion enveloped me. Lethargy stole over me; I slept.

My eyes flickered open; I felt an overwhelming sense of loss.

I stood up, the door of my coffin shaped iBed slid open, its amber coloured liquid ran down my body.

'Good Morning Ángel Castillo' a voice greeted me. The window gradually cleared from its opaque state. I squinted my eyes at the increasing light.

'How long have I been under?' I asked it, scraping the liquid from my body passing gently over my injuries.

'You've been under two and a half hours, equivalent to five hours of normal sleep,' it replied in a disapproving tone. 'The medical prog wants you to use it at least five hours per night for the next seven days.'

'Oh Shut up,' I headed for the shower.

'Your itinerary is ready at the breakfast table,' the computer continued when I emerged from the shower.

'Turn on the news' I ordered.

The beach view in the kitchen window switched to headline streamers. One of the headlines expanded into a video clip when my eyes remained too long on it. A man ran through a shopping mall, glancing desperately behind him. Mall guards chased him, tasers gripped tightly in their hands. Normal shoppers froze, their hands at their open mouths. The man fell and slid along the floor, smoke came out of the jack by his left ear. Two wires led to the crouching guard holding the taser. The headlines screamed '3rd MAN DIES VIA NEW TASER!'

'Where's the itinerary?' I asked gulping my yogurt. My eyes scanned down the screen and stopped at the item informing me that I had a meeting at 8am. Damn it, I had half an hour to get to the office.

I made my way forward and sat in the cockpit of my spinner, the room behind darkened, automatically powering down.

Strapped into my seat, the flight computer displayed my current sleeping flight path on the front screen window. At top speed, my office lay twenty minutes away.

'Computer, lay in a course for the office to arrive by 07:50 hours.' The flight computer displayed the indicated course, and a flashing icon on the screen flashed at me, 'CONFIRM COURSE'. I clicked yes on the touch screen. I hesitated and took off in manual, the engine noise felt only through the vibration on the control stick.

I looked up from the screen catching a glimpse of my reflection. I looked away, my fingers compulsively went to the Keloidal ridges over my left eye, the last souvenir of another life. All those good looks wasted by those surgically embedded claws that had opened my left cheek and nearly cost me the eye.

Oh leave it alone, I thought and went back to watching the scenery. Stupid eye watered anyway.

I grimaced and studied the scenery, the raindrops streaked on the windscreen. Air traffic seemed light for the time of day, vehicle lights flashed white, amber and red. A collection of various commuter vehicles, flew back from the Great Sleeper Circuit located off the coast of Brighton at ten thousand meters altitude. The Great Sleeper Circuit became the first airborne sleeper park established fifty years ago due to the lack of viable land and population pressure.

London's skyline gradually came into view. I spiraled down from the east following the set flight plan. The financial district of London's forest of towers gleamed in the rain, each mega-building sparkled at its highest point. A white flashing navigation beacon winked at me, warned me not to approach too closely.

In the distance, I saw my destination; 'The Mushroom,' the City of London Arcology with its mushroom shape towered over the rest of the city, its depths lost in the flooded landscape of London Town. The park, domed over, flashed by.

I descended thirty levels to the parking levels and hovered, the artificial horizon glowed green on the windscreen. I slowly side-slipped over the edge of the landing pad, the computer counting off the remaining meters. Touch down.

'GOOD MORNING, CDA, HOW can I help you?'
'Good morning, CDA, How can I help you?'
'Good morning, CDA, How can I help you?'
Eve the office A.I. can handle up to fifty simultaneous conversations. Jacked into her parallel circuit, Amber's eyes fluttered closed, the dust motes hung in the air; almost asleep. She learned the ropes fast, but boredom ate away at her. I watched her for a moment. Two weeks into the job and she made coffee just the way I liked it.

Eve wore a classic professional-looking avatar, she had a low cut grey suit that hinted at her nudity under it, her blond hair tied back in a ponytail. A circular receptionists desk separated Eve from the rest of the room. A burst of flames in front of Amber startled her awake, a person wearing a demon avatar had arrived.

Along the walls, armchairs with little coffee tables dotted the room. Digital artwork depicted 21st century London scenes.

'Coffee, black,' I instructed Amber walking before disappearing into the conference room. All the others waited inside.

The smell of freshly made coffee permeated the room. Amber sat the coffee mug on the table by my left elbow; everyone else already had their morning drinks in front of them.

'There was a murder in Croydon old town,' Lexi said. 'The Police are referring it to the Guild for specialist investigation due to the nature of the death.'

'I wonder if we'll get that? Hmm, that's nice,' I felt my lips smile with the first sip of coffee.

'We'll have to wait and see,' Lexi replied.

'Today should be historic! Come on guys, let's jack in,' I added sitting at the head of the table. 'You too, Amber.'

The translucent cable glistened on the table, coiled like a serpent waiting to strike. It slotted behind her right ear. Amber's avatar, a beautiful Geisha of ancient Nippon, stared from the screen. She blinked rapidly and closed her eyes, leaning back in the chair. I hear that something like déjà vu comes over them when they assimilate into the net. I jacked in last, fitting an old fashioned headset over my eyes. It's not the same for me using the headset. There's a barrier against the full sensory experience that they have when you jack in directly. I prefer to remain in control of my brain. They probably think me hopelessly outdated.

Lexi and I stood side by side in the cyber conference room. My avatar didn't have the scar and appeared sixteen years old, Lexi wore white skin-tight jeans and a see-through blouse showing off her well-endowed charms. Kiya, a specialist in tracing people through the net, wore an avatar of an American Indian with the head of a wolf, alternating with his own head. He flanked his cousin Alexandro. Alexandro's avatar, an anime boy vampire.

Eve gestured us toward the portal at the far end of the room. One by one the others went through, I brought up the rear with Eve.

We stepped into the Guild, short for the Professional Investigators Guild.

'Hoink, hoink' Kiya chanted as he walked past the logo. The street knew us by the derogative 'PIGS'. We filed in and joined the fifteen other agencies gathered there. People gathered in small groups; a quiet murmur the only sound. The senior partner of each agency sat down at the big round table in the middle of the room.

Two ten foot tall griffins flanked Erik Withers, the Chairman. Their eagle heads shrieked in unison. The murmuring immediately stilled.

'This is the one hundredth and forty-fifth meeting of our Guild,' he said. 'You are all here by direct invitation, this session's restricted to members only. It's been thirty years since the Police stopped investigating serious crime because the overall rate of violent crime outside of controlled habitats became too much for them to handle. They made the decision to concentrate on public order and easy-to-investigate crimes. This is where we came in. Our specialized skills and combined resources meant that murders and other such crimes were properly investigated. From today, the Guild is the official special investigatory arm for the entire planet.'

An amazed murmur went through the room with everyone speaking at once.

'So what happens now?' a voice shouted out.

'The Guild will forward any requests for assistance from the police to the relevant agency in the area. It will be an automated process managed by the Guild's AI, the Twin Griffins. Assuming the first test cases are carried out in a professional manner, It will mean more work for everyone.' Erik continued, 'Please have your agency AIs sync with the Twin Griffins who will give out the assignments.'

Dotted around the room, agency AI's synced with the Two Griffins, blinking blue in unison. Windows winked opened in front of them; assignments scrolled down.

'I wonder how many new assignments we'll get now?' Kiya asked no one in particular.

The meeting soon broke up with people filing out and disappearing from the ante-room like so many cheap genies in a bottle.

'I have to have a word with the heads, so you guys head back to the office, Lexi will give out the assignments,' Ángel instructed us.

An hour later, they gathered in the conference room around the briefing table listening to Lexi when I came out from under and stood up,

'What's there for me, Lexi?'

Lexi turned and smiled, 'There's a murder down in Croydon that looks interesting. The victim is down at the Freezer, and a CSbot has secured the crime scene. What do you want to do first?'

'You and I cover the crime scene first. Has the coroner released a report yet?' I brought up the case files and sent the gruesome images and video clips from the crime scene to the wallscreen.

Kiya leaned in and stared in morbid fascination at the first video of a man, his naked corpse tied to a chair. Kiya motioned with his hands and the image filled the screen. The dark brown blood had dried on his body where it dripped down his face and onto his shoulders and chest. The view panned downward following the streaks on the victim's torso.

His whole torso criss-crossed with deep cuts, created a pattern on his body where a razor sharp instrument had flayed him open, in places it looked like the perpetrator had dug into the body like he had tried to root out some kind of parasite, exposing the muscular structure of the body. The camera continued to pan down, and it became clear the killer had spent some considerable time, maybe hours working on the victim.

END

JORGE SALGADO-REYES is a Chilean and British sci-fi/cyberpunk author, private investigator, and photographer. Born in Temuco, Chile, Salgado-Reyes left his country of birth at age seven in 1975 with his family driven into exile by the Pinochet dictatorship. Subsequently brought up in the United Kingdom, he changed residence frequently with his family as a child. Salgado-Reyes became somewhat of a loner who read science fiction from an early age. After spending his adolescence in Mozambique, he returned to the UK where he completed his education.

In 2011, Salgado-Reyes began writing his first novel, *The Smoke in Death's Eye*, a work still in progress.

In 2012, Indie Authors Press published Salgado-Reyes' first reference book, *British Process Servers Guide*, written in collaboration with Stuart Withers and Helen Withers.

Salgado-Reyes can be contacted on Facebook, Twitter, or through his Amazon Author Page. Further information can be found on www.salgado-reyes.com/wiki/jorge-salgado-reyes-2/.

AFTERWORD

WE WOULD LIKE TO personally thank you for buying and reading this book. Producing this anthology has been, and continues to be, quite fulfilling for us and we hope that it is enjoyable for you as well.

Please consider taking a little extra time to help others find this book by leaving feedback where you purchased it. Your opinion about this book truly matters, both to our authors who have contributed to the anthology and to other readers.

If you have any questions, comments, suggestions, or just want to say hello, please visit our publisher's website on Indie Authors Press, www.salgado-reyes.com, and follow our publisher's Twitter: @Indie__Authors

Indie Authors Press